HIS SCANDALOUS LESSONS

HIS SCANDALOUS LESSONS

Private Arrangements
#1

Katrina Kendrick

HEAD
ZEUS

An Aria Book

First published in the UK in 2023 by Head of Zeus,
part of Bloomsbury Publishing Plc

9 7 5 3 1 2 4 6 8

A catalogue record for this book is available from the British Library.

ISBN (PB): 9781837930975
ISBN (E): 9781837930968

Cover design: HoZ / Meg Shepherd & Jessie Price

Typeset by Siliconchips Services Ltd UK

Printed and bound in Great Britain by
CPI Group (UK) Ltd, Croydon CR0 4YY

Head of Zeus
First Floor East
5–8 Hardwick Street
London EC1R 4RG

WWW.HEADOFZEUS.COM

For the women still finding their voices.

∽ 1 ∽

LONDON, 1872

Anne Sheffield's father had always trained her in the art of obedience.

He repeated his rules so often that she could recite them by rote, each designed to strip Anne of her sense of self – a gradual erosion of her opinions and desires until she became little more than his creature.

Then there were Stanton Sheffield's three most important edicts:

1. Never leave the house without her father, a bodyguard, or a chaperone.
2. Offer no insights beyond the safe topics of weather and ladies' fashion.
3. And never, *ever*, let slip all his dirty political secrets.

In short, Anne was not to give the impression she was anything more than a decorative object.

Beautiful, but hollow.

Her father's allies in Parliament praised him for the daughter he had raised. She was perfect, they declared. *Perfect* meant shallow and empty – nothing more than a gilded trinket to grace the mantelpiece.

But Anne had ideas, carefully hidden from prying eyes – dreams of a future that was her own.

Plans of escape.

For months, she'd studied the servants' movements and planned for every contingency. After her father stepped out for a late meeting with other members of the Conservative shadow cabinet, she seized her chance. His staff were as efficient as a ship's crew, their steps marking the hours until her freedom.

Tonight, Anne Sheffield was going to break her father's rules.

Anne donned her most modest gown, tiptoeing through the familiar halls of her home. As she reached the garden, she discreetly made her exit through the back gate and into the darkened streets of London. The rain, a gentle mist, clung to her cloak like tiny droplets of dew, providing the perfect cover for her to hide her face beneath the hood. She shuddered as the chill of the early spring air seeped through her bones. Determined not to let the weather slow her down, she tightened the cloak around her and hastened her pace.

Not too fast.

Reason and instinct waged war as Anne made her way onto the busy main road. She must appear confident in her purpose. If anyone saw her acting suspiciously and recognised her—

Anne shook off that thought. In three months, she would be a duchess – trapped in a gilded cage with no means of escape. This was no time for doubt or hesitation.

Determined to stay the course, Anne hailed a nearby hackney cab. The driver cast her an appraising look, but she met him with a serene assurance and supplied him with her destination's address.

She sounded calm; her heart was rioting.

The hackney cab jolted to a stop, sending Anne's pulse racing with a mixture of apprehension and uncertainty. As she stepped out of the conveyance, she was met with a charming townhouse that was not at all what she had expected. Its rustic brick façade and white-trimmed windows were more suited to a peaceful countryside abode than the lair of a rogue. It was almost... *quaint*. The front steps, lined with a riot of colourful flowers, only served to heighten her unease.

She did not like surprises.

Anne inhaled deeply, taking in the night air – and a steadying breath of courage. She plastered on the most confident expression she could muster and strode forward to knock.

As the butler swung the door open, Anne braced for his inevitable disdain. After all, she was a woman, daring to darken the doorstep of a bachelor's residence in the late hours of vice and debauchery. But to her surprise, the man maintained a politely bland countenance. She supposed many a lady had arrived to this particular house before her.

"May I help you?" he inquired, his voice smooth and professional. Anne couldn't help but admire the man's composure, and she wondered just how well Mr Grey compensated him for his unwavering demeanour.

Anne lifted her chin. "I'm here to see Mr Grey. Is he at home?"

"And whom may I ask is calling?"

"Please tell him Miss Anne Sheffield is here to speak with him urgently."

"Of course," he said and stepped back from the door – graciously opening it wider for her to enter. "Shall I take your cloak, Miss Sheffield?"

Anne shook her head, determined to keep her cloak firmly in her possession for a swift escape. "No, thank you," she said firmly. She wanted him gone before she could change her mind.

The butler bowed slightly, motioning her in the direction of the front parlour. "Very good, Miss Sheffield. If you'll wait here, please."

Anne couldn't help but appreciate the finely appointed room. Gleaming furniture was complemented by a plethora of landscape paintings – each presented as if it belonged in a gallery. She would have said it had a woman's touch, but perhaps that was to make Mr Grey's usual guests feel at ease. From what she knew of him, based only on snippets of gossip, he was renowned as a charming lover. Attentive, and – they whispered – as handsome as the devil. Anne had witnessed more than one lady blush when confiding tales of his dalliances.

Outside the bedchamber, Mr Grey was known as a generous philanthropist, donating to causes such as women's suffrage and workers' rights.

But Anne's father despised him. Stanton Sheffield deemed Mr Grey nothing more than a manipulative scoundrel who used whatever means necessary to push progressive bills through Parliament, seeking to alter the fabric of

British society. Bribery, threats, intimidation – whatever it took.

Mr Richard Grey, renowned lover and most notorious rogue in London, was a Machiavellian schemer to rival Anne's father.

And that was precisely the sort of man she needed.

Anne stared up at one of the paintings on the wall, mustering her bravery. The colours splashed upon the canvas were bold and striking, painting a picture of a tranquil beach at dawn. Yet, the serene vista failed to soothe her nerves. She inhaled deeply, attempting to steady herself as the sound of her breathing echoed in the chamber.

Then footsteps echoed behind her, followed by a voice as rich and thick as warm honey.

"Miss Sheffield."

Anne turned and went entirely still.

Rumours had not done him justice. She'd heard Mr Grey was handsome but didn't expect him to be as beautiful as some Biblical seraph. Like warrior angels in paintings, his hair gleamed like spun gold, and his eyes were the most startling shade of blue she had ever seen. It wasn't their colour that surprised Anne, but the intensity. He frankly and shamelessly assessed her as if Mr Grey envisioned her stripped bare and vulnerable.

A heated look, to be sure, but more than that. Astute and analytical, as if he were an inventor examining a strange contraption, trying to determine where he might place her – or how he might use her.

But Anne had grown accustomed to men using her.

She planned to use this one back.

Anne looked away first, back to the painting of the coastline. The name signed at the bottom was Caroline Stafford, who Anne recognised as the Duchess of Hastings. Her Grace's artworks were all the rage among the *beau monde* for their distinctive style and vivid colouring.

"You enjoy the duchess's work," she murmured, still trying to gather herself. His proximity did not help matters. "You have several of her paintings."

Mr Grey moved to stand beside her. "Do you like them?"

"The strokes show a lack of restraint." Then, with a slight smile, she added, "But the duchess does this deliberately. It adds to the wildness, the..." He was staring at her now, and Anne tried not to squirm under his scrutiny. Her smile disappeared. "... The atmosphere," she finally finished. "They're extraordinary. But I suppose she must hear that often."

"I'll still be certain to let her know what you think," he said. "But something tells me you didn't come to my home in the middle of the night to compliment my choice of art."

Anne exhaled heavily. "No," she replied with a note of resignation. "No, I didn't."

How did Anne begin her audacious appeal for his aid? It was scandalous, immoral, even – but she was desperate.

Mr Grey broke in on her thoughts. "Shall I ring for tea?" he asked, as if he could sense her distress.

Anne had no patience for pleasantries. "No, I don't want tea."

"If I may be so bold," he said, rather gently, "the easiest

option in this circumstance is to plainly tell me what it is you need."

"You weren't the least bit flustered to find me here," she murmured, almost to herself. "But I suppose I'm not the only woman to show up on your doorstep."

"True enough," he admitted. "Can't recall any being the daughter of a standing politician, though – that's a first for me."

"What about the daughter of a man who despises and curses your very existence?"

Mr Grey smiled slowly. "Not a first for me. I have something of a reputation among fathers who would rather see me hanged than breathing."

"For your wild ways," she stated with a nod.

"Indeed," he replied, his grin growing wider. "For my wild ways, my wicked heart, and my habit of fucking their daughters."

Anne inhaled sharply as that word passed Mr Grey's lips – a vulgarity she'd never heard before. Surely it wasn't something one uttered in respectable company.

"Are you trying to shock me?" she asked, her spine straightening into resolve. *It won't work.*

"I have a talent for shocking people, whether I intend to or not." When she didn't say anything, he added, "But if it's debauchery you're after, I have principles against debutantes."

"A rake with principles." Anne studied him with interest. "How astonishing."

Mr Grey raised a brow. "You wouldn't believe the sort of mayhem I'd cause without them."

"So you possess a glimmer of integrity – though it should have been obvious, given your partiality for progressive politics. You have an impressive habit of annoying my father."

He inclined his head, and a spark of humour lit his eyes. "Ah, now we're making progress. It's my life's mission to aggravate Tories. My *raison d'être*, as it were."

A reluctant smile tugged at the corners of her lips. She still couldn't look at him directly. Her father had always spoken about not meeting a man's gaze – it assumed equality when none existed, he claimed. He'd told Anne to maintain her downward attention out of humility and respect – a habit she despised even as it became second nature.

But then Mr Grey reached out and lifted her chin with a gentle finger, coaxing her eyes to meet his. Anne jerked away with a soft gasp at the sudden contact.

He dropped his hand and gave her an apologetic look. "Easy," Mr Grey said, his voice deep and calming, as if he sensed her inner turmoil. He dropped his hand. "I'm so sorry. I should have asked permission before I touched you."

All at once, Anne felt the humiliating sting of hot, unshed tears. How strange it was to speak to a man who regarded her as important – who sought her consent.

It surprised her that Mr Grey, the cunning manipulator that he was, understood such things better than anyone she'd met.

"Yes," she whispered. "You have some integrity despite your habit of blackmailing politicians."

Mr Grey scowled. "If you're here because you want me to blackmail someone for you—"

"On the contrary. It's your skills in seduction I require." She straightened, determined to show no hint of vulnerability. "I need your help to find a husband."

Rivulnerability - was too delicate to mock.

∽ 2 ∽

Richard stifled a laugh. Miss Sheffield's face – that bit of vulnerability – was too delicate to mock.

"Miss Sheffield, as we've already established, I'm a rake. Marriage is not for me."

Her finely arched brow rose. "I said I need your help to find a husband, not that I want to marry *you*."

This time, he let his amusement show. "Finding a suitable husband for an eligible debutante is not the usual purview of a rake."

Though he appreciated a beautiful woman as much as the next man. Anne Sheffield was lovely, with graceful curves and fragile features, and that hair – it was so red and vibrant, it seemed artificially enhanced. Her eyes surprised him most: they were wide enough to be innocent but filled with an awareness he hadn't seen in many debutantes.

When their gazes locked, his world had tipped. And he did something too damn bold – he'd reached out and touched her without a second thought: no manners, no permission, just raw, reckless instinct.

Like an idiot.

But he was on edge. What the hell had possessed Anne to come to him? Stanton Sheffield despised him with a fervour reserved for only the most loathsome pests. And Richard returned the feeling tenfold. The mutual contempt between the two men was enough to incinerate whole cities.

It was Sheffield who had taught Richard that politics was a brutal game. Progress required lying, cheating, and stealing, because bastards like him wouldn't let the country move an inch without a vicious fight. And Sheffield fought dirty, with no qualms about using his influence to crush anyone who opposed him, and no regard for honour or ethics.

Richard doubted Sheffield treated his daughter any better than his opponents in Parliament – otherwise, she wouldn't be there talking about marriage.

Richard had to hand it to her, though: it took brass neck to take a risk on a man with his reputation – and in the middle of the night, no less.

"We've already established that you are not just another rake, Mr Grey," Miss Sheffield remarked, her tone as composed as the paintings of the seaside that graced his walls. "You're a master strategist with enough political secrets to put the Vatican to shame, I suspect."

His smile lingered. "Perhaps. But you're not here for secrets."

"No, I'm here for your very pretty public face," Anne said, her voice edged with impatience. "You're an expert in matters of seduction, yes? Assuming those rumours weren't all lies." She turned her gaze back to the painting, as if to veil her embarrassment at what she was about to propose. "*Fucking*, I believe you called it when you attempted to shock me earlier. I'd like you to teach me."

Bloody hell. Was he dreaming? Or had his life taken some wild turn and this woman who knew his underhanded dealings came for lessons in lovemaking? Good God.

He swallowed hard. "Miss Sheffield. There is a world of difference between marriage and tupping. Otherwise, I'd already have a wife. I understand you're something of a sheltered young—"

Anne glared daggers at him. "Do *not* condescend to me." Her temper lit like a candle, nearly singeing him with the heat of her outrage. "I know what I want – to learn everything about seducing a man. I intend to make him so desperate to marry me that he'll risk my father's wrath and procure a special licence to wed me without his permission. That is what I *need*, Mr Grey. That is what I require from you. I'm not so sheltered and naïve to think this will be a simple task, which is precisely why I'm here in the middle of the bloody night asking a man reputed to be the most notorious rake in London for help."

The air crackled between them like fire sparks. They were almost touching, and her breaths came in short, shallow rasps beneath her cloak. What would make a woman so desperate? Unless...

"Sheffield intends for you to marry the Duke of Kendal, yes?" he asked carefully. At her startled look, he made an impatient noise. "Information is a currency I accept. You didn't think I managed to manipulate associates of your father without learning a thing or two, did you?"

Miss Sheffield lifted her chin. "We're to wed in three months."

"I also understand," he continued, "that he is considerably older than you—"

She laughed, but it had no joy – just rancour and bitterness. "Sir, if a man were kind and treated me well, I'd marry one twice the duke's age."

Richard went still. "I see," he said softly.

He had some sense of honour, as crooked as it was. His sister, Alexandra, was an authoress who wrote about the injustices women endured behind closed doors.

At first, he read her writings solely to impress a widowed countess who was a fervent advocate for women's suffrage and saw him as nothing more than a handsome face and a physique suited for her pleasure. Even after their affair ended, he continued to peruse his sister's work, but now to argue on behalf of those causes with men of influence who, otherwise, would never have cared.

One such cause was the belief that women were little more than property. His sister would probably kill him if he let Miss Sheffield leave tonight without assistance, and he'd never forgive himself.

"You see what?" Miss Sheffield asked him in a tight voice.

"He's hurt you. Kendal."

She stilled, her expression cold and detached, though Richard noticed how tightly she clutched her cloak. "I don't wish to discuss my betrothed. Will you teach me or not?"

Richard attempted to be gentle in his approach. "As much as I'd like to help, what you propose is risky for me. If we were caught, I'd consider it my duty to wed you."

"Oh, if only it were that simple," Miss Sheffield

murmured. "The duke could find me naked in the arms of another man and still meet me at the end of the aisle in three months. No, I require a husband with influence, and I've no intention of asking you to interrupt your cherished existence of debauchery and intrigue." She cast a glance in his direction. "I suppose it's easier to indulge in corruption outside the halls of government than within them."

Richard shrugged. "I won't deny it."

"And so I am here" – she continued, as if he had never spoken – "to ask for lessons and to propose a bargain."

His suspicion sparked to life at once. This was a daughter of Stanton Sheffield, after all. "What sort of bargain?" Richard asked warily.

Miss Sheffield's lips twitched with a smirk that formed the most alluring damn dimple on her left cheek. "My word, what a look that is. I'm not offering you a poisoned chalice, Mr Grey. I've heard you're seeking support for a bill allowing common men the right to private ballots. My father opposes it – landlords find it convenient to control tenant voting. And he believes if the Irish vote privately, they'll force the issue of home rule."

He stiffened, but kept his face stoic and unreadable. "I'm aware of that. What are you proposing?"

"I'm privy to the intelligence my father has against members of Parliament to influence their decision on this," Miss Sheffield continued. "So I'm offering a trade: your lessons for that information."

"You want to help me blackmail people?" Richard asked doubtfully.

Miss Sheffield lifted a shoulder in a delicate shrug. "How you use the material is up to you. But I assure you:

that bill won't be brought to vote. If Gladstone forces the issue, members of his party will cross the floor and face the consequences to hide worse scandals. My father would love to watch the disaster unfold."

Richard exhaled a deep breath and studied Miss Sheffield. He had men in his employ from Whitechapel, and the MPs for the East End counted among his friends. To say nothing of a few other palms he kept greased if he needed information. And he'd promised to do whatever it took to get the bill brought to vote and passed.

It would be easy to let this woman walk out the door and say he'd done what he could, but it would be a lie. Politics didn't come easily to him. The game was ruthless, cut-throat, and dishonest. And Stanton Sheffield played it better than anyone.

"How do I know you're telling me the truth?" He couldn't quite bring himself to trust Sheffield's daughter. "What politician would ever entrust his daughter with sensitive information?"

A tense silence filled the air, rife with unspoken suspicion. Then, just when Richard thought she meant to take her leave, she released a gentle breath and began.

"Your foyer has a small shelf of books – thirty-three in all. It appears you favour the classics, despite the disorganised state of the bookshelves. Six volumes on the decline of the Roman Empire – though you're missing the second volume, which I find rather egregious, as it contains some remarkable tales from religious clashes. The remaining five are on philosophy, two of which are *A Discourse on Inequality* in both French and English—"

"Stop. *Stop*." Christ, his head was throbbing. "Are you

trying to tell me your father uses you as some sort of... personal record-keeper?"

Her lips twitched in a half-smile. "Yes, Mr Grey, that's precisely what I am saying. Do try to keep up – I'm in something of a hurry. Do we have a deal or not?"

He was tempted to ask for more time to consider her proposal, but he doubted she'd offer it twice. He'd never have another opportunity to glean information that would destroy Stanton Sheffield; it was his daughter or nothing.

"Fine," he said, almost reluctantly. "We have a deal."

Miss Sheffield nodded, as if she'd expected the answer, but it gave her no pleasure. "Then we'll start tomorrow night. I'll come by again—"

"Not here." He couldn't chance the possibility of anyone seeing her. At her questioning look, he said, "I need to speak to a friend of mine, a lady with an impeccable reputation. She'll issue you an invitation for a long visit, so this will appear to be a proper arrangement."

Her expression darkened. "Mr Grey, I don't think you understand my predicament. My father won't permit me to leave the house unaccompanied – for any length of time. Even to visit ladies of impeccable reputation."

Richard leaned closer, pausing only when he heard her quick intake of breath. He wasn't certain if it was attraction or fear, and he had no desire to encourage either. "He will not refuse this invitation, I assure you."

She searched his gaze for a moment, as if she were about to argue, but she only nodded once. "Fine. I will await your word."

As she started for the door, he called out, "Shall I arrange a carriage for you?"

She paused. "No. If I don't hear from you, I'll enjoy this hour of freedom while it lasts. I've no authority to force your compliance, and I wouldn't use my father's methods even if I had. All I ask is that you don't lie to me."

Who was this woman with such strength in her voice? What experiences had honed her resilience? Richard wanted to know – he wanted to know *her*.

Before he could answer, she swept out of the house, past his butler.

The door clicked shut, and his home seemed to sigh into stillness. And Richard felt as if his world had just tipped on its axis.

∽ 3 ∽

"If you could turn towards the light, please."

Richard stood stark naked in a well-lit chamber as Caroline Stafford, Duchess of Hastings, scrutinised the canvas before her. He shifted closer to the window, gritting his teeth against the pain in his back and legs. It was no surprise that she wanted him in such a position – it displayed his muscles to their best advantage.

The duchess was known publicly for creating serene landscapes of the English countryside. Under the *nom de guerre* Henry Morgan, she created extraordinary, scandalous pieces of the male form – with Richard as one of her many subjects. Caroline obscured the visages of her models, but the stares of thousands of art patrons had feasted appraising eyes upon every inch of his body. He'd been told of women so charmed by his physique they were rendered senseless.

Richard couldn't deny the admiration was a balm to his vanity, but standing still was a special sort of torture.

"Not a twitch," Caroline declared from across the studio, her paintbrush suspended expectantly. "You're starting to fidget."

"Caro," Richard drawled, "I'm standing here with my arse on full display for your painting whims. Surely you can show a little mercy for my aching muscles."

She gave a delicate sigh of concession. "Very well, but only because you're so pretty. And, unlike my other models, you have the good sense to know when to be quiet."

He laughed as he adjusted his pose slightly. "Is that your way of telling me to shut up?"

She leaned forward, making deft strokes with her brush. "When I want you to shut up, I'll say it. Lift your arm higher… Yes, just there. Perfect."

He hadn't expected this consequence of his visit today – standing for hours while the duchess captured his likeness on canvas. When inspiration struck, Caroline proved a most formidable force. Her eyes lit up as soon as she imagined him in a scene from one of her paintings – envisaging a new angle of his body to explore, a different character for him to play.

At present, the duchess had appointed him as a hunter: stringing his bow and nocking his arrow.

He had grown accustomed to being Caroline's "muse" – a role she strictly limited to professional bounds. Her husband's extended absences presented Caroline with ample opportunity for romantic dalliances, but she never took advantage. Sadly, when her husband returned to London, the couple kept their distance from each other.

Caroline told Richard it had been seven years since she last saw Hastings.

Seven years wasted, Richard thought, trying not to stare down at the attractive woman sitting before the easel.

If Richard had a wife like Caroline at home, he'd spend half of every day in bed with her, not gallivanting around the world, ignoring her. Despite Caroline's cheerful façade, Richard knew loneliness drove her to art and patronage work to fill the void left by her absent husband.

"You still haven't given me an answer about Miss Sheffield," Richard said.

A house party at Caroline's sprawling country estate was the perfect cover for Miss Sheffield's scheme. While her guests were occupied with the witless japes and trifling chatter of the high society, Richard would teach Miss Sheffield in the privacy of the garden cottage.

He was looking forward to the instruction. But the house party? He'd rather drink hemlock.

"Stop making that face," Caroline said. "You look as if you're about to murder someone."

"It's a house party," Richard said. "I just might."

Caroline shook her head. "I hope the information Miss Sheffield offers you is worth the trouble. I can't imagine what it is since she seems as daft as a post. She could talk for hours about her hat collection."

Richard had never met Miss Sheffield until she appeared on his doorstep, so it surprised him that people claimed she had more beauty than brains. He assumed being Stanton Sheffield's daughter had compelled her to conceal the caustic wit she displayed in his parlour. Her father was notorious for his ridiculous views on how women should act: obedient, biddable, and silent.

Stupid, Richard finished the thought with a scowl. It had to be galling for her.

"She's not daft," he stated firmly.

"Oh?" Caroline stopped and looked up quizzically. "Well, that's interesting. But makes sense when I think about it."

"How so?"

Caroline shrugged and bent close to make some fine brushstrokes. "Sheffield watches his daughter intently at social events," she said. "It's quite uncomfortable to witness."

Now that Richard knew Miss Sheffield was privy to political secrets, he wagered Stanton wanted to ensure they never saw the light. *Cunning bastard.*

"Is that a yes, then?"

"Richard," the duchess said with an impatient flash of her eyes, "you're asking me to assemble a house party with very little notice at the beginning of the season. Are you deliberately trying to drive me mad?"

"I thought you enjoyed a challenge."

A long-suffering sigh escaped her lips. "I didn't say I *couldn't* do it, you odious man. You know I am perfectly willing to do whatever you ask, short of murder."

"*Whatever* I ask?" He flashed a wolfish grin. "To the bedchamber, then."

Caroline simply ignored him and continued to paint, undaunted by his attempts at flirtation. "Still married, dearest."

"Didn't stop you from asking me once before."

It was how they'd met. Two years after her husband's abandonment, she had propositioned Richard to be her lover. She couldn't go through with it, of course – so she asked him to pose for her sketches instead. He consented on a lark – and before long, they had become fast friends.

Caroline's smile was rueful. "And now I'm convinced I'd probably break you. You're not for me."

"Is that why the duke spends all his time away? Did you break him, Caro?"

Her lips drew tight as she leaned back in her chair. "Something like that," she said, rather curtly. "I'm done for the day, I think."

Richard reached for his dressing gown and shrugged it on. "I'm sorry. I've offended you, haven't I?"

Caroline yanked off her gloves, dragging her hands down her face in a weary motion. "No," she replied, her voice as thin as a thread. "It's Hastings. He's on holiday in Edinburgh, so I expect him to return shortly and resume his favourite pastime."

"Debating in the Lords?"

"Avoiding me like the plague."

Richard winced. "Ah."

"Right. Unless his sense of duty finally prevails, and he gives me a baby."

He hesitated, then ventured, "Why does he keep eluding you?"

Richard recalled Caroline's debut; her beauty and charm had made her incomparable, despite her lack of dowry. When the Duke of Hastings hastily married her, the *ton* raised eyebrows – and when he abandoned her after the wedding vows, even more tongues started wagging.

Richard had met Hastings many times, and the man

hadn't seemed a fool – but surely only a complete and utter lackwit would dodge a woman like Caroline for seven long years.

She forced a smile. "Perhaps I'll tell you one day." Before he could ask anything else, she gestured towards her easel. "Well, what do you think? Is it horrid? Should I burn it?"

Richard stepped closer to look. In the scene's centre, a bold hunter stood with his bow in hand, ready to strike. His powerful form had begun to take shape beneath Caroline's brushstrokes. She'd painted his sinewy legs and defined arms, even crafted the veins on his hands with exquisite detail. As always, her work was stunning.

"I wish you'd take credit for these," he said quietly. "Not use a man's name."

Caroline huffed a laugh. "Don't you know? If a man paints a naked body, it's art. When a woman does it, it's pornography." She began packing away her supplies. "I'll send the invitations and the letter to Miss Sheffield's father. I hope you comprehend what you're doing."

4

S tanton Sheffield's eyes narrowed as he read the letter. "What is this?" he asked Anne, resting his hand on the back of the oxblood leather chair.

The air was heavy with the pungent scent of cigars and the faint musty smell of old books lining the shelves. Anne focused on the mahogany desk, where a glass inkwell sat atop a stack of papers.

Because she wouldn't have been able to hide her delight.

Mr Grey had done it. The invitation was more than Anne had hoped for – her father couldn't turn down a summons from the Duchess of Hastings. Despite the political disagreements between the duke and Anne's father, the duchess was renowned for her grace and poise.

How in the world had Mr Grey convinced *Caroline Hastings* to assist in their scandalous endeavour? Anne hoped he hadn't blackmailed a duchess.

Her father's deep voice snapped Anne from her reverie.

"I didn't realise you were on such familiar terms with Caroline Hastings."

Anne's cheeks burned under Stanton's scrutiny, sweat pearling at her temples. The fire blazed in the hearth, casting golden light across the room and reflecting off Stanton's coal-dark eyes.

He was a towering figure, even by the lofty standards of their class. His broad shoulders were clothed in luxurious velvet, and his stare was as hard and unyielding as his ambition.

Wealth, power, and the desire to maintain them had been the only constants in his life. He'd married for money, gained political influence through intimidation and deceit, and become richer still through bribery.

Anne managed a tight-lipped smile. "We met at a few social events, and I was taken with her paintings when we visited Rivington Estate last year," she said, her voice carefully controlled. "Do you recall, Papa? I asked your permission before writing to her to say as much."

Her father had permitted a sojourn to the countryside to soften his image for a bribe. They donned their respective parts: she, the submissive daughter, content with the trifling pursuit of hat shopping and nothing more. And he, the affectionate patriarch who would do anything to ensure his daughter's happiness.

It was all too easy to fool society – no one wanted to delve any deeper into what lurked beyond their gilded prison walls.

Stanton waved away her explanation with an impatient gesture. "What does she want?"

Anne bit her lower lip, her hands trembling as she fiddled with the fabric of her dress. If he refused, she had no options.

No future except the one he decided for her.

She chose her words carefully. "Kendal and I are to be wed in three months," she murmured. "And as his duchess, it's my duty to ensure his happiness in all things—"

"*And?*"

"—so I hoped to ask Caroline Hastings for advice on how I might be the perfect wife for him."

Anne summoned the courage to meet her father's eyes. He stared at her with an intensity that seemed to pierce through her, searching for any indication that something wasn't quite right in her story. She quickly looked away, her pulse skittering.

"Kendal has given you instruction on how to please him. He has for years now," Stanton said.

Anne suppressed a shudder. From the moment Stanton declared her betrothal to the duke, Kendal had been a spectre over her shoulder. Her personal phantom, never letting her forget that her life – her every choice – was his to decide. With marriage, she'd be passed from one man's grasp to another – an exchange of ownership.

What joys would she be allowed? What dreams might she pursue? What happiness would she ever know?

But she already knew the answers.

None.

You will be nothing.

Taking a deep breath, Anne forced a smile onto her lips. "Yes, Papa. The duke has told me what a man expects from a wife. I'd like guidance from a duchess on succeeding in the role she's filled so well."

Stanton tapped his finger against his desk, absorbing her statement carefully. "No. I can't accompany you," he finally said. "I'll be gone for a few days before Parliament reconvenes. Pressing business up north."

Anne's heart sank. Every moment he stayed away from London was precious to her, but his servants would report any suspicious activity. Her scheme had to happen now or never.

She tugged at the lace of her dress, averting her gaze in a show of mock embarrassment.

"It's only that other women have mothers and aunts to guide them before marriage," she said in a small voice.

Stanton's attention swung back to her. "Ah. I see." He let out a breath, considering her words. "Very well. Seek the duchess's counsel. I think Kendal will be pleased you're receiving advice from a woman so far above reproach. Were it anyone else, I wouldn't be so lenient."

Relief crashed over Anne as she realised he was letting her go. She had to bite her lip to keep herself from outwardly expressing her joy.

"Thank you, Papa."

She would not fail.

⌒ 5 ⌒

Anne had no choice but to obey her father's command to take a maid with her.

She nestled into the cushions of the private train compartment as the other passengers boarded, the rustle of her silk dress barely audible. The luxurious surroundings of velvet drapery, gilded fixtures, and mahogany panelling faded into the background as she grappled with the weight of her father's control.

Mary – her maid and Stanton's informant – peered up from her book with a smile that offered little comfort. The walls seemed to inch closer, suffocating Anne in the small space as her mind worked. She clenched her jaw as she struggled against the rising wave of fear. She had to get rid of the girl before they arrived at Ravenhill. But Mary wouldn't leave – Stanton had made sure of that. Maybe Anne could buy her silence?

Then the compartment door opened with a jolt that froze Anne in place.

It was none other than Mr Grey.

Even among the bustling passengers of the train's corridor, he stood out – and Anne couldn't look away. Her thoughts scattered like a flock of startled birds. How could one man demand such unwavering attention with seemingly no effort? Who was he to have such an influence over her?

"Mr Grey," she said with forced civility. "What an unexpected pleasure."

His gaze sought hers and held it. She'd forgotten the full force of those astute blue eyes – the full force of *him*. His bearing was as confident and commanding as ever, and his attire spoke of effortless sophistication – dark grey trousers and a matching overcoat, a fitting ensemble to enhance his broad shoulders. Mr Grey's body was made for confrontation and pleasure, not leisure. His dishevelled golden hair hinted at other pursuits – or other beds.

Anne's mouth pressed into a thin line. Unbidden, her mind conjured a vision of him frolicking with some other woman between satin sheets. She pushed the image away in a rush of displeasure.

Mr Grey could not hear her thoughts, but his slow, wicked grin suggested he *read* them just fine.

Anne tore her gaze from his, feeling the weight of his scrutiny like a physical force. She couldn't endure it for long – no more than one could withstand a relentless siege. In mere moments, he had launched an assault on her senses, stripped her bare, and left her exposed.

It was alarming.

"Oh, I'm *full* of unexpected pleasures, Miss Sheffield." His sultry glance quickened Anne's pulse. "You'll understand that in time."

Mary watched them both shrewdly. She undoubtedly recognised Mr Grey's name from Anne's father's rants.

His notice shifted to her maid with an imperceptible narrowing of his regard. "And who is this?" His voice dropped an octave – deep and smooth, warm honey poured over velvet.

Her maid stood and curtsied nervously. "Mary, sir."

"Miss Mary," he purred, like a tiger coaxing its next meal. "If I may speak to you for a moment?"

Ah, poor Mary. Lord, but Mr Grey set his charm to work, it was a dark art no different from witchery.

He smiled an utterly beautiful smile and beckoned. The girl drew closer, helpless to resist. Anne watched in fascination. She wondered if she ought to find it distasteful how quickly he could enthral a woman. But wasn't that why she sought him out? Wasn't this the lesson she wished to learn? With only three weeks to snag a husband, Anne had little time to ponder the ethics of it.

He leaned down and murmured into Mary's ear.

"Oh, I couldn't possibly!" she protested.

Mr Grey whispered something else. Good grief, was he trying to seduce Anne's maid?

Then he took a fold of bills out of his pocket and thrust it into the girl's hands. "Yes?"

"And I'm off," Mary said brightly. She winked at Anne. "Enjoy yer holiday, miss."

Anne could only sputter a reply as the girl snatched up her shawl and bounced out of the carriage. Mere heartbeats later, the whistle blew and the train lurched into motion.

Without a word of explanation, Mr Grey claimed the seat across from Anne. He removed his hat and gave her a look so heated it could start a forest fire. He reclined with his ankles crossed and one arm lazily draped over the back of the bench. Tension thrummed in the air, palpable as a physical force.

Anne's cheeks grew warm. That compartment was not big enough for him. He took up an excessive amount of space, more than was humanly possible, as if he had somehow managed to squeeze in additional inches. No, she didn't like this. There was... too much of him.

Too much of *everything*.

Anne fought the urge to huddle into the corner and tuck herself away. She had to regain control of the situation, even if it meant buckling under his scrutiny.

"What did you say to my maid?" she demanded.

Mr Grey shrugged. "I offered her a post with a friend of mine," he said evenly. "Higher wages, holidays, and a more kindly employer than she has at present. Then I gave her some money for incentive."

Anne's lips parted in surprise before she could school her expression back into neutrality. "How did you know my father isn't kind to his servants?"

"Simple," he murmured as his gaze sharpened on hers. "Because he isn't kind to *you*."

Anne's every muscle jolted in response. She concentrated on the passing scenery, her fingers curling hard into her palms. As the train continued to chug forward, ever closer to their destination, its steady rhythm offered her no comfort. Her breath came in quick snatches – too fast.

Mr Grey seemed to find something amusing in Anne's distress, and his mirth only intensified her discomfort.

Forcing a calmness into her voice she didn't feel, she said, "We will establish rules, you and I, if we are to work together."

"Rules," he repeated, eyebrows lifting slightly. "What sort of rules?"

"For how to conduct ourselves, of course. First, I would prefer not to discuss my fiancé or my father unless it's necessary for your efforts." Her chin rose a fraction of an inch. "Do you understand?"

He nodded once. "Quite."

"Second: in exchange for each lesson, I'll provide information about my father's colleagues, including men he's purchased and blackmailed. Their identities will be at my discretion. At the end of the house party, I intend to deliver you a complete dossier regardless of whether I've successfully secured a husband."

Mr Grey tilted his head slightly. "You would give me so much, even if you fail?"

Anne pressed her lips together. Perhaps she should not have made such an early concession. If she were a man, Stanton would have lectured her on showing her hand too early. One cannot make demands when one had given the game away.

But Anne was not her father. She was not heartless, and she would not be ruthless, either.

"My father's allies force tenants to vote against their best interests or risk being thrown into the streets. They deserve to have their say in a private ballot. I couldn't live with myself if I didn't do everything possible to right that wrong."

Mr Grey studied Anne, his expression unreadable. He finally broke the silence with a low, "You care about this?"

"My father might be a monster, sir, but I'm not. All I ask is that you treat me with integrity and honesty."

"Is that rule three?"

"If you like."

Mr Grey extended his hand, pausing mere inches away from her. Offering her an unspoken request for permission. As if she were a skittish creature he meant to soothe into trust. Anne slid her palm into his but was surprised when he proceeded to remove her glove slowly, one finger at a time.

"Rule four," he said, his voice low and gentle. "Nothing happens between us without your consent. Is that understood? Will you allow me to touch you for lessons?"

His bare skin pressed against hers, firm yet tender. No one had ever asked Anne's permission before. It left her exposed, vulnerable.

Her throat felt tight and dry. "What if I don't like it? You touching me?"

He withdrew his hand at once. "Then I'll stop."

The silence hung between them, charged with the raw, electric tension of something about to break. Anne's heart thundered in her chest, a wild, unbridled thing that threatened to break free of its confines. She was too afraid to look at him now, too scared to ask her next question.

She took a deep, fortifying breath and whispered, "What if I don't want you to stop?"

He hesitated, ever so briefly, before his fingers returned to her face. Featherlight and tenderly exploring the curve of her jawline, then down the line of her neck and over the wings of her collarbone. "Then I'll continue."

Anne shivered beneath his touch, a pleasure so exquisite it was anathema to her. She leaned back, her skin on fire, torn between wanting him to stay and wanting him to go. The dizzying sensation threatened to overwhelm her.

It was too much.

Anne caught his wrist, exerting just enough pressure to keep him at bay.

"Ah," he said softly. "I believe that ought to be our fifth rule: consent can be withdrawn at any time."

The oppressive stillness was broken only by the rattling of the train, a monotonous rhythm slower than Anne's pulse. Her attention fell to his hand. He'd been in a fight – the evidence was made plain by his knuckles, bruised and scabbed, flecked with dried blood – but it hadn't been he who'd taken a beating. He'd done the pummelling.

"Have you hit someone, Mr Grey? Several times, from the look of things."

"No one who didn't want to be hit." At her confused expression, he offered a smile. "My brother and I are in the same boxing club. He was in a mood to punish himself yesterday."

She shivered, not understanding why any man would inflict such brutality upon another. "Over what?"

Mr Grey shrugged. "He's besotted with a woman."

"I don't understand."

"Can't say I do, either." He traced her knuckles with his thumb. "Your skin is so smooth, unscarred. You've never dealt violence." He paused to meet her eyes. "I hope you'd feel no qualms about using it if someone ever threatened you."

Anne's body shook with an exhale that seemed to rattle her frame with a force that rivalled the train beneath them. Could he hear her heart? She hoped not.

"Rule six," she said, gently pushing his hand away. "You'll be honest with me about my suitors. I don't want…" At his frown, she cleared her throat. "I don't want a younger version of my fiancé. To trade one prison cell for another."

34

"I can't attest to how they treat women privately, but I'll do my best to advise you. Caro will, too."

Anne drew back slightly. He must know the duchess well to use her given name so freely. She trailed a finger along the wooden edge of the window as the train barrelled through the countryside.

"Caro? Is the duchess your lover, then?" The words slipped out before she could weigh the wisdom of such a question. "Sorry, never mind." Anne waved a hand. "I only wondered how you convinced her to entertain my scheme. She's aware of why I'm here?"

Mr Grey's lip twitched. "She is." He sounded amused. "And no, Caro and I aren't lovers. We're friends. The rest is not my secret to tell."

"I see," Anne said, not truly grasping the situation. But it didn't matter; he was only in her life for a short time. "Rule seven," she continued. "At the end of this fortnight, we'll return to being strangers. No one can learn about—"

"I assure you," he interjected, "I'll be discreet."

"Allow me to finish. I know how politics operates, Mr Grey. The cut-throat tactics and the lack of ethics. I'll provide you with enough information to bring down my father, but you must not ruin *me* to do it. Do you understand?"

His nod was resolute. "Yes."

She sat back. "Good. Then I believe we have an equitable arrangement."

The Duke and Duchess of Hastings' residence, Ravenhill, was a magnificent display of opulence and grandeur, like something straight out of a fairytale.

As the carriage approached the estate, Anne's breath caught in her throat. The sprawling grounds were a veritable wonderland, with towering spires that reached for the heavens and gleaming turrets that seemed to pierce the azure sky. The gazes of numerous stone gargoyles kept watch as the horses came to a halt at the main entrance.

But despite the beauty of the estate, Anne couldn't shake the apprehension that gnawed at her gut – a nervous energy, a mix of excitement and trepidation that made her heart race with a fierce, restless longing. The imposing towers cast their long shadows over her, making her feel small – and quite intimidated.

"The duchess herself isn't nearly as formidable, I assure you," Mr Grey said with a hint of amusement, as if he'd heard her spoken thoughts.

Anne tried to relax, unable to meet his gaze. "We've met. I doubt she was particularly impressed with me."

"What makes you say that?"

She forced a shrug, though it felt more like a shudder. "You know something about public roles, don't you? Mine was to impersonate an especially shallow idiot."

To put it lightly. Anne would have preferred to avoid speaking at social gatherings. Being introverted was preferable to appearing foolish. However, her father would not allow her to remain quiet at balls; she had a specific role to fulfil.

Mr Grey shot Anne a pitying glance, but she spared him no notice. She was here today, determined to save herself.

The Duchess of Hastings greeted them with a smile as they descended from the carriage. Anne had always admired her grace and poise – and that singular independence she craved.

The duchess took both of Anne's hands in her own. "Miss Sheffield, it's so lovely to meet you."

"We've already met, duchess," Anne replied with a hint of amusement. "At Lady Blythe's garden party – though I don't suppose you remember me?"

I was the ninny prattling on about her hat collection.

"I believe I encountered another debutante there of similar size and stature. But from what Richard told me, that wasn't *you*, was it?"

Oh, the duchess could not understand what those words meant. Anne was more than just a dolt with a fluttering fan and expensive silks.

Anne could finally act like herself.

"No." She swallowed the emotion in her voice, trying to sound calm. "It wasn't me."

The other woman smiled. "Come. I'll show you to your room, and you can tell me all about yourself."

"And me?" Richard asked jovially, a devilish twinkle in his eye. "Do I not get a greeting?"

The duchess fixed him with an arched brow, but amusement danced in her gaze. "Oh. Hello, Richard," she said sweetly, dry wit seeping from every syllable. "So nice of you to drop by – *again*."

Anne laughed in surprise.

"Do you see how she speaks to me, Miss Sheffield? No salutation. No offer of refreshment or—"

"Yes, yes," the duchess said dismissively. "Because you'll eat my entire kitchen as you always do, I expect. Come along, Miss Sheffield. Richard can look after himself." As the other woman led her towards the house, she leaned in. "And please call me Caroline. I have the feeling we'll soon be fast friends."

6

As the evening began, Anne took her place beside Richard at dinner, a vision of serenity in Caroline's lavishly appointed dining room. The polished mahogany sideboards gleamed, their rich hues casting a warm glow refracted by the crystal glasses catching and scattering the flickering light of the candles like stars.

The duchess eyed Richard from across the table. "The servants will no doubt discuss this peculiar arrangement, but tonight, let's pretend we're having a dinner party with guests. Anne, address Richard as though you are meeting him for the first time."

Amusement flickered in Richard's face as he straightened in his chair. "Are these my lessons or yours?"

"Oh, do excuse me," the duchess said wryly. "I'd forgotten that you fancied yourself an authority in the art of small talk." She took a delicate sip of her wine and leaned back, as if waiting for a performance to begin. "By all means, impress us with your wit and charm."

Richard shook his head with a short laugh. "All right, Miss Sheffield," he said, striving to keep his voice light and easy. "Speak to me as you would a dinner companion. Where did you grow up? London?"

Anne stared fixedly at her plate. What was going on in her mind? She had shown a surprising boldness by coming to his house in the dead of night, but now she seemed utterly rattled by a simple dinner conversation.

She briefly looked up to meet his gaze before returning her attention downward. "No," she replied, barely above a whisper. "In Dorset. We lived on my father's estate until he went into politics. He's the MP for Dorchester."

Richard's frown deepened. Anne avoided meeting his eyes, as if she longed to be anywhere but there.

"Do you miss it there?" he asked, hoping to draw her out.

A becoming blush crept up Anne's face. "Not at all. My father loves London."

"And what about you, Miss Sheffield?" Richard leaned in closer, scrutinising her profile with a curious expression. "Do *you* love London?"

The question hung between them, casting a pall of awkwardness over the table. Richard watched as a deepening flush coloured Anne's features, wondering if it was sincere or a carefully calculated act.

"Of course," she said, her voice pitched so low that Richard had to strain to catch it. "I think it's a remarkable place."

But the hollowness in her words was unmistakable, devoid of any genuine emotion or joy. It was as if she were reciting a memorised script.

Still, he persisted, intrigued to see how far she would take this game of pretence. "What do you like most about the city?"

Anne paused, as if collecting her thoughts. "The social life," she finally said.

Well, that was the whole point, wasn't it? Any woman with half a wit came to town with one goal in mind: to make a good match. "*And?*" he prompted, his tone heavy with sarcasm.

Anne appeared to be caught off-guard by his line of questioning, searching for an answer that wouldn't give her away. "The…" she trailed off uncertainly. "The parks."

Richard's eyes narrowed. A London park was a pitiful imitation of the lush, verdant countryside landscapes. A dreary, soul-sucking pit of filth and despair, where the smatterings of greenery were no more than a cruel tease for those trapped in the squalor.

"So you take pleasure from the parks and from being seen," Richard remarked, sarcasm lacing each syllable. "How positively mundane. Imagine being so easily satisfied."

Anne's eyes flashed with irritation, and her lips tightened into a thin line. She was no fool; she was catching on. "What's wrong with being easily satisfied?" she retorted, a hint of defiance in her tone.

"I suppose nothing," he admitted, the words spilling from his mouth before he could stop them. "And do you find anything else of interest in London?" he asked, his voice laced with incredulity. "Perhaps the theatre?"

"I've never been," she said curtly. "But I do enjoy the weather."

His patience, already stretched taut, snapped. The weather? Of all the vapid responses she could have given, she chose the weather?

Richard couldn't contain his frustration any longer. "Enough lying," he said flatly, his gaze boring into hers.

Anne's eyes widened with surprise, the flickering candlelight reflecting in their depths. "I beg your pardon?" she dared.

She likely expected him to keep playing along while she parroted every fluff and fabrication to hide her true character. But he was here to instruct her – and even a dim-witted fool could see that she was being dishonest.

Caroline cleared her throat. "*Richard*," she warned sharply, gesturing for the servants to serve the next course.

"My lesson," he reminded Caroline. He turned his full attention to Anne. "Are you telling me the truth or what you think I want to hear?"

The corner of her mouth curled up in a grimace. "People like London," she said, her voice dripping with disdain. "A *lot* of people do. It's a popular destination."

His eyes narrowed. "You admitted your father likes the city, not you. And no one – and I mean *no one* – likes it for the damn parks or the weather. You grew up in Dorset, for heaven's sake. I'm not a complete idiot."

"Fine." Anne's hands rose in an exasperated flourish. "London is horrible. It's smelly and dirty and crowded and ugly. Should I describe everything else I hate to potential husbands? Would *that* satisfy you?"

Her eyes blazed with a familiar spark, and Richard was

relieved to see it. Here was the woman who had come to his doorstep in Belgravia with a spirit as bright as a flame and a mind as sharp as a knife, refusing to be left at the mercy of fate.

"No, it wouldn't," he said. "Back to the lesson. Do you miss Dorset?"

"Yes." Anne sighed. That sound was the most honest thing he'd heard all dinner. "I miss Dorset."

A forlorn note lingered in her voice, a wistful emotion of a heart tugged in two directions. She missed Dorset. She would never truly find pleasure in the cut-throat society of London, not as long as the rolling hills of her childhood home still whispered her name.

"What do you miss?"

A flush spread across Anne's porcelain cheeks as she glanced pleadingly at Caroline. But Richard was not one to be deterred. He waved his hand insistently, determined to get an answer out of her. "Let her speak, Caro." His attention remained fixed on Anne's face. "It's a simple question."

The room descended into a hushed silence as Anne swallowed. She was clearly struggling to find the right words. "It was so warm there in the summer," she said. "The gardens on the estate were charming."

But Richard wasn't fooled. He sensed the longing in her voice, the way she wrapped herself in comfort and familiarity. He knew Anne had been taught to use lies as a shield against the truth, for she was the daughter of Stanton Sheffield, a man who valued deceit above all else. To her, lying was as natural as breathing, a necessary survival skill.

"And did you have any hobbies?" he asked, hoping to draw Anne into a more engaging conversation. "Riding, gardening, anything like that?"

Anne seemed taken aback by the question, her features rippling with indecision. "Occasionally, I'd shop for ribbons and fabrics, frocks and hats. I should tell you all about this exquisite—"

But Richard was not in the mood to indulge her. He rubbed his forehead in frustration. "That's enough," he said curtly. "Stop speaking. Do not utter another word."

Caroline gave him a scathing look. "*Richard.*"

Anne's cheeks flamed scarlet. She scooted back from the table, her entire meal forgotten. "Forgive me. I must be more tired than I realised. I'll just—"

But her sentence remained unfinished, for she had hurried out of the room. Richard watched her go, his heart sinking with a pang of guilt that he couldn't shake off.

Caroline's eyebrows shot up, her voice dripping with sarcasm. "Yes," she drawled, "your conversational skills are positively remarkable. You managed to charm Miss Sheffield so thoroughly that she fled the dinner table like a scalded cat."

Richard's face twisted into a grimace of self-disgust. 'I'm aware,' he said through gritted teeth. He was the biggest cad ever to grace Caroline's dining room.

"She was only trying to oblige you with small talk, the sort she's been trained to use her entire life. And it was like watching you shoot a sparrow out of the sky. Or kick a kitten."

God, but it was like kicking a kitten. "*I know.*"

The duchess's eyes narrowed. "Then why are you still here, you beast? *Apologise*."

Richard wasted no time. In an instant, he was on his feet to follow Anne.

∽ 7 ∽

Richard rapped his knuckles on Anne's bedchamber door.

"Thank you, but I don't need any help tonight," came the muffled response from within.

He turned the knob, startling Anne as he entered her room uninvited. "And yet, here I am, ready and willing," he said with a smirk.

Anne gasped, leaping up from the window seat. "You can't be in here! This isn't—"

"Proper?" Richard finished for her, shutting the door behind him with a decisive click. "How quaint coming from a woman who brazenly strutted into a bachelor's residence after midnight."

A charming blush spread across her cheeks, and Richard couldn't help but admire the sight. She was a study of untamed disarray, her hair a riot of curls, her dress all askew. For a moment, he imagined what she'd look like without all that corseted restraint. Was there anything more enchanting than a lady caught off-guard?

"That was different, and I did not *strut*," she said. "You told me to—"

"I was a fool," Richard said. "A complete idiot."

Anne's eyebrows shot up in surprise. "I – I mean. Well, yes, you were," she said, clearly taken aback by his candour.

"And I apologise."

She shook her head slightly and resumed her post on the window seat. "I can't say I blame you. I should have mentioned my father's rules."

"Rules?"

Richard sat beside her, careful to keep a proper distance. She may have given him leave to touch her, but he had no intention of taking advantage. She deserved more respect than that.

"Yes. He has many of them," Anne said bitterly. "He determined I should never talk about anything but the weather and fashion."

He made an incredulous noise. "Why the hell not?"

Her gaze met his before skittering away. "He didn't want to risk me sharing political information. So I was to give none at all."

Richard cursed Sheffield for treating Anne like a figurehead in his machinations. How could someone do that to a child – to his own family? Richard hated the man for smothering his daughter, and he admired Anne all the more for not yielding. He could scarcely imagine the courage it took to defy her father and come to his enemy for help.

"Let's start again, then," he said softly, reaching for her hand. Her palm was warm, smooth, so small compared with his own. "What do you miss about Dorset, Miss Sheffield? Tell me the truth this time."

"Truth, Mr Grey? I'm not sure I remember what that is."

His lips curled into a rueful smile. "You gave away the answer the moment you mentioned the countryside. Your voice gentled, almost as if you were homesick. What was it for?"

The corners of her mouth softened, and she closed her eyes. "The cliffs."

Ah, that was something. "Describe them to me."

"When the skies were clear, I would walk along the bluffs, feeling as if I could see the entire world before me. On stormy days, I watched from a distance as the rain swept in from the sea. The waves changed with each gust of wind. Have you ever seen such a thing?"

He shook his head. At that moment, he would have given anything to share in her reverie, to have taken the time to appreciate the simple pleasure of a summer thunderstorm. A lifetime of politicking had left Richard with the sense of a life half-lived, a world of chaos, from which he had forgotten how to savour the smallest pleasures.

Richard regretted it now as Miss Sheffield gave a small, fond smile at the memory. "No? It seems a shame. Nothing is more beautiful than the scent of the sea during a storm."

She spoke in a voice like smoke, low and almost husky. She had him mesmerised.

"Tell me more," Richard murmured, wishing she would keep going – sharing her stories, her secrets, her soul. "Did you walk each day?"

"No matter the weather," she confirmed. "I love the rain.

I find it invigorating." She peered at him inquisitively. "Do you?"

He instantly understood why she often kept her eyes averted. The rich umber of her irises shimmered in the candlelight, hinting at a soul so deep and warm a man might drown in its depths if he wasn't careful.

Richard studied her face, entranced by the beauty of her delicate features, and he swallowed. "I prefer it to sunshine."

The admission seemed to surprise her. "That's unexpected. May I ask why?"

He paused, his jaw tightening as he wrestled with painful memories. "My mother died on the nicest day I can recall."

"Oh," she whispered.

Anne closed the space between them, never breaking eye contact. In the silence, she raised her hand, offering comfort.

He hesitated and then, ever so slightly, nodded.

As her fingertips brushed his cheek, a jolt of electricity shot through him, igniting a fire that burned like a brand. His pulse quickened, and his breathing grew shallow as he became acutely aware of every sensation – the gentle warmth of her palm, the silky texture of her skin, and the lingering touch that seemed to spread heat through every part of his body.

"I'm so sorry for your loss."

Richard swallowed. "It was a long time ago. I barely remember her."

But he did. Lady Kent had been too consumed with punishing the earl for his infidelities to care for her offspring. And their father had been just as selfish, returning only to attend his wife's funeral. Richard had grown up with two parents more intent on hating each other than loving their children.

"Even so," she said, "it has made you dislike sunny days. It seems a shame when they're so rare."

He had never noticed how beautiful her voice was, how kindness echoed in its timbre. He could listen to her speak for hours.

"What of your mother?" he asked. "I know little about Sheffield's personal life."

Anne dropped her hand from his face and looked away. "She died when I was an infant. She and my father were in a carriage accident. He lived; she didn't."

"It must have been difficult without a mother," he said, thinking of his sister and her struggles.

"Perhaps it would have been easier," she murmured, "if I had a father who loved me as much as he loved his money."

"Miss Sheffield—"

"Don't apologise," Anne said, her voice as resolute and unyielding as the night he'd first heard it – steel against stone, a blade forged from determination and strength.

"I didn't intend to," Richard replied. "I was going to say that your father's a damned fool."

He looked at her in admiration. How could a woman so fierce invite anything but awe?

She lowered her head, but not before he saw her smile. "Thank you." She reached for the small table beside her to collect the stack of papers there. "These are for you. Information on Mr Charles Alston. His reputation in the shipping business is, to put it lightly, shady. He hides his dealings with false names."

Richard stared down at her neat handwriting and glanced

through the pages. "These are impressive. You remembered all the details?"

"Of course." Anne straightened up. "My father couldn't risk his documents getting into the wrong hands. So I became the repository of all his secrets. He relies almost entirely on my memory." She lifted her chin, a challenge in her gaze. "And I remember *everything*."

Richard's mouth curved in admiration. She had told him Stanton used her memory to document his activities, but this was remarkable. Here was the entire history of one man, stored in Anne's extraordinary mind. No wonder Stanton kept her close; she was a living, breathing record of his blackmail tactics.

When Richard remained silent, she inquired, "What will you do with it?"

"I need to send this to Thorne," he muttered, skimming the carefully detailed dates, amounts, names.

"Thorne?" she echoed. Confusion flickered over her features. "The East End gaming hell owner?"

"The same. Most of his dealings in Parliament go through me, and Nicholas Thorne has a great deal of influence in the criminal underworld. He's the one who helps me remind men of their loyalties when bills come up for a vote."

"I see." Her lips pressed together. "Then you must tell him to take care. If my father catches word—"

"I know." He reached out and clasped her hand. "You must trust me."

"I never learned how to trust people, Mr Grey." Anne sighed.

"Richard," he corrected. Gently, he stroked the back of her knuckles with his thumb. "And I'll teach you."

∽ 8 ∽

Anne had arrived at the breakfast room hours before, keen to begin the day's lessons. However, Richard had yet to make an appearance, and there was no indication from the servants that he had even stirred from his slumber. Anne's patience was wearing thin.

She stabbed at her eggs with her fork, muttering under her breath. "Where on earth is that foolish man?" she grumbled, her frustration mounting.

Men are useless, Anne thought. *Rakes worst of all*.

The Duchess of Hastings was perched at the other end of the long mahogany table, her eyes fixed on the paper in her hands. She sipped what Anne was sure to be her fifth cup of coffee – or possibly her sixth. She had given up on counting.

"Hmm?" Caroline looked up. "Did you say something, dear?"

"Mr Grey," Anne said, the name itself enough to sour her mood further. "Richard. He's absent."

Caroline shot Anne a sardonic look. "Absent? Yes, that's

one way to describe him before the clock chimes at noon. A bit like calling the sky *azure* and this coffee *essential*."

Anne pinched her nose, despairing. "Don't tell me he does this every day."

"Every single day," Caroline replied with a rueful shake of the head. "It's astonishing, really. You'd have better luck prying a dragon from its hoard than dragging Richard out of bed before noon. It would be like me getting struck by lightning – right now – in this very breakfast room. Unheard of."

Anne set down her cup of tea and leaned back in her chair. "I have sixteen days to find a husband. He ought to understand how difficult that is. Most of them are so useless they can't even tie their bootlaces, let alone muster up the courage to propose to a lady."

Richard should have warned her about his tendency to behave like a roguish reprobate. How on earth did these men get anything done?

Caroline's grin was a wicked thing. "You should go wake him up."

"Yes, yes, I should," Anne said through gritted teeth. "The scoundrel."

"Burst into his bedchamber and demand he stop lazing about."

"Yes, I—"

"And if he resists, offer him no mercy," Caroline continued, her voice growing more enthusiastic with each word. "Tug open the curtains and force him to face the day. Serenade him with a rousing ballad."

Anne raised an eyebrow. "You appear to be unduly excited for me to do this. Why?"

"Because I take great pleasure in tormenting Richard,

53

and he won't leave that bed unless you give him hell. Good luck." Caroline settled back, looking rather pleased with herself. "Let me know how it goes."

Anne marched towards Richard's bedchamber, her spine rigid with indignation.

She was paying him with inside information, and Anne expected him to uphold his side of the agreement. Not one of those lazing-about-until-the-afternoon sorts of bargains. What dastardly political schemer loitered in bed until noon, anyhow?

She flung open the door, a demand on her lips – but the words died unspoken.

Oh. My goodness.

Richard was simply mesmerising. Sunlight slanted through the closed curtains, casting a golden hue over his tanned and chiselled skin. His blankets hung low, exposing the lines of his hips.

She understood why the ladies at every garden party indulged in shameless, breathless sighs whenever they spoke his name. Noblemen, as a rule, were rarely so attractive – usually plain, so soft and arrogant and stupid, puffed up with their money and titles.

But Richard's body was a masterpiece of musculature, of tone and strength and dexterity. It certainly didn't help that – right now – he was unguarded and vulnerable, just as he might be after lovemaking.

Fucking, Anne corrected. That was what he preferred.

The word suited his state of undress, a display so sinful it seemed to be an invitation for iniquity.

For heaven's sake. Attraction was a nuisance, a waste, a distraction she couldn't afford.

"Richard," she called out.

"Mmm?" came the answer, thick with sleep.

"*Richard.*"

"*Mmmmmmmmm?*"

"Stop making that ridiculous sound and look at me."

Richard opened one eye and peered at her, his hair sticking up in every direction. "What time is it?"

"Time to wake up," Anne retorted.

He glared at her. "The *hour*?"

"Half-past ten in the morning," Anne replied with annoyance.

"You devious vixen," he muttered, pulling the pillow over his head. "It's too damn early. Come back later."

Anne made a frustrated noise and approached the bed. "Do you *really* lie in until noon every day?" she asked incredulously.

"Every day there isn't a hellion pestering me," Richard grumbled, his voice muffled. "Go away, Miss Sheffield," he added.

"I shouldn't have to remind you I am in a precarious position," Anne reminded him. "I need a husband. You're here to help me. I refuse to indulge your... your... rakish whims." When he didn't respond, she patted his shoulder. "This is an emergency." Anne heard him mumble something from beneath the pillow. "What was that?"

He uncovered his head and looked at her. "I asked if the building was on fire."

"Of course not."

"Is the duchess injured badly enough to suggest her death is imminent?"

Anne crossed her arms. "I can't believe—"

"Are you, personally, dying?"

"No. But I'm about to commit a murder."

Richard smiled a slow, lazy grin at her. "You're so feisty in the morning, Miss Sheffield." Then he shoved the pillow back in place and muttered, "It's excessive. Go away."

Anne curled her hands into fists and stared down at him. If he thought she was about to walk out of that door, he didn't know how stubborn she was.

Anne strode up to the window and yanked open the curtains. A blinding ray of sunshine assailed Richard as he cowered beneath a pile of pillows.

To make matters worse for him, she began a raucous rendition of 'Rule Britannia'.

Richard tore the pillow off his head. "What the devil? Stop that, this instant."

But Anne only smiled wider and belted out the second verse.

"You sound like a cat howling in the street," he shouted over the singing.

"Better get up then, or I'll sing it again," Anne replied, her voice soaring to a higher octave.

"All right, *all right*. I'm awake." Richard rolled over and stared up at the ceiling. "You absolute menace."

"Wonderful." Anne grinned. "I'll send up the valet to get you dressed."

"I liked you yesterday, but I do believe I may hate you now, Miss Sheffield," Richard grumbled, still blinking sleep from his eyes.

"If you're going to curse me," she said, "you might as well use my Christian name."

"Curse you, Anne," he muttered, climbing out of bed. "Curse your firstborn and each one after until the end of time. May you all never know the comfort of peaceful slumber. I hope every morning brings a cacophony of caterwauling cats and wretched women singing 'Rule Britannia' like caterwauling cats."

"It got you up, though, didn't it?"

He hurled his other pillow at her. Anne ducked and laughed as she swept out of the room.

9

"First, you woke me up, and now you're going to make me walk?" Richard's gruff tone trailed behind Anne like a recalcitrant child. She walked ahead, leading him down the winding garden path. "There's a perfectly adequate cottage on these grounds for our use."

But Anne loved the rare autonomy Ravenhill afforded her. Caroline had regaled her with descriptions of the stunning walks and woodlands at breakfast, and Anne couldn't wait to explore. After years of being watched and monitored every moment, it felt positively luxurious to roam on her own, free to speak her mind without fear of punishment.

"I don't want to spend the day inside," Anne said, tilting the wicker picnic basket in her hand. "Surely courtship is more than sitting around in a stuffy parlour."

"At a more respectable hour," he grumbled.

"I'm rather surprised at you," she told him. "A man with a reputation as a political terror, and you're quite pitiful when your sleep is interrupted."

"Madam, I'm not pitiful. I'm ferocious."

Anne couldn't stifle a smirk. "Ferocious? I'd expect someone of such cunning to be out making threats at dawn."

Richard's posture exuded nonchalance as he leaned against a tree, his hands tucked in his pockets. "A good night's rest is essential for plotting and scheming," he drawled, his eyes glittering with mischief. "Manipulating people is an art, after all. Like painting, but with words and trickery."

Anne studied him, taking in his relaxed posture. It was easy to forget the danger he represented when he appeared so at ease. Richard Grey looked like a rake. He spoke like a rake, smiled like a rake, walked like a rake, and stood like a rake.

Even then, he grinned at her in that lazy fashion of scoundrels, like a man whose foremost concern was his own pleasure and nothing else.

"I see why politicians underestimate you," she said, studying him. "You appear non-threatening. Your reputation is deliberate."

"Politicians think one glance at a half-naked woman is enough to distract a rogue – to make him forget his purpose." He gave a casual shrug. "It's a convenient façade when it suits me."

Her eyebrows knitted. "And when it doesn't?"

"The people of Whitechapel have real problems to worry about," Richard said, his tone serious as he pushed off the tree and stepped towards Anne. "They don't care how I stretch the truth to help them. They need food, shelter, wages, and a council that gives a damn about their struggles. It's easy for me to play the part of a scoundrel when there are people who have it much worse."

Richard reached for her, hand drifting to Anne's cheek, his touch gentle and reassuring. "And you?" he asked, his voice low and smooth. "In the carriage, you spoke of your own performance. What was it you called yourself?" He paused, as if he could sense how his words burned her. "*An especially shallow idiot?* Is *that* an effortless role for you to play?"

Anne's throat constricted. It was like asking if one could dance with a shattered limb. She had performed her duties so often that she could do it with closed eyes, but it was agony every time.

More impossible every day.

Anne's fingers clasped Richard's wrist, intending to push him away, but the contact kept her as steady as an anchor.

"No." Her chest ached with a profound longing she didn't understand. "It's an obligation. That's how my father demanded I behave. Easiness has never been a part of it. What I do is not noble."

Richard's expression softened. "So Sheffield is aware of your clever mind?" he asked. "I'm not just talking about your memory. Your wit, your honesty." At her silence, he let out a disapproving noise. "I take it he's not, then."

"It's easier that way," she said, forcing herself to release his hand. "I couldn't plan my escape if he knew all I was capable of. I had to play the fool for everyone."

Richard shook his head. "That's the difference between us. I have friends with whom I can be myself. Who do you have?"

The intensity of his gaze was almost too much to bear. This was the truth behind that rakish façade – he was too astute, too keen. He missed nothing.

Anne glanced away. "I have you," she murmured. "Don't I?"

"For now," he said softly. "But what of your future husband?"

She didn't answer. Turning, she started down the path, saying, "I won't have one if we don't have our lesson."

10

Richard sat within the ruins at the crest of Ravenhill, his gaze locked on Anne.

She stood framed in the archway of the jagged chapel remains like some wild goddess, auburn hair escaping her coiffure to frame her face in a fiery halo.

What he experienced surpassed desire – more than just a simple craving. It was a primal impulse he couldn't comprehend, a voracious appetite gnawing at his very essence.

He had felt flickers of attraction for Anne before, of course. When she spoke of the sea the previous night, he had been tense with the urge to kiss her – but this was different. Insatiable, a hunger that consumed everything in its path. A thirst so powerful it penetrated every inch of his being.

"Pass me something from the basket for the ravens, won't you please?" Anne's voice was a whisper like silk on the breeze, her gaze sweeping over the birds perched on the ruins.

His lips parted, a breath he couldn't catch.

The sun blazed around her, a corona of molten gold. His blood burned with a searing need, a yearning so intense it scorched his soul. Richard fought to ignore the heat that stirred in his groin, aching to touch her. His imagination unfurled, a vivid tapestry of what could be: the texture of Anne's skin, kisses trailing down her curves, tracing unseen secrets that the sun's rays had already touched. Pleasuring her beneath the stars, whispering in her ear in the darkness.

"Richard?" Her voice broke him from his reverie. When he focused on her, she tilted her head, a fiery lock of hair escaping from its restraints. "What were you thinking just now?"

He battled against the surge of heat in his veins, pushing his insatiable thoughts back into the shadows.

"Don't feed the ravens," he said resolutely, leaning on the blanket. He crossed his legs and took a grape from the basket of food.

"And why not?" she asked with a beautiful smile.

"Because." He struggled to control his voice, a tremor in his reply. "They're smart, tricky, and have fickle manners."

Anne's lips curled with amusement. "Rather like you, then? You were staring at me with the strangest expression, as if you were…"

"Yes?" Richard held his breath for her answer.

"Oh, nothing." She shrugged, settling down beside him on the blanket. "Never mind. But you told me you would teach me to flirt today, and I regret to inform you I don't know what it is."

Richard gave a rueful grin, grateful for the change in

subject. "Surely you know what flirting is? You own a dictionary, don't you?"

Anne narrowed her eyes at him. "If I recall correctly – which I do, because I'm *me* – its definition was simply: playing at courtship; coquetry. So unhelpful, a man must have written it."

"It's a dictionary, not an instruction guide."

"Then be my guide. How does one flirt?"

The challenge lit a spark in his chest. She wanted to learn how to make advances? Very well, then.

"Flirting," he began in a low, husky voice, "is a skill. How can a man express his interest without actually saying so? How does a woman do the same? They engage in a dance."

Richard shifted closer to her so she experienced the full force of his attention, but not so close that it was intrusive. He knew the effect his gaze had on a woman. He'd show her what it was like to be on the receiving end of a scoundrel's smouldering—

"What if she isn't attracted to him?"

The query derailed Richard's train of thought. He sat back and blinked. "Sorry?"

Anne drank her wine as if Richard hadn't, moments before, given her his best smouldering scoundrel look. "What if it's an unrequited interest, and he's the one flirting? And she's the unwilling participant?"

Well, this was certainly not the question he'd expected. "If she physically distances herself, it indicates she's not interested. God willing, he'll understand the message if he's not a buffoon, a villain, or a complete imbecile."

Anne nodded thoughtfully, her gaze intent on her glass. "Space is involved with flirtation? How?"

Richard's carefully thought-out instructions proceeded to crumble. "If both parties are amenable, they'll usually commune through physical contact. She might lay her fan across his arm, for example. Weren't you taught the language of fans?"

Anne sighed, a sound both weary and bitter. "What use is that to a woman betrothed from the age of twelve?"

Twelve? What cad would agree to such an arrangement? What sort of father allowed it?

Richard's jaw tightened with barely contained anger. "I wasn't aware you were so young," he murmured, feeling a surge of hatred for the Duke of Kendal. Richard never ignored his intuition, and the duke had always made him uneasy.

"My father was determined to keep Kendal from marrying before I came of age," Anne said. Richard despised how her gaze slid away. "So he granted the duke a degree of influence over my upbringing."

A shaft of fury struck Richard low. "What influence?"

Anne shuddered. "He trained me to become his perfect wife. But no matter what I did, it never satisfied him. Kendal's always resented me."

Richard's fists clenched, his knuckles turning white. If there existed no word for the red-hot blend of rage and sorrow he was feeling, he'd have to invent it. He wanted nothing more than to pummel the duke and her father until they were bloody.

Since he couldn't act out his impulses, he'd choose another route: obliterate them socially.

"Resented you?" he echoed in a low growl.

"Yes." Anne's gaze remained on the ground. "But never

mind that. So, tell me: what if the man in your hypothetical scenario doesn't respect the woman?"

Richard's expression softened. "Then he's an absolute bastard, not fit to breathe the same air as her. Understand? If a man doesn't respect you, he's worth nothing."

A flicker of warmth touched her cheeks, and a wry smile curved her lips. "Thank you. Please continue with the lesson."

"First, let's assume both participants very much want to be there. Flirting is all about conversation. Respectful, playful discourse." Richard scooted a few inches away, creating a polite distance between them. "Friends," he said, motioning to the gap between them. "Now ask me a question – anything you want to know."

She laughed and considered that. "All right. What are your siblings like?"

"Ah, good question. Friendly. My brother James is more practical than me, as an earldom involves a great deal of work. In my father's near-complete absence from our lives, he raised my sister and me. Alexandra, in contrast, would probably conquer the entire world if only she were marginally more organised. She's an authoress who writes essays about women's issues and the working classes. Exceedingly dull, idiotic people think her ideas too extreme and unladylike."

"How lucky you are." Her expression gentled. "They sound so lovely."

"They are." Richard shifted his position, moving slightly nearer to Anne and gestured between them again. "Flirtation. Ask me something else."

Anne smiled and took another sip of wine. "Where did you grow up?"

Richard let his desire for her show on his face this time. "Have I told you where I call home?" he asked, his voice low in its intimacy. "Hampshire," he murmured, leaning ever closer. "My brother has an estate near a charming village called Stratfield Saye. But I love London, too. All sorts of mischief to find and pretty ladies to see," he said, his grin widening. "Some knock on my door after midnight."

She laughed. "I see now what flirting is. It has an element of teasing, yes? You do it well."

"I'm not done yet." He closed the distance until their thighs touched. "This kind of closeness only works in private – between lovers who already understand the rules between them." He lifted his hand and caressed her jaw gently, his eyes hooded and inviting. "One last question. Ask me anything."

This was how lovers exchanged secrets in the dark. They spoke with their lips almost touching, for there was no question of propriety. In the privacy of their chambers, they were free to express their desire and behave as they wished.

"What were you thinking about earlier?" she asked quietly. "When I was standing under the archway?"

He considered telling her something harmless – that she was breathtaking in her newfound freedom, that her stare was still steel-hard but no longer filled with suspicion.

But he had promised her honesty, and he had no intention of going back on his word.

His thumb slid over her cheek. "I imagined what it would be like to undress you slowly," he admitted. "And brush my lips against every bare inch of your skin."

Anne's breath caught. He thought he saw desire in her gaze, but a mischievous grin swept the emotion away. "That was excellent. No wonder you've charmed so many women. You're quite good at this."

Richard dropped his hand and reached for the picnic basket in distraction. He bit into a grape, tartness resting on his tongue. Of course she believed he was merely playing the part. *Of course*. He contemplated correcting her, but what would be the point? She hadn't come here to be seduced.

"Let me try now." She shifted until her skirts draped over his trousers.

He paused. "Try what?"

"Intimate talk. I should know this, shouldn't I? If I'm ever alone with a man I fancy?"

He wondered if he'd made some mistake, but as God was his witness, he couldn't identify it.

So he only cleared his throat and said, "Yes. Quite."

Anne's expression changed to solemn concentration. She leaned closer, her palm flat against Richard's chest, then slid her other hand to his nape. Her gaze dropped to his lips, just a few inches away – the perfect distance for a kiss.

"The words of intimacy are foreign to me," she whispered, "but I know a few things. Like how I dream of pressing my lips right here" – she slid her finger over the pulse that beat wildly beneath his skin – "and tasting you. How would you sound if I did that? If I take your clothes off and kiss my way down—"

"*Anne*," he groaned. Christ, now he was hard.

The little hellion leaned back and laughed. "You look as though you've swallowed a plank of wood. Was I that bad?"

"You were..." *Too good. Too damn good.* "You learn quickly. I'll say that for you."

She sipped her wine and smiled – a devastatingly slow, utterly beautiful smile with a single dimple.

Yes, he'd made a mistake. A grave mistake.

He wanted her.

∽ 11 ∽

The following afternoon, Richard escorted Anne to a charming cottage on the estate grounds. Whitewashed and decorated with azure window frames and a matching front door, it boasted a fairytale charm that the climbing roses on the trellis would further enhance come summer.

"It's lovely," she breathed. "Does the gardener or gamekeeper occupy it?"

"Neither," Richard said, drawing closer. "This is Caroline's private studio. She's cleared it out for us."

Anne's cheeks were rosy from the afternoon's stroll, her smile content. Freedom suited her – he'd noticed, on their walks, how her eyes warmed, and she looked at him now with a glimmer of trust. It filled him with a warmth he dared not name.

She pushed open the wooden door, and Richard followed her inside.

Caroline had had the entire place scoured and scented with lemons. The furniture was soft and inviting, made for ease and relaxation. The duchess had crafted it as a refuge, a haven to work without interruption. A small bedchamber was tucked away for rest between sessions. Richard knew Caroline came here when she needed to flee – a sanctuary for her soul.

And now, for a time, it would be his and Anne's.

"How incredible," Anne murmured, admiring one of Caroline's paintings.

It was from her Henry Morgan collection, depicting Eros and Psyche embraced in the nude, their bodies twisted in pleasure. Caroline's signature brushstrokes caught the moonlight streaming through the window to highlight the couple in their ecstasy. The canvas was so large it covered nearly half the wall.

"I wish I could still paint," Anne said wistfully. "Not that I was even a fraction as talented," she hastened to assure him. "But I enjoyed it. I used to attempt watercolours."

"Used to?" Richard cocked his head. "Isn't that a standard hobby for ladies?"

Anne's expression hardened. "Kendal didn't like the mess I made of my clothes, so my father threw out my work." As Richard thought of something to say, she brushed her fingertips along the frame. "Henry Morgan. I remember his art at the National Gallery. I felt as if I spent hours admiring each one."

He smiled. "*Her* art."

Anne spun to face him, her brow furrowed. "Sorry?"

"Henry Morgan is Caroline's pseudonym."

"My word," Anne said in surprise. "Why wouldn't she claim credit for these? Everyone loves them."

"Because the scandal would overshadow the quality of the artistry. People would call them perversions." At her confused expression, Richard shifted closer. "You understand the limitations society imposes on women. Even duchesses aren't exempt."

Anne nodded in understanding. "Because the figures are nude."

"That's certainly part of it. There's also the content." He dipped his head toward hers as if to impart a secret. "Eros is a demigod, and Psyche, a mere mortal. But notice how his gaze is reverent?" he murmured. "He worships her as if she were a goddess."

"Is that so terrible?" Anne asked.

"No. But this is an intimate moment. He's pleasuring her. Don't you see the ecstasy in the way they're grasping each other?"

He heard the way her breathing changed. But if he had expected her to blush, he was wrong. Instead, she only smiled.

Then she said something that surprised the hell out of him: "They're both enjoying it. How lovely."

Her eyes seemed to hold a secret as they feasted on the painting, as if Anne herself was Psyche, head thrown back as her winged lover pleasured her.

Richard felt a surge of lust, a crackling jolt of electricity. He couldn't fight it any more than he could deny she'd twisted his every fantasy and desire with nothing but a look. He craved the sight of her, the sound of her, the feel of her, when she shattered into release beneath him, trembling and gasping with the force of it.

What would her expression be in that moment? Would her lips part in a scream of bliss? Would she call his name?

He yearned to see every last moment of her pleasure as

he buried himself deep inside her, heart thundering in his ears, fierce and raw and overwhelming.

Breathe, he thought, forcibly putting some distance between them. "Now you understand why there would be a scandal."

He tried to find solace in the space he'd created, but her gaze had shifted to the portrait beside it.

Worse still, it was a painting of Richard – Achilles with sword and shield, standing before the gates of Troy, daring Hector to battle. It was among the first Caroline had ever attempted of him, and one of her favourites.

And here was Anne, staring at his naked body.

God help him.

"I only wish she didn't have to hide it," Anne said with a sigh. "The level of detail is astonishing. So different from her landscapes. She certainly chooses beautiful subjects."

Richard's smile was slow. If she was going to admire his form, he might as well enjoy it. "Like it, do you?"

"I love it." She raised her hand to the painting, not quite touching. "Look at the shadows here. The way she's captured his muscles, the veins along his arms. I remember several women swooning over this at the gallery – or, at least, pretending to."

"What about you? Did you pretend to swoon?" He was being an underhanded, vain bastard now, but he wanted her to keep talking.

A laugh bubbled up from her chest. "To maintain my performance. We debutantes rarely have the chance to see men in the nude before marriage, so we have to claim it's shocking, or people will realise we like it too much. These are so very realistic, as if painted by a lover."

"Caroline remains devoted to her husband. Certainly, she's never bedded this particular subject."

"Oh?" She arched an eyebrow. "How do you know?"

Richard's grin turned wicked. "Because this is a painting of me."

Anne's jaw dropped. She looked from him to the painting, back to him... to the painting. And her cheeks pinkened.

Nothing was more beautiful than a blushing redhead; that was damn well for sure.

Then, unexpectedly, Anne smiled. "This is what you didn't want to tell me about on the train? I thought this secret wasn't yours to share."

"It wasn't until you admired my naked backside. Then I couldn't help myself."

She was laughing now, clearly not embarrassed that he'd caught her looking. Quick of wit, full of surprises; he liked that about her.

"You're so arrogant, Richard." Anne shook her head. "She ought to paint you as Narcissus."

"So you say. Admit it, Anne. You're only looking for another opportunity to see me in the nude," he said with a wink.

"I have dozens of opportunities, don't I?" Anne's gaze drifted back to the painting, her expression devilishly unashamed. "Whenever I want to look at you naked, I need only revisit the gallery."

Richard's ears were warm as he hungrily drank her in. She was a sight to behold – and he was dangerously close to adoring her. "You're trying to shock me."

"A talent I learned from you," Anne replied with a mischievous glint in her eye. "You always try to shock me with the words you use. So I thought I'd return the favour. Tit for tat, Richard."

"Ah, now we're speaking of tits, are we? This conversation just got more interesting."

Her mouth fell open. That was another word she'd only overheard in whispers. She shook her head with amusement. "You're such a scoundrel. Shall we begin a lesson?"

He held out his hand, and she didn't draw back. Obediently, she grasped his fingers and stepped closer, until her gown brushed against his leg.

"Let's begin with a dance."

The proximity did nothing to ease his desire, but he was a man of control and restraint. He always had been.

Anne wrinkled her nose and shot him a sceptical look. "A dance?"

"You dance, don't you?" he asked, wrapping his fingers around hers.

She raised a single eyebrow. "I played an idiot, not an incompetent," she retorted.

A swell of admiration filled his chest. He'd expected Anne to be as diffident as a wallflower, but he was rapidly appreciating her sharp humour and quick tongue.

"Good. The house party will formally begin with a ball when the other guests arrive. That's where you'll make your impression. Now place your hand on my shoulder."

Though her eyes held a hint of challenge, Anne obeyed, her fingers curling lightly against the fabric of his coat.

An unexpected jolt went through him at her touch. This wasn't the usual embrace of a woman, confident and practised. Hers was soft, almost hesitant. A gentle blush coloured her cheeks, and she lowered her gaze.

At that moment, Richard wondered if she'd felt it, too. A spark between them that had the potential to grow to a conflagration.

He pressed his other hand to the small of her back and drew her against him. "There, easy enough."

Richard heard her breath catch, but Anne swiftly regained her composure. "I already know how to dance," she reminded him. "And there's no music."

"We don't need any. Watch." He began the steps of a waltz, and she followed, reluctantly at first. She was a fine dancer, light on her feet. Graceful. "Seduction begins here," he murmured close to her ear.

The scent of roses clung to her like a promise, and he wanted to bury his face in her neck, press his lips to her pulse.

"With a dance?" She sounded almost amused. Beguiled.

Look at me, he thought. *Look at me.*

"Yes," he confirmed. "And a conversation. A touch. Just enough to leave them wanting more."

Little things amounted to so much. Richard could have told her she was proficient at bewitchment without trying. Anne had woven a spell around him, with nothing more than a few words and a coy smile – set his blood on fire, made him crave her touch and imagine her arched beneath him in bed.

"How do I do that?"

Her question drew him from his reverie. *Focus, Richard.* "Look at me."

He felt her release a breath before she locked her gaze with his. Christ, God. Her eyes were extraordinary – a rich brown with specks of emerald, deep enough to hold a universe of secrets. She required a husband who could meet them directly.

"That's all it took," he whispered.

Her lashes fluttered as she lowered her eyes once more. "Kendal and my father said men want—"

"Men like them," he finished. "Not men like me."

"Very well. Men like you, then. What do you want?"

"Shall I be honest with you? In frank language?"

"Yes. Always."

He couldn't help but press his cheek to hers, a whisper of a touch. "I want to meet a woman's gaze. When I converse with her and when I fuck her." He felt her start. "I've shocked you, haven't I?"

But her smile was the most beautiful thing he'd ever seen. Each one was a triumph. Richard had already won so many smiles from her and was still desperate for more.

And he had no right to her mirth. Another man would bring her joy – her future husband.

"Not shock," she told him. "I'm not accustomed to such plain speaking. I like it." She chuckled. "Does that make me scandalous?"

"Yes. But I enjoy a bit of scandal, don't you?"

Her laugh was low and husky; it sent a fresh wave of lust through him. Freedom agreed with this woman. She fairly glowed with independence.

"I'm beginning to think I do."

"Be warned," he said. "Caro's guests will be on their best behaviour. No plain speaking." He saw her smile flee and leaned in closer. "You'll just have to get them to drop their guard."

A scratch at the door interrupted their lesson. "Sir?" The

butler. "Her Grace has asked that I inform you dinner will be served in two hours."

"Yes, thank you," Richard called out. He lifted Anne's chin. "Until tomorrow."

Her hands clung for a heartbeat longer on his shoulders.

12

Anne and Richard strolled the grounds, a mosaic of hues and aromas.

Vibrant wildflowers burst through the earth, and the trees waved in the wispy breeze. The birdsong echoed through the air, and the sweet smell of spring filled Anne's senses.

But Anne was entirely focused on Richard.

He was witty and attentive, his lessons the highlight of her days. With every passing day, she learned from him the art of conversation, his parries in discourse as deft as a swordsman's. The ease with which he shifted topics often left her so engrossed in the discussion that she forgot she was meant to be performing.

Though she paid him handsomely in information, Richard's company was worth the price.

"What are you looking for in a husband, apart from a title?" he asked as they meandered along the winding path.

Now that Richard knew of Anne's proclivity for walks,

they spent more time exploring the myriad paths around Ravenhill than they did inside.

Anne carefully skirted a rosebush, the thorns ever-ready to catch her skirts. "The title wouldn't be important if I could marry without delay and the need for a special licence." She glanced up from beneath her lashes, her gaze inquisitive. "Unless you know of any unmarried MPs who require a wife? They'd need to be kind and respectful. That's all I ask."

Richard's attention shifted to her, his eyebrows arching in surprise. "That's all you want? Kindness and respect? No other stipulations?"

"My standards are low," she said dryly. *And desperate.*

"Low?" His lips curved ever so slightly. "You might as well have buried your standards in the ground."

"Then the question is, who will dig them up?" she asked, chin lifting in a challenge. "You tell me, then. What should I look for in a husband?"

"Someone who makes you laugh," he began, gaze sweeping across her face. "Who listens to you, and who—"

But Richard never had a chance to finish his thought. A torrent of rain suddenly unleashed from the heavens, pelting them with cold droplets.

Anne laughed, her voice rising above the din of the downpour. "We'll have to end our walk early."

He reached for her hand, entwining their fingers as he grinned. "There's a gazebo on the other side of the hill. Shall we run for it?"

They took off in a madcap race, their laughter ringing through the air more loudly than any peal of thunder.

By the time they stumbled beneath the shelter of the arbour, they were both soaked to the skin and breathless.

Anne leaned against a column to admire the copse of trees illuminated by nature's choreography. "I missed this about the country."

"Isn't London rainy enough for you?" Richard asked.

She shook her head wistfully. "Not the same. In the city, the noise muffles the raindrops as they fall from the trees. It's the silence I miss."

Anne forced her gaze away from the tempestuous scene beyond the gazebo to find Richard watching her with burning sapphire eyes. His look was fixated, almost feverish. As if he were bewitched, and she was the unwitting sorceress. As the rain continued to pelt against the gazebo's roof, a crackling energy charged the air between them – a fever dream forged in the flashes of lightning.

Then Richard stepped forward and ran his hand along Anne's cheek, sweeping aside a lock of rain-lashed hair. His fingers lingered on her skin, tracing down her jaw and over the curve of her neck.

Anne's breath caught. She didn't understand this dizzying sensation that flooded her veins. A ravenousness that seemed almost bottomless. She never wanted him to stop touching her.

He swallowed hard. "Your hair came undone." His voice was low and husky – like smoke on the wind, it fired her blood.

"It's always been a problem to tame. I—"

"It's beautiful." His hand cupped the back of her head, cradling it against his palm. "God, look at you," he whispered, as if to himself.

"What?" She was half breathless with anticipation and half terrified of what he might say next.

"You ought to marry a man who could be in a room full of people and only see you, who burns for you alone." His thumb dipped to brush her lower lip. "And if he doesn't, he's a damn fool."

"Richard..." Anne swallowed. "You promised you would be honest with me."

She heard his breath hitch, as unsteady as her own. It gratified her, somehow, that he was as unbalanced as she. "Yes. Yes, I did."

"I can't explain my feelings, almost like I'm..." Anne trailed off, her heart pounding. She wanted things she had no right to ask for. Summoning her bravery, she said in a shaky voice, "I want to touch you. And do other things."

Even saying it out loud made her blush. She had spent many nights dreaming of intimacies she was too scared to put into words. Each fantasy was different, and she knew that once alone in her room tonight, she'd imagine licking the droplets of rain from his skin, pressing delicate kisses over his lips, and, if her courage allowed it – undressing him.

A sound reverberated in his throat, as if he read her thoughts. "Desire, sweetheart. That's what it is."

"No one has ever been gentle to me." Her heart struggled to contain a volatile combination of shame and yearning. "I don't understand how a husband should be intimate with his wife. Will you show me?"

"Christ," Richard breathed.

"Please," Anne whispered, feeling exposed by her boldness. She despised begging for a scrap of tenderness because it was so foreign. "Just... just don't kiss me on the lips, all right? I don't like it."

Kendal had kissed her there, punishing her. He told her he hated her – and then had bitten her lip, drawing blood. He had—

Richard eased his fingertips beneath her chin and gently lifted her face toward him. "Where did you go just then? In your memories?"

Anne's mouth twisted, and all the words she couldn't say shoved back into the shadows of her thoughts. "They have no place here," she whispered.

Richard knew the silent language of her longing, for it was his native tongue. As if he could interpret her innermost wishes, he discerned what Anne desired: his lips pressed against her neck like a whisper of moth wings, his hands sliding down the slopes of her shoulders until they rested upon the neckline of her dress.

Anne sensed his hunger, the echo of an ache that consumed her. She dared not tell him about her need for his lips, branded on her flesh like a prayer for salvation. But he understood it already, as if by fate, and lowered the muslin to kiss her exposed skin.

"This is how a husband should touch you," Richard murmured, sweeping kisses across the tops of her breasts in reverent motions. "As if he can't get enough of you. As if he'd die if he stopped."

Heat ignited between them as Richard pressed Anne against one of the gazebo's columns. His movements were precise, deliberate, as if he were testing her resolve. But she no longer craved the security of the familiar; she wanted something else – his tongue, tracing fire lines over her skin to memorise her. To learn a new language of passion and become as fluent as him.

Anne tipped her head back in encouragement and whispered, "What else?"

"Your husband should always ask you a single vital question." Richard's gaze scorched her with heat. "What do you want?"

Anne froze. No one had ever asked her that before – not in a way that it mattered. That query was reserved for women with freedom and agency who could name their feelings and identify their wants.

But Anne? She didn't have the vocabulary. She could not voice the feelings surging through her; they were too fresh, too unfamiliar.

She gathered all her courage and whispered, "What if I don't have the words for what I want?"

"Then allow me to teach them to you. I stop when you tell me." Richard's hand moved to the back of her dress. "Do I unbutton?"

The tension in the air was thick as Richard waited for her answer.

She drew a steadying breath, and a single word escaped her lips. "Yes."

He glided his fingers over her bodice, unfastening each button until the sodden cloth sagged with its weight. He slowly peeled away each layer of fabric until her bare breasts were visible.

Richard made an appreciative noise that sent a shiver of heat through Anne, an electric pulse that was almost too much to bear. *Lust* seemed too tame for it – *desire*, too pretty. No, the impulse she had was savage and feral.

"You want me to kiss you here?" His fingertips brushed her nipple, sending sparks through her veins.

"Yes," she said in a strangled voice, scarcely believing what she was agreeing to.

He leaned forward and set his mouth upon her, stroking her nipple with a hot flick of his tongue.

She gasped, arching against him. "*More*. Please, more."

"Show me where else I should touch you. Take my hand."

Before she could change her mind, she took hold of his palm and guided it down the curve of her hip. Then, taking a deep inhale for courage, she placed it between her thighs.

"Here," she said, her cheeks burning.

A low groan ripped from him, primal and sincere. His breath seared her skin. "Honest language?" he rasped against her breast.

"Always."

"Cunny," he murmured, sinking to his knees before her. "Quim. Pussy." He groaned, and his hands were beneath her skirts, tugging down her drawers so slowly that Anne trembled with anticipation. He looked up at her with a fire and hunger so intense his eyes seemed almost bottomless. "Shall I kiss you here?"

Something raw and desperate in his voice matched the deep craving inside her.

"Yes." Her assent was barely audible above the pounding of her heart.

He responded with a groan, his lips finding the slick heat between her thighs.

A gasp lodged in her throat. Her fingers tangled in his hair as he explored her with his mouth and tongue, every touch and lick igniting a wild desire more feral than human.

She yielded to the unfamiliar and exquisite pleasure, her body no longer her own.

Richard's finger plunged into her, sending a jolt of ecstasy surging through her. His name tore from her in a frantic cry, drawn against her will. She was insatiable – his to command.

His to take.

Anne shattered beneath his ministrations, the world fracturing into a million pieces as an explosive wave of sensation surged through her. She found herself weightless, her lungs unable to draw in air. All she could do was utter his name again in a desperate plea, the sound tearing from her like a prayer.

Richard stood, embracing Anne in his arms as she steadied herself. They stayed in that moment of stillness, hearts beating in unison. Their breath slowing.

"Thank you," she whispered against his chest, "for letting me experience that."

He pulled back suddenly, as if her gratitude had scalded him. Then he adjusted her clothing with brisk efficiency, avoiding her gaze as if he had shut off any emotion he had felt earlier.

"Of course," he murmured coolly. "Our lessons are done for the night. The rain stopped, so we should return to the house now."

Without another word, he clasped her hand in his own and led her away, out of the gazebo and into the soft light of the evening.

∽ 13 ∽

The air between Richard and Anne changed after their rendezvous in the gazebo.

Where before they'd stolen light touches and exchanged knowing glances, now Anne couldn't help but notice the way he pulled away. Courtesy had replaced the passion that simmered between them. His touch was no longer reverent and hungry, but polite and professional.

As though he'd erected an invisible barrier between them – a boundary of propriety.

A wall she wanted to tear down.

When other guests arrived, and Anne made the necessary introductions, she tried to keep her gaze from wandering to Richard. He was only being a gentleman – reminding her gently that she wasn't meant for him. If she were wise, she would be grateful for his kindness.

But Anne was not wise – at least in this regard.

She hated it.

On the night of the ball, Anne braced herself for

disappointment. She'd socialised well enough with Richard, but this was an entirely different challenge.

Find a husband in twelve days or become a duchess in a gilded cage.

The maid worked on Anne's hair as she attempted to still her racing heart. No time for nerves – the ball had already begun.

Twelve days.

Twelve days to find a husband or surrender her fate.

Anne turned as a soft knock sounded at the door. "Enter."

The Duchess of Hastings swept into the room, every inch the regal lady of class and refinement. A string of rubies glimmered at her throat, accenting her resplendent crimson dress. The low neckline displayed the creamy expanse of her chest, and the cinched waist exhibited her curves to their utmost advantage. Next to Caroline, Anne felt utterly homely in her plain gown.

"I came to see if you needed anything," Caroline said politely.

The duchess had kept her distance in all matters relating to Anne and Richard's lessons, but in the evenings, she had opened to Anne with astonishing warmth. Her beauty was matched only by her charm; she was truly lovely in all regards. Anne adored her.

"I'm so nervous," Anne admitted in a breathy rush. "Sorry for being late—"

"My love, you don't need to apologise," Caroline said kindly. "I'm here to help, not to lecture."

The other woman examined Anne's gown with her discerning eye. Anne knew it was not so much fashion-forward as a fashion frozen – her father's preference for modesty had left Anne with nothing but plain gowns. It was the loveliest she owned.

"This is what you plan to wear?" Caroline asked.

Anne felt the heat rise to her cheeks. "It's the best dress I have."

The duchess inclined her head, expression thoughtful. "Charity," she said, turning to the servant. "Go into my wardrobe. The green silk will do nicely. With haste."

Anne opened her mouth to demur, but the maid had already taken leave of the room. "But I couldn't—"

Caroline stepped forward and took Anne's hands in her own. "I want you to understand something." Her voice was soft and confident. "You're magnificent no matter what you wear. But I believe the green would look splendid with your complexion. We're close in size; it should only require a few alterations."

With a light rap on the door, Charity's arm was outstretched with a dazzling length of emerald silk. The exquisite fabric shimmered in the candlelight like a precious gem, its plain cut and understated adornments nothing short of regal.

Anne's fingertips grazed the divine material with reverence. "Do you think it's too much?"

Caroline's smirk was fierce and resolute. "No, dearest. Anything approaching *too much* exactly what you need."

Anne nodded, a silent acceptance of Caroline's words. The oppressive weight of her father's spectre lingered at her shoulder, threatening to overpower her will to explore what could be. She would have to exercise unorthodox strength, courage, and daring to free herself from the life she had been born into.

She was determined to break away, no matter the risk.

Anne took a deep breath and steeled herself. "Very well."

The duchess smiled, a glint of mischief in her eyes as she turned to Charity. "Shall we?"

Time flew by in a flurry of activities, punctuated by the snip of scissors and the sound of pins clinking against the floor. Another maid arrived to adjust the dress to Anne's precise measurements as Charity meticulously arranged her hair and carefully tucked small white flowers between the tresses.

When Anne finally stepped back and surveyed the results of Caroline and the maids' careful handiwork, a feeling of satisfaction filled her. The emerald gown the duchess had chosen for her was masterful, its vivid hue heightening the allure of her fair complexion and rosy cheeks. Its silhouette was crafted with a daring hand, exposing just enough of Anne's collarbones and shoulders to reveal an enticing glimpse of cleavage.

It was exquisite; an act of rebellion that would've earned Anne a scolding from her father and a frown of disapproval from Kendal. But she trembled with excitement instead of apprehension.

This was how she would escape – by being visible. By being herself.

Caroline's voice cut through the stillness, and Anne felt her arm encased in a friendly grip. "Now we'll make a grand entrance together," Caroline said, beaming.

Anne blushed, embarrassed to have kept her friend away from her guests. "I apologise—"

"Shh." Caroline leaned in, as if to impart a secret. "My dear, what's the point of being a duchess if I can't break the rules from time to time?"

Anne smiled at that. She had wanted to break the rules for her entire life – and she was going to.

Everything on her own terms.

⚬ 14 ⚬

The night stretched long and wearisome, leaving Richard's patience in tatters.

He was practically counting the minutes until he could escape this dull gathering. He'd stepped into the ballroom, heart thundering with the anticipation of seeing Anne, but he'd been thrust into an interminable sequence of dances.

After enlisting Caroline's aid in tracking Anne's whereabouts, the duchess also disappeared. Where the devil were they?

He gritted his teeth and plastered on a mask of politeness as he guided Miss Cecil through their endless waltz. He'd only just met the woman because the Earl of Montgomery approached him in uncharacteristic distress and insisted he pair with her.

"Miss Cecil is the bane of my existence," the earl had hissed with agitation. "Dance with her. Keep her the hell away from me, and I'll throw money at any bleeding heart cause you please. And if you know of an interested lady, send her my way for a quick shag. I need a distraction."

Though Montgomery was a friend and much praised for his affability in public, Richard couldn't understand what possessed Caroline to invite him. He knew the beast beneath that grinning mask – not one fit for Anne. He made a mental note to warn her to stay away from the earl at the earliest opportunity.

As he danced with Miss Cecil, his thoughts ceaselessly returned to Anne – awakening a hunger that no amount of polite conversation or obliging dances could soothe.

Last night, he'd slumbered fitfully and hard, his body twisted in frustrated desire. Richard had palmed his cock and imagined making love to Anne again and again and again in the gazebo – dragging his name from her lips with each climax.

When exhaustion finally did yank him into sleep, she'd haunted his dreams.

"Are you enjoying yourself tonight, Mr Grey?" Miss Cecil's voice pulled Richard from his reverie. She was beautiful – it was only fitting that he should pay her due attention – but his thoughts were elsewhere.

Imagining a future that didn't exist.

Richard gave her a polite smile. "Of course," he said. "I'm enjoying myself immensely."

Enjoying myself so immensely that I'd rather be anywhere else.

"Splendid," Miss Cecil murmured, clearing her throat. "Well, I—"

A flash of emerald on the stairs drew his notice, and all his breath left him in a harsh scrape of a sound.

Bloody hell.

Anne was a vision in that dress. The rich emerald fabric flowed around her like a waterfall, shimmering in the light. Its expert cut accentuated her gently curving hips, while the bodice hugged her slender waist. The sleeves showed off her delicate arms, while the neckline plunged just low enough to tease the eye. It perfectly contrasted with her auburn locks, which seemed to be styled with deliberate intent: to make men think of a boudoir and all the carnal pleasures that lay within.

Richard couldn't help but imagine running his fingers through her hair, tugging on those delicate strands as he ravished her deep and hard. In the imaginative realm of his mind, her breathing grew ragged when he uttered those lustful words he'd just taught her: *cunny, quim, pussy.*

He swallowed hard to contain the groan that threatened to escape his lips. *She is not for you.*

If Richard's hasty assessment of the other gentlemen was correct, each man had succumbed to a similar fantasy.

He didn't like it.

Anne's gaze flicked towards him, and she gifted him a clandestine smile that nearly stole his breath before Caroline began taking her around the ballroom.

The woman in his arms said, "She seems lovely."

Richard's attention returned to Miss Cecil, who fixed him with a stare that was too fierce and knowing – razor-sharp and blazing with intelligence. He had judged her too soon.

The corner of his mouth twitched. "I'm sure she is." He tested her, gauging her response.

"I beg your pardon," Miss Cecil murmured. "It seemed as if you knew her. Well."

He quirked an eyebrow. "How did you come to that conclusion?"

"The way you looked at her." She shrugged, not breaking eye contact with him. "And the way your hands tensed around me. I'm not completely oblivious, sir."

"No, you're certainly not, Miss Cecil." A widening grin accompanied his words.

"So you do know my name." Her expression was warm, but Richard detected a hint of challenge in her eyes. "I thought Lord Montgomery may have failed to mention it when he approached you in a blind panic and convinced you to join me for this awkward waltz."

He blinked, taken aback by her insight. "How did you—"

"As I said," she replied, "not oblivious."

The waltz concluded, and Richard made a short bow, pressing a brief kiss to her hand. "Monty is an imbecile, by the by. Any gentleman would be lucky to have you."

She sighed as he led her to the chaperone who had been minding her all evening. "That's what I'm constantly being told," she mused quietly.

"By whom?"

Her smile was fleeting. "Everyone. All the best with your lady, Mr Grey. You may not be in the market for a bride, but you're no fool, I gather. She won't remain a debutante long." With a nod, she rejoined her chaperone.

Richard scanned the room for Anne, muttering, "No fool? I'm the biggest damn fool in all of England." Finally, he spotted her standing among a group of ladies, chatting with Caroline.

As Richard started towards her, Lord Montgomery

appeared by his side, holding a glass of champagne. "Who is that? Do you know her?"

Anne, of course. Montgomery's gaze was so intent, Richard felt a surge of protectiveness – especially after pleasuring her in the gazebo. The memory still sent a shock of sensation through him.

"She's not for you," Richard said in a voice that was sharper than he'd intended.

The other man's smile was slow and dangerous. "Claiming her for yourself?"

"That is Stanton Sheffield's daughter. One would be wise to secure her hand in marriage before claiming her."

Montgomery seemed undaunted by this information. "At this point, I'd take any distraction from Miss Cecil."

Richard experienced a slight pang of sympathy for the young woman he'd danced with earlier. "I found Miss Cecil delightful and intelligent, a far cry from your usual taste. So if you've ruined her and have plans to do the same to Miss Sheffield, mark me, I'll rip out your throat with my bare hands."

A spark of something dark ignited in Montgomery's eyes, lurking beneath his angelic charms. "Don't act so self-righteous. Miss Cecil's exceptional intellect has nothing to do with it; she's harboured a longstanding infatuation since childhood that I've no intention of reciprocating." He glanced at Anne, a hungry gleam in his gaze. "I need a method of disengagement that makes it clear I am no longer available, and she needs to find an appropriate suitor."

"Listen to me, Gabriel," Richard hissed, pressing closer. "You won't use Miss Sheffield to break Miss Cecil's heart."

Montgomery's smile was sharp, like a blade. "How noble of you. Do you care about this one?"

Years of Richard's backroom dealing and skulduggery threatened to crumble. His reputation demanded a certain level of debauchery and vice, which he'd been happy to supply for his causes, but Montgomery seemed driven by something darker – an ugliness that had pushed him towards the bottom of a bottle and then into the arms of any number of women long after Richard had called it quits.

That darkness made Richard want to bundle Anne up and take her away from it all. She'd seen more of the devil in men than any woman deserved.

"Don't make me regret our friendship, Monty," Richard said in a low voice, almost like a growl. "We have rules. We don't toy with debutantes."

But Montgomery's brow rose in surprise. "So you *do* care for her." His eyes found Anne across the ballroom. "Any reason, or is your newfound integrity a by-product of the same reckless behaviour you were ready to rip my throat out over?"

An image of Anne flashed in Richard's mind – her head thrown back in rapture as she gasped his name. Fire licked through his veins as he fought the pull of his emotions like an undertow, clenching his teeth until they ached.

"Forget the question," he growled. "Forget you've seen her. There are at least two lonely widows here if you fancy a dalliance. If Mrs Hunt and Lady Baden don't suit, find some village girl eager to warm your bed. If you'll excuse me, I need to speak with our lovely hostess."

Richard strode across the ballroom determinedly. Caroline was in a circle of ladies, presenting Anne to the Marquess of

Granby. He seemed decent enough – a courteous, dignified gentleman who'd bend to Anne's every whim. Dull, but not a degenerate like Montgomery.

Anne flicked her gaze at Richard before returning her attention to Granby.

Good. Let him think nothing else is worth noticing.

She was the perfect pupil, so why did Richard yearn for her regard? Why did he crave for the moments when he could speak freely, feel her skin, whisper secrets against her throat, pleasure her?

No. She is not for you, Richard reminded himself yet again with a tightness in his chest.

"Mr Grey," Caroline said, snapping him from his thoughts. "Do you remember Lord Granby? He was at my art exhibition last Michaelmas."

And the bloke liked art. Staid, boring. Perfect. Good for Anne.

Jolly good.

Richard forced a smile. "I recall. Wonderful to see you again." He returned his attention to Caroline. "Duchess, may I have this dance?"

Anne gave Richard a shrewd look, which he decisively ignored. Let her converse with Granby – she was smart enough to realise that among the throngs of men here vying for her affections, Granby had the rank, influence, and wealth to be her ideal match – and he wasn't an absolute reprobate who would take up a mistress after they wed.

The grand ballroom thrummed with the din of a hundred conversations and lively fiddles. Richard gripped Caroline's gloved hand as if he were strangling a gryphon and dragged her onto the waxed parquet. Her gown whispered beneath their feet, and the light of a thousand glittering candles loomed around them.

"What's wrong? Why are you flustered?" Caroline's murmur was nearly lost in the swell of the music as they began their Schottische.

Richard scowled. "What insanity drove you to invite Montgomery?"

Ever the perfect hostess, she did not so much as glance in the gentleman's direction. The duchess shot Richard a withering look. "He's a friend of yours, isn't he?"

"Friends like him are why I don't have debutantes at my parties," Richard said through gritted teeth.

Caroline raised an eyebrow. "Oh. So this is about Anne."

"Of course it's about Anne," he snapped. "Montgomery is a cad, a blackguard, and a scoundrel. What were you thinking?"

The duchess's lips curled into a smirk. "I'm sorry. Did you say something? Must've been lost in the irony fog of you criticising someone else for being a scoundrel when you traffic in extortion and bribery on a daily basis." She gave him a chastising look. "Furthermore, Gabriel's my cousin, and you demanded I assemble a house party at the drop of a hat. I was rather hard-pressed for options."

Richard's expression hardened as he spoke, his voice laced with frustration. "Too hard-pressed. I may be a miscreant, but I do it for the right reasons. Can he claim the same?"

The amusement faded from Caroline's face like a stone falling from a cliff. "Would it make a difference if I told you he's changed since his travels?" she asked. "He hardly even resembles the man I remember from our childhood. And Anne is..." Caroline's eyes flicked to Anne, and her voice softened. "Well, she's beautiful. Maybe she could be exactly what Monty needs."

Richard's jaw tightened as he spoke firmly, "She deserves better than to be what some man needs. What about what *she* needs?"

This answer seemed to surprise the duchess. Her gaze snapped to his. "She'll decide that for herself."

Realising he may have overstepped, Richard's head lowered slightly as he added, "Just keep an eye on him, Caro," as the dance ended, and he escorted her off the floor.

"I'll tell her of Monty's scandalous habits," Caroline agreed. "But I won't smother her, Richard. Please excuse me." She pulled her arm from his grasp and made her way over to Anne. "Miss Sheffield, let me introduce you to a few more people I think you'd like."

Richard watched as Caroline deliberately led Anne away, and there was nothing he could do.

ᴄᴍ 15 ᴍᴄ

Anne waited for the corridor to fall silent.

She'd retired early, the other guests fading into a conspiratorial symphony of creaks, whispers, and laughter. House parties were notorious for debauchery and dalliances, the air saturated with the perfume of intrigue.

Anne paced, her heart thundering in her ears. She strained for the faintest rustle of sound – a groan of a floorboard, the distant voices from outside, the whisper of trees against the windowpane.

When the silence stretched like a shroud, Anne dared to move toward Richard's bedchamber. She placed every footstep as if it were an offering. An exhale snagged in her throat as she passed darkened doorways and sleeping nobles.

Any mistake and she'd be sent home with a reputation in tatters.

Finally, she reached her destination. Moonlight crept

through the hall window, gilding Richard's door with a pale glow that seemed to mock her wavering courage.

Anne cursed her beating heart as she twisted the handle, half expecting it to be locked. To her relief, it opened without a sound, and Anne stepped inside.

The faint scent of sandalwood perfumed the air. Darkness greeted her, broken only by the fall of lunar light slanting through the curtains and falling on Richard's form in the blankets – his beautiful body adrift in languid dreams.

A long, ragged exhale left her.

He was stunning in repose, his grace and power displayed in that unguarded moment. The sheets had slipped to his hips, revealing an expanse of smooth skin Anne longed to feel beneath her fingertips. She wished she'd been brave enough to ask more from him back at the gazebo.

Had she been bolder, would he have obliged? Would he have fixed her with that gaze of his, framed by raindrops and lashes, and surrendered himself to her touch? A hundred erotic fantasies filled her mind of what they could have shared, each one haunting her thoughts.

And here she was, trespassing on his dreams.

Anne straightened her shoulders and turned to leave.

"Coward." That rough voice, laced with sleep and amusement, shattered her composure.

Heat streaked through her veins.

"I thought you were sleeping," Anne replied, astonished at how steady and controlled her words sounded while her body trembled. "You're ferocious about it, remember?"

"Was sleeping. Heard the door." When she didn't reply, Richard added, "Contrary to my ferocity earlier in the week, I'm a light sleeper when I'm agitated."

The question was out before she could stop it. "Agitated?"

"Haven't fucked in a while." Though it was too dark to see her flush, he must have noticed her head dip. "Honest language," he said, as if in apology.

"Yes. I gathered."

Anne's skin was on fire. How could she look at him now? Would he understand how his answer thrilled her? How she burned not from discomfort but a longing to soothe his agitation – for she was unsteady, too?

"Anne." Richard's voice softened, a quiet rumble that seemed to caress her like velvet. "Turn around and tell me why you came. I'm perfectly harmless."

She swallowed and slowly turned.

Good heavens.

Anne's body jolted with a forbidden thrill as she beheld Richard sprawled across the bed, staring at her, his tousled hair and sinful smile threatening to unravel all her defences. His mere presence unleashed a storm of want inside her.

No. Stop this.

He was beyond inappropriate. How dare he be so tempting? It was obscene. Outrageous. It should be outlawed for indecency.

Anne steadied herself and forced her gaze away. She had to stay focused on her task.

Eleven days.

That was all she had.

Gathering the utter tatters of her resolve, Anne marched towards the bed. She wouldn't allow herself to linger on memories of his touch in the gazebo; she had a task to fulfil.

"I require your guidance."

Richard's brow arched in amusement. "At this hour?"

"Yes." She steeled her voice against his charms. "Granby invited me to a morning stroll, and you were clear about not rising until noon. This couldn't wait."

"Let me guess: Granby is the type who would leap from his bed at dawn. Perfect, utterly dull Granby," Richard said with a sigh.

What was wrong with him? "Are you drunk?"

"God, I wish I were." He patted the mattress next to him. "Come here."

Anne licked lips that suddenly felt too dry. "Do you think that's wise? After what happened in the gazebo?"

Richard fixed her with a searching look, his eyes darkening with some emotion she couldn't identify. "Do you regret that now?"

Stillness fell like a shadow. Could a single query overthrow her defences so easily? She'd just started to build walls against him, and he'd already broken them down with one bullet of a question.

No, she could never regret such an exquisite moment. Even when she married Granby – or whoever else – she would still remember it as her first taste of tenderness, thoughtfulness, passion, and longing. But no one could ever compare because this man had branded her with his touch, left his mark.

What do you want? he'd asked.

Didn't he understand the weight of that? How four mere words turned her life upside down?

"No," Anne said in a whisper that barely extended beyond the darkness. "How could I forget it when it haunts me in my dreams every night?"

Richard's expression grew heated. He reached for her. "Anne—"

"No." She caught his hand and held it in her own. "I have only eleven days. Do you understand?" She heard a ragged breath escape him before he nodded. "Good. So how do I speak with Granby? This isn't like a dance – I'll have to spend an hour or two in his company without making a complete cake of myself."

Richard gave her a half-smile. "You've managed to avoid mortification in my presence for two or more hours. That has to be a point in your favour."

Anne waved a dismissive hand. "You don't count. You're the one I can mock and do silly things around without consequence. Come now. You're an expert in small talk, aren't you? A virtuoso of verbiage, a paragon of conversation?"

"While these are exceedingly nice compliments to me, they don't bode well for Granby," Richard said.

"I'm not here to flatter Granby, am I? It's you I must praise excessively tonight for favours, Narcissus."

"Oof." He pressed a hand to his heart. "You wound me. Very well, I'll play." He shifted in bed to sit up. The movement did strange things to his muscles – made them flex – and—"Granby's keen on horses."

Anne blinked, tearing her attention from his magnificent torso. "Horses? What?"

"Large creatures. Four legs. Good for travelling—"

"I know what a bloody horse is," Anne said impatiently. "What I *don't* know is anything else about them."

Richard quirked an eyebrow. "Granby has more

experience with equines than ladies. Flutter your lashes at him, give him that one smile you do, croon compliments about his preferred species, and he'll be eating out of your palm by nightfall."

Anne stared at him, bewildered. "The smile? What smile?"

His expression shifted to exasperation. "You know perfectly well which one."

"I'm afraid I don't," she said, her lips curving into a small smile despite her efforts to appear serious. "That's why I asked you to tell me."

"The one with the dimple," he said gruffly.

Anne couldn't quite contain her laughter any longer. "You noticed my dimple?"

He cleared his throat, the hint of a flush dusting his cheeks. "It's comely. No one could deny your dimples are an endearing feature."

"Do you have dimples?" she asked, trying to sound idle and offhand. "I can't recall."

"No."

"Will you smile so I can judge for myself?"

"No."

She reached for him. "I think you do." Richard danced away from her reach, but she kept coming after him, crawling toward him on the bed. "I know you – have a dimple right – there – aaack!"

Anne crashed into Richard, her soft curves melding into the hard planes of his body. His frame was honed by muscle and warmth, and the steady thrum of his heart beat against her chest like a caged bird. Somewhere in her scramble, their fingers entwined, blurring the line between embrace and lust.

She longed to break every rule and kiss him. She thrilled at the rigid proof of his desire against her hip, for it meant he was as much a victim of this madness. A fragile enchantment blazed between them, spreading like wildfire through her veins.

But it wasn't enough. Their bodies could be coaxed into a feverish passion with just a moment's touch; Richard's mind perplexed her – did he imagine her in the darkness? Did he ache for her when night fell? Did his skin yearn for hers?

"Do you dream of the gazebo?" Anne asked recklessly.

Richard breathed a single word into the void between them. "Yes."

A shiver of pleasure thrummed through her – gratification and sadness in equal measure. For that day no longer seemed real.

Madness or enchantment? Anne could think of no other explanation for why she leaned forwards, grazing her teeth along the shell of his ear before asking, "In your dreams, do we stop?"

A sanguinary blaze flared in his gaze then – raw and wild – feeding the craving that consumed her.

"No. We don't stop."

That answer ignited her – she was on the cusp of exploding – but when she reached for him again, he drew away.

The distance in that movement – so infinitesimal as to be nonexistent – was as much a shock as standing on a cliff's edge. It left her dizzy. The fire in his expression was gone, smoothed over. Controlled. She envied him that, for she remained hot all over.

"Time for you to go to bed, sweetheart," he said. "You have an early start tomorrow."

"Yes," she said, her fingers still wrapped tight in his. "I do."

"Horses," he reminded her.

"Horses," she echoed.

Richard released her. "To bed, Anne."

She stumbled to the door, off balance from the encounter. When her hand brushed the knob, she was assailed by a strange need to confess. "Richard?"

His breath sounded like a groan of resignation. "What?"

"I wish we hadn't stopped that day."

Before he could reply, Anne slipped out of the bedchamber.

∽ 16 ∽

Anne stifled a yawn as she and the Marquess of Granby circled the pond.

He spoke of horses with such fervour and passion that it made her question if he loved his stallions more than any woman he'd bedded. Oh, for goodness' sake. Horses weren't even interesting. All anyone had to do was give them a pat on the nose, and they'd be content.

Anne forced herself to pay attention as he instructed her in the finer points of rearing and backing horses, but her mind kept straying.

But maybe she was wrong. Perhaps he knew more about women than he let on. Maybe he knew exactly how to rear and back them, too.

Despite his unending soliloquies, Caroline warned Anne that Granby was one of the most influential and independent gentlemen at Ravenhill. The others were too young, more eager to engage in dalliances than marriage, or didn't strike her as strong-willed enough to withstand Stanton's machinations. This would all be pointless if she ended up with a man her father could manipulate.

So she summoned every ounce of wit and allure and pretended to be interested.

"I can't believe you never learned to ride," he said. "I thought most country girls were practically raised in the saddle."

Anne couldn't bring herself to tell him that Stanton forbade her from riding, considering it too bold a pursuit for a young lady. It afforded a woman far too much freedom.

"I suppose I'll have to learn now, won't I?" she said, flashing Granby a sultry smile – the same one that Richard had described to her the night before.

And its effect astounded her: Granby blushed and coughed, looking down at his feet. "I'd be happy to teach you." His smirk was bashful. "Tomorrow, if you'd like?"

Anne felt a pang of guilt for thinking him boring; he may not have been as exciting as Richard, but he was kind and dependable. A partnership with Granby might lack passion, but it would provide safety and security – something she desperately craved after being betrothed to a man like Kendal.

"Would you?" she asked with a coy grin.

They were approaching the gardens now, which meant their walk would be at an end. But Granby was proposing another outing, and that was a small victory.

"Of course. If you'd care to try your luck at equestrianism, there's a stable's worth of nags that the duchess keeps—"

"Miss Sheffield!"

Anne looked over to see the Earl of Montgomery striding across the path towards them. He radiated power and confidence, from his broad shoulders to the decisive manner he approached them.

Anne stiffened, uncertain why he was approaching so rapidly. She couldn't quite shake off the apprehension that gripped her. Though they had shared a dance the night before, his gorgeous face and clever wit were mere trappings that masked something darker.

His charm was as beguiling as a siren's song, but he didn't fool Anne. She'd grown up surrounded by such games in her father's household.

Anne's lips stretched into a practised smile as he closed in on her, hiding the turmoil beneath. She spoke with a voice sweeter than honey, masking her unease. "Good morning, my lord," she greeted him with false warmth. "How do you fare?"

Montgomery, despite his faults, cut a dashing figure. Dusky hair that was somewhere between auburn and the brown of fine port. And those eyes – as emerald as a spring meadow and every bit as vibrant. Despite possessing a less grand title, she could see why many ladies considered him a better catch than the Marquess of Granby.

"Very well, Miss Sheffield," he purred in his melodic voice. He gave Granby a nod. "Good day, old chap."

The marquess nodded in greeting. "Montgomery."

"Keeping Miss Sheffield to yourself? Can't say I blame you." Montgomery's smile suggested secrets and mischief. "She's lovely. The garden brings out the green in her eyes."

"My eyes are brown," Anne replied with saccharine sweetness.

Granby laughed.

"Quite," Montgomery murmured, with no hint of mockery. "And how do you find the property?"

"It's wonderful. Lord Granby and I were just discussing horses," she said, hoping to divert his attention. "The duchess has a stable full, as I understand it."

"Does she?" He glanced over her shoulder, and she saw a strange emotion clouding his gaze. She could only guess at its nature, but before she could figure it out, he turned on the charm with a winning grin. "That's fascinating. Very fascinating. We were about to begin a game of croquet. Can I tempt you out for a set?"

Before Anne could answer, Granby spoke up from beside her. "I think I'll head in for a respite before tea. You both go without me."

"I'll look after her splendidly," Montgomery said with a clap on the marquess's shoulder. "See you at dinner, old chap."

Anne's irritation grew as Granby walked away. The earl had an overbearing presence that could make a timid man like the marquess avoid her if he thought she wasn't worth the effort.

She couldn't let herself be diverted by someone with no intention of marriage, nor be manipulated by yet another clandestine gentleman with a skill for concealing his true feelings behind a cheerfully curved lip.

No, this would not do.

"Tell me the truth," she said, her voice sharpening against her will. "Were you lying about croquet, my lord?"

Montgomery feigned affronted dignity. Of course, that charm was nothing more than a clever sham. "I? Deceitful?" At her raised brow, he confessed, "The duchess has proposed croquet for tomorrow on the west lawn, and I desired Granby to leave in haste. Knowing his aversion to sport, I uttered a minor untruth."

"Also known as a lie."

He seemed both impressed and surprised by her forthrightness. But Anne had spent several days with Richard and found plain speaking refreshing. She had no time for nonsense now. Granby, despite his single-minded passion for horse racing, did not play games.

"Bravo, Miss Sheffield. Most of the other ladies would have pretended not to notice."

Anne narrowed her gaze. "I'm not interested in pretending. Nor am I unobservant. Whatever you intend to use me for, know that I'm unwilling."

But when she thought that might have angered him, Montgomery only smiled. "At least you kept up your end of the act with Granby. Deftly done, considering how dreary his hobbies are."

"I owe you no explanation, sir. Excuse me." She started away along the garden path, hoping he would take the hint to leave her alone, but the earl only followed her like a predator stalking its prey.

"I see why he's besotted with you," Montgomery murmured. "I wondered if he'd lost his bloody mind last night, but... yes, now I see it."

She stopped and regarded him over her shoulder. "I beg your pardon?"

Montgomery's mask slipped, and his gaze sharpened like a rapier's point. He surveyed her as if she were a militia standing ready for battle. "Grey," he said, as if it should be obvious. "He made it clear I wasn't to trifle with you."

Anne should have been annoyed, but Richard had promised. He wouldn't allow her to exchange one cage for another. She believed him.

"Enemies, then?"

Montgomery's lip curled in more of a grimace than a smile. "No, friends. Of a sort."

"Of a sort?"

He gave a wry noise that hinted at frustration. "Friendship doesn't come easily to me. So I take Grey's advice seriously."

Anne tilted her head, attempting to unravel the enigma that was this man. "This is not permission, you understand, but what did you want to use me for? What prompted you to approach so quickly?"

Montgomery scrutinised her for a moment before responding. "Very well," he said. "I'm trying to evade a certain someone, and I needed a quick diversion."

Anne's confusion multiplied. They were in the garden, brazenly exposed to the eyes of the house and any other guests. To her right, other ladies strolled and laughed.

"We're clearly visible to everyone, in case you hadn't noticed."

"Oh, I had every intention of being seen with you." His lips curved in a sly, secretive smile. "When one wants to avoid an unwelcome romance, an unmarried woman in one's presence should do the trick nicely. Make it clear that I am unavailable."

"I see," said Anne, a bit taken aback by his cavalier tone. "Who are we speaking of?"

He smirked and gestured to someone beneath the willow tree. "The bane of my existence."

Anne started to turn her head, but he caught her arm before she could.

"No. Don't look. You'll only attract her attention."

But Anne couldn't resist stealing a peek at the object of his disdain – not as Anne had expected, a beast with teeth and claws, but a delicate young woman with brown hair who was rather conspicuously not looking their way.

And Anne could identify it plain as day – the same need that settled heavily on her own heart. A yearning she recognised all too well. It occurred to Anne that perhaps women would not be so weighed down by longing if things came easier. If they could move about as freely as men.

Anne, after all, would not be desperately seeking a husband if she had such independence.

She whispered, "I fail to see why you're so scared of that girl. She appears to be entirely inoffensive."

"The ones that appear inoffensive are always the most dangerous," Montgomery muttered. Then: "But it occurs to me you would know about that, lying to Granby the way you have."

She smiled at the amusement in his voice. "You may consider me harmless if it suits you."

Montgomery looked her up and down. "Bloody hell, it's a pity you've set your sights on Granby. You'd make a better match with Grey. Did he teach you how to be this ruthless?"

"I was raised in a political household, my lord. Deception is second nature to me."

"So you admit it then?"

Less than a month ago, she would have denied it. But now? Ruthlessness had become her weapon of choice. Not the kind her father had wielded, like a cat toying with its prey, but a means to an end. She had learned to be cunning out of necessity, to survive in a world where men had all the power. Her father's lessons in manipulation and subterfuge had been hard, but they were paying off. Now she was using those talents to escape her former life and start anew.

Such skills were all some women had.

"Perhaps," she said in a low voice. "But you seem to know something about ruthlessness, don't you? I was warned about your reputation."

Montgomery's lips quirked into a lazy smile. "Caroline's been talking about me, has she? What did she say?"

"Oh, nothing of substance. She referred to you as a rake, a rogue, a libertine, and a blackguard. All rolled into a single charming package. I found it rather amusing."

"Ah, yes, my cousin compliments me quite prettily, doesn't she?"

Anne laughed. "And it's almost comical that such a scoundrel is terrified of one woman."

Still pretending not to notice the lady in question, Montgomery now directed his dazzling grin at another debutante across the garden. Her cheeks reddened, and she whispered to her friend, the two bursting into giggles.

"Lydia Cecil's been infatuated with me for years. I'm trying to protect her."

"From you?" she quipped.

"From herself," he corrected. "I'm not interested in marriage, and it wouldn't do to give her any hope."

"Nor me, I suppose."

He seemed surprised again by her honesty. "That's what I like about you, Miss Sheffield. Get beyond those lies, and you're refreshingly candid."

Anne leaned over to stroke a pink rhododendron on the path. The garden was overflowing with them, their scent filling the air. "If you value candour, then I'm afraid I must inform you I'm here for a husband." When his amusement faded, she flashed him a grin. "Calm down. I've no intention of pursuing any gentleman with no interest in a bride. Especially not one who is hiding something."

Montgomery didn't bother to correct her. He only gave a faint smile. "Granby, then?"

"Granby," she confirmed softly. "But please don't tell him."

He seemed almost puzzled. "He's not – Miss Sheffield, I doubt he'd appreciate your directness. The marquess isn't…"

Anne laughed. "No, he's not ruthless," she finished for him. Now he was warning her, too. For a man who inspired such obloquy from the duchess – rake, rogue, libertine, blackguard, indeed – Montgomery was shockingly considerate. "He doesn't have to be, does he? Sometimes we don't have the luxury of choice."

Before he could ask what she meant, Anne backed away.

She could not stay in his presence a moment longer without sparking the kind of speculative gossip that would occupy everyone at the house party.

"If you need a diversion again, find someone else to use," she said over her shoulder. "Or try your luck with the truth."

∞ 17 ∞

Richard had barely seen Anne all bloody day.
The Marquess of Granby, Lord Montgomery, and Caroline devoured her attention while an endless parade of debutantes commandeered his.

Richard attempted to snatch a conversation with her at dinner, but Granby monopolised her focus. Then, just before the second course, her fingers ghosted across his knuckles – a private message that sent a jolt of heat through him. Later, when everyone retreated to the drawing room for games and frivolity, Anne's quick smile in his direction promised another late rendezvous.

So he waited.

Finally, long after the house settled and quieted, a rustle in the hall drew his notice. A note slid under the door, and Richard grinned like a damn fool.

Cottage. 20 minutes.
– A

★ ★ ★

Richard's boots crunched on the gravel path. The cottage glowed in a golden hue that seemed incongruous in the oppressive darkness of the trees. He paused at the threshold, allowing Anne's presence to wash over him. He inhaled the faint scent of her perfume that lingered in the air, committing the floral redolence to memory.

Rule six. At the end of this fortnight, we'll return to being strangers.

A painful breath left him.

Richard berated himself for his foolishness – for permitting himself to drift too close to her, for desiring her with such need and intensity that it squeezed his chest tight. He was no fool; he knew Anne wasn't his.

Were Richard a superstitious man, he would have suspected enchantment, witchcraft. A curse. But those were only words for the sort of longing that seemed, at first, to be inexplicable. It wasn't magic that had compelled him to come here tonight. The truth was so much more straightforward: it was the most natural thing in the world to want her.

Anne's voice whispered through the window. "Richard? Is that you?"

He let himself in. "Yes. My apologies for being late."

When she smiled, Richard was almost felled by the beauty of it – it was the same smile he'd spoken of in bed... so dizzyingly lovely it could make a man forget his name.

"That's all right." She held up a garden mallet. "So how does one go about playing croquet, anyway?"

Richard couldn't help but laugh. "Croquet? At midnight? That's why you brought me here?"

"Cottage croquet," she corrected, her voice as soft as the moonlight. "It's too dark outside, and Caroline has us scheduled for an afternoon session – she said we could borrow the equipment for practice tonight."

"You've never played?"

"No." She dropped her gaze and shifted the mallet in her hands. "Father wasn't one for games. Aside from political ones, of course. Waste of time and all that."

"Anne." He closed the distance between them. "Even I don't know how to play croquet. You needn't have worried about looking foolish."

She shook her head, auburn curls bouncing around her shoulders. "I can't focus on learning when I'm supposed to be charming. Not when—" She looked away.

"What?"

The corners of her mouth tugged downward. "If the gentlemen here are interested in finding a bride, I'd need more than a few days to convince them. Montgomery at least had the courtesy to be upfront about it. Matrimony is the last thing on his mind."

Richard was glad he didn't have to threaten the earl with bodily injury. That had a way of ruining a friendship.

"I'm so damn sorry, Anne."

She lifted her shoulders in a helpless shrug. "This simplifies matters, I suppose. Granby is in the market for a wife. A bit of a dull conversationalist, but he's kind and safe. Decent enough. So I'll redouble my efforts there."

"Decent enough?" Richard cut in, his tone incredulous. "That's your bar?"

"Yes," she said quietly. "Low standards, remember?"

Richard's heart clenched tight at her words. Her

requirements were such simple requisites – the bare minimum of what a wife should expect – yet she regarded them as exceptional.

Did she not understand that she deserved more? The night sky of stars above the cottage was a reminder of infinite possibilities, and a single glance was all it took to know that this woman was worthy of each and every one.

"Do these standards include any passion? Desire? Intimacy?" Richard couldn't help but ask. "Or are they too extraordinary?"

Anne dropped her gaze away from his. "They're appreciated but ultimately unnecessary."

"Unnecessary?" Richard echoed, unable to keep the disbelief from his voice.

"Don't sound so put out with me, Richard. My marriage won't require those things. I've told you what I'm looking for. I've been very clear."

No wind stirred the trees outside; no rain pelted the roof. The night seemed to roar with its silence, and Richard's mind raced with anger and heartache that this woman – this beautiful creature who deserved all the stars – was so willing to settle for so little.

"Very well, if that's what you think." Richard cupped the back of her neck softly with his hand. "If you don't believe you need passion and desire…" He breathed out a rueful laugh. "We all have our delusions, don't we?"

He'd have to prove to her just how damn necessary they were.

Richard heard her ragged inhale as he drew her closer. And when her breathing eased, he lowered his head and pressed a tender kiss to her throat.

Anne's eyes fluttered closed. A sound of helpless capitulation rose from her lips as her hands tugged at his garments. Her mouth, hot and searching, moved to his jawline, nipping and tasting as she explored its angles.

Her croquet mallet clattered to the floor, forgotten.

The moment shifted. Anne pushed him back against the column and clawed at his shirt and jacket, ripping fabric and scattering buttons. Her teeth sought purchase on the skin of his shoulder, bereft of the gentleness of before. She was wild, desperate; Richard matched her ferocity. He shoved up her skirts and gripped her backside. With his free hand, he found the slit in her drawers to where she was slick with desire.

God, she was so wet.

The thunderous staccato of a sudden downpour slashed through the roaring silence.

Anne jolted, her lungs releasing a soft gasp against his neck. Abruptly, she pulled away from him, straightening her skirts with trembling hands. But her swollen lips, tousled hair, and his own fingers, still damp with evidence of her want, were proof of what they had done.

Irrefutable.

"If you thought to make a point," she said shakily, "you failed."

"Failed, did I?" he drawled, lifting his fingers to his lips and licking them languidly to savour every last drop of pleasure. "Tastes like desire to me."

Anne's mouth fell open. Her pupils dilated with the unmistakable glaze of lust, but then she looked away and snatched the cloak she had hung over the chair. "I'm going back to my room," she said breathlessly. "Don't follow."

But Richard intercepted Anne before she reached the door. His frame quivered with a potent blend of longing and rage. "I never took you for a coward."

Her lips flattened. "Call me whatever you like. You won't change my mind."

"No? You can't tell me you don't think about the gazebo," he snapped, his voice brutal and raw. "That you don't go to bed and dream of me between your thighs, licking your cunny and teaching you honest vocabulary."

Her small gasp was a confession forced out against her will. "Richard—"

"You can't tell me," he continued relentlessly, "that you don't touch yourself there at night and wish it were my hand making you climax. That you don't whisper my name in the darkness and wish I'd whisper back."

Anne shut her eyes tightly. "You don't understand."

"No?" Richard closed the space between them, their bodies flush against one another. His chest tightened with a bizarre pleasure as she trembled. "Feel that? Want honest vocabulary? That's my cock, and it's hard every damn time I look at you. You asked me if I dream about the gazebo, and here's the truth: every night, I dream about fucking you there. I'll regret not asking for it for the rest of my life. So yes, I understand."

She shook her head, those beautiful, wild curls coming loose. "*No*. Stop it."

Now Richard's anger was threatening his composure. He kept it coiled tight because he would not frighten her. Never would he do that. "Then tell me, Anne. Explain to me why you think I can't possibly comprehend why you don't want passion in marriage—"

"*Because I'd pretend it was you*." At his stunned expression, Anne repeated, "I'd pretend it was you. Your earlier point was not a victory, Richard. Not a triumph. It was a reminder of what I can't have."

Richard was silent as she threw open the door and strode out of the cottage.

18

Anne should have been a siren, with her emerald gown that complemented her skin like a kiss from springtime.

Richard gritted his teeth as she flirted outrageously with the Granby during her croquet set, her dazzling laughter ringing over the lawn, fingers touching the marquess's arm as if they were old friends. The other gents' eyes hungrily followed her, but Anne swiped away their clumsy advances with an expert hand. Her attention always drifted back to Granby – her mark, her fool.

Her unwitting dupe.

No, Richard shouldn't use the word *dupe*; it implied a cunning deception leading to a terrible end. But if anyone had struck gold that day, it was Granby – he likely knew it, too. She was a catch.

Hell, she'd even cajoled the marquess into playing croquet – something he despised and for which he'd never shown one ounce of interest before. There was no question he was besotted.

Anne's smile was dazzling as Granby sent his ball through the hoop with aplomb. Richard's heart lurched at the sight of her joy, the ache in his chest threatening to tear him apart.

He hadn't been able to sleep last night after she'd left the cottage, not after her confession. That sentence pierced through Richard like a thousand tiny blades.

I'd pretend it was you.

He didn't deserve rest, not after what he said to her.

"Don't stare too long," Caroline warned, appearing next to Richard. "Or you'll put Anne in an uncomfortable situation."

"I'm not staring," he objected, watching as another lady took her turn and missed the hoop entirely. "Granby is being pretty forward, don't you think?"

Caroline skewered him with a pointed look. "He's a perfect gentleman with her, Richard. I think he genuinely likes her."

"I know." His laugh was dry and humourless. "That's why I hate him. I'm being an utter bastard, aren't I?"

"You're far from the only one," Caroline said, observing the Earl of Montgomery and Lydia Cecil – engaged in a heated argument near the thorn bushes. Cecil wielded her mallet like an avenging angel, her fury palpable even from afar. "Lydia and Gabriel were once friends, but now he's treating her like a plague carrier."

"She's probably fortunate since his only skill seems to be in breathing, and she deserves a damn sight better," Richard muttered. "But Monty might benefit from being knocked on his arse by a woman."

Caroline watched them with a wistful expression. "Perhaps. But she should tread lightly. Nothing good comes of pushing someone into loving you. It doesn't work that way."

"Know a thing or two about that, do you?"

Caroline's lips flattened into a line. "I married an unwilling husband only to have him walk away from both me and our friendship and avoid my existence for seven years. Yes, I comprehend romantic catastrophes all too well."

"Caro—"

She shook her head sadly. "Let it go, Richard. It's done now." Then, the air reverberated with the sharp crack of a mallet striking a ball, and Caroline mustered a pleasant façade. "Well struck, Miss Sheffield!"

Richard looked over as Anne's ball sailed through the final hoop and came to a rolling stop. Her face bloomed into a victorious grin, her entire being concentrated on the man standing across from her. Richard felt something inside him twist and turn, dark, ugly, and unrecognisable. Jealousy? He did not like it. She was not his.

I'd pretend it was you.

Anne's gaze flickered to his own, as if sensing his emotions, and he offered a weak smile in return. He clapped in a show of applause. A silent acknowledgement that he had been a fool again, and he was sorry.

Anne seemed to understand, and her lips curved up ever so slightly in response, expression conveying an almost tangible sentiment of regret. *I'm sorry, too.*

∽ 19 ∽

Anne was falling in love with Richard Grey.

The clock on her bedchamber mantel ticked relentlessly, like a despot counting her remaining moments of freedom. Four days to convince Granby to propose. Four days left before she must don a mask of indifference and pretend Richard was nothing but another acquaintance.

But clocks were just cold metal and mindless machinery – gears and cogs and springs whirring away without conscience or care. The urgency Anne felt was all its own invention, an emotion crafted by her heart and mind, far more intricate and abstract than any machine.

Love was like that, wasn't it? It was a human prerogative beyond reason or logic; once it had its hooks in you, it was almost impossible to let it go.

But Anne resolved to wring every last drop of joy from her remaining days in Ravenhill.

No arguments about marriage or the future, or thinking about what her life might be like after she left. These were more than mere nights; they were an interlude, a respite from the world, a moment of bliss carved out of the relentless march of time.

For four more nights, Richard was hers.

When Anne entered his bedchamber, the door clicked softly closed behind her.

"Thank God," he murmured, stirring in his sleep. "The odds had narrowed to near zero that you'd show up."

"Would you have braved the hallway and snuck into my chamber?" A strange yearning filled her chest when she asked it.

"Absolutely." She heard the smirk in his voice. "I wouldn't have let you escape me that easily. I was prepared to give you a full seven minutes before I came searching – glad you saved me the trouble." The following silence stretched for eternity. When he spoke, it was a barely audible whisper. "Anne? What is it?"

Fear lodged in her throat. "I only have four days left," she whispered.

A soft exhale drifted across the room like smoke from an extinguished candle. "Come here, sweetheart," Richard said.

He sat up in bed and opened his arms to her. His features cast in silver by moonlight, broad shoulders and strong chest displayed in all their glory, his masculinity so achingly beautiful. Anne stepped into Richard's embrace. Solid and reassuring, he welcomed her with a protectiveness that promised safety.

Nuzzling his neck, she drank in his scent of rich soap and brandy, overlaid with something uniquely Richard: a faint sweetness, as if marked by some wayward magic. That same enchantment had made her fall in love against all reason.

His lips laid a tender claim upon her forehead, a gentle and comforting benediction. "Granby's a fool if he doesn't make you his wife."

Anne nestled against him, the heat of his skin on her cheek like a prayer. "It's not just him."

Richard kissed the top of her head. "What, then?"

It's you.

I'm scared of losing you.

And I can't have you.

"Will you kiss me?" she asked, her voice a sigh. "On the lips?"

The moment expanded until it seemed to fill the entire room. The only sound was the steady beat of their hearts, the sudden rapid pace of their breath.

Finally, he let out a soft groan as he tightened his hold on her. "Anne."

"Kendal is the only man who has, and…"

He gently pushed her back so he could meet her gaze. "And what?"

Anne shuddered, visions of Kendal's vicious embrace washing over her; the burning sensation of his punishing lips as he left bruises on her shoulders. A reminder that she was nothing more than a pawn in her father's game, a tool to be used and abused at will.

"It hurt," she breathed. "Is kissing supposed to hurt?"

The muscles in Richard's jaw tensed. "No," he growled. Soft but adamant. "Kissing is not meant to be painful. Ever."

The words hung in the air like smoke, their voices barely above a hush, as if they were exchanging secrets. Richard's fingertips traced a soothing loop on Anne's back, his silent assurance of support taking away some of the pain.

"What's it supposed to be like then?" a fractured whisper escaped her lips.

Richard nudged his forehead to hers and exhaled his warmth onto her lips. All the rage drained from him as quickly as it came. She wanted to close the gap between them, that small yet infinite space that separated them. But she left it up to him.

He cupped her cheek. "A kiss should always leave you wanting more."

"More of what?" she asked, a quiet plea for more than what had been taken from her.

He paused – right before their lips met – and uttered his response with a single breath. "Everything."

Richard kissed Anne with the certainty of a long-lost lover, as if their bodies recognised each other. They moved together like the tides, each seeking the deep, dark places of the other. A wild affirmation of everything forbidden and denied. This kiss was not the start of something, but the middle of a confession, an explosive clash of desire.

Every touch of his tongue, every whisper spoke secrets to her soul, secrets she'd never known. Each moment was a million unheard words.

Beautiful and terrible, that kiss. It changed her, shattered her world into pieces she could never rebuild.

It changed everything.

"More," she gasped.

She found herself pinned beneath him as he took control. Her nails clawed against his flesh, a silent invitation to join her in reckless abandon. He gave a soft assent against her lips, and the pair tumbled into the abyss with nothing to rely on but pure instinct.

A frenzied fervour consumed them, their kiss a desperate language of nipping teeth, grasping hands, insistent kisses.

Need driving every movement.

"Please," she whispered.

She had no words to articulate the hunger that burned within her. Nothing she knew could penetrate the searing heat of her desire other than the single phrase he had taught her – the first word he'd spoken that still scorched her like a conflagration—

"Fuck me." A reckless benediction.

Richard tore free from her with a shuddering gasp. His gaze was unfocused, and his chest heaved as he tried to get his breathing under control. "We have to stop."

Anne touched his arm. "Richard—"

He pushed back from her with a strength she had not expected from him, his gaze more distant than the stars. "You need to go." He closed his eyes, as though he could no longer bear to look at her. "You're not for me."

Words like daggers. She scrambled out of bed. How could she ask this of him? Why hadn't she considered it would be as difficult for him as it was for her? "Richard, I'm—"

He made a soft sound of resignation, and Anne's heart cracked open. "Just go, sweetheart."

Anne fled the room.

20

"I've enjoyed our morning rambles and riding lessons," Granby said, guiding Anne around a gnarled tree root. "I look forward to them every day."

"Yes," she said, trying to quell the storm of emotions raging inside her. "I agree."

Relieved that he didn't notice her distraction, Anne's thoughts kept returning to the kiss she shared with Richard the previous night. The fire that ignited in her heart dismantled all sense of propriety and restraint, leaving her craving more than a mere kiss. She yearned for something deeper and darker, a rapture almost too beautiful to bear.

"Miss Sheffield," Granby said, interrupting her thoughts. He surprised her by coming to a halt and taking her by the shoulders. Anne felt his gaze like hot metal on her skin. "I've the feeling we could be more than friends. Do you agree?"

No.

Anne wanted to scream it, push him away, but practicality held her back. Wasn't this what she longed for more than anything? Freedom meant everything – and Granby stood offering it all in a breathless moment.

But something hollowed in the depths of her soul, a darkness that whispered this was wrong. *This was wrong.* As if her father was there with them, pushing his manipulations onto her; she felt twisted, like a broken tool in his hands.

"Yes," Anne said, hating herself for allowing even that word. "I... very much enjoy your company."

Granby lifted her chin with a finger, and the air shifted like static before a lightning strike. As if she stood on a precipice about to fall. "I'm glad. I've never treasured a woman's companionship the way I have yours. I feel as though you truly listen to me."

Anne almost laughed bitterly at the notion. She had barely heard him this morning as she let Richard's kiss dominate every thought, every sensation, every ache in her soul. She was a villain – a fraud.

"And I think," he went on, "we may be well-suited for one another. So..." He chuckled – an easy, carefree laugh that seemed to melt off his tongue and float in the surrounding air. "What I am trying to ask is – will you be my wife, Miss Sheffield?"

Anne hesitated, her pulse thudding in her ears. In any other life, she'd have leapt at the opportunity, thrown herself into his arms and laughed with relief – but now she quailed, a strange foreboding gripping her chest.

But she wasn't an idiot. This was her chance, and she had to take it. So she forced a brilliant smile and said, "Yes. Yes, I will."

Granby grinned, leaning forward to brush his lips across

hers. It was a fleeting moment and cold as winter, with none of the searing heat that had consumed her with Richard. All that remained was a faint tinge of disappointment.

"I'll ask Sheffield for permission when I return to London," he said.

Anne's heart cracked like ice on a lake. "There's something you should know."

He looked puzzled. "What is it?"

"It's my father. He—" She let out a rattling breath, unsure if this would drive him away – yet a traitorous part of her almost hoped it might. "He's determined to marry me off to the Duke of Kendal."

Granby frowned. "I'm sure that once he sees how well-suited we are, I can sway him to reconsider."

Anne couldn't believe how kind he was. She didn't deserve him; he merited a wife who was not a liar, a swindler, a cheat – a woman who could come to love him.

"He's not a man who convinces easily. I've been promised to Kendal since I was twelve." At the sharp inhalation of his breath, she added, "I know. I should have told you. But I found that once we were together—" No, she could not lie, not even for this. She wasn't talented enough. "That wasn't my choice. But you would be."

Granby seemed to consider her words, his jaw muscles twitching. Then he nodded slowly, as if coming to a decision. "If I can arrange a special licence, will you promise to wed me?"

"Without hesitation." She smiled warmly at him.

His lips curved up in response. Then he pulled her close and held her for a moment.

Anne glanced over his shoulder and spotted Richard emerging from the nearby shrubbery. His gaze raked over them, and something unreadable flickered in his expression. When their eyes met, she gave him a single nod of confirmation.

Richard offered her a gentle smile and turned back the way he'd come.

⌒ 21 ⌒

Anne found Richard alone in the library while the other guests enjoyed tea in the garden. Granby had invited her, but she refrained, her façade threatening to crumble at her feet like the ash of wildfire.

Richard didn't turn as she closed the door behind her. He stood at the window, motionless, his chiselled features cast in sharp relief by the vibrant colours of the sunset. Anne felt the dagger of longing sink and twist deeper as she took in every detail of his masculine frame, from the broad shoulders that strained against his shirt to the strength in his muscled forearms.

Every day she'd fallen more in love with him, and now she couldn't imagine her life without him in it.

Words failed her as she spoke his name. "Richard," she whispered, the sound barely audible in the deafening silence of the room.

What more could be said? Nothing seemed adequate – no apology, no thanks.

He replied with a single sentence that shattered the stillness like broken glass. "I suppose congratulations are in order." His voice was emotionless and unfamiliar, like he'd been rehearsing it for days.

"No," she said softly. "They aren't."

His laugh was dry. "And why not? You came and accomplished what you set out to do. You received an offer from a marquess. That has to count for something. Granby will make you a good husband."

The disdain in those words nudged the blade deeper. Did he not notice how it hurt her?

"Will he?" Anne barely dared to hope for a different answer.

Richard answered with no hesitation. "He's everything you wanted: kind, safe."

He didn't have to say the rest, but she'd heard that unspoken sentiment as clear as a bell, and it angered her.

Boring.

Anne made a noise of frustration. "Damn you, Richard Grey." His surprised gaze flicked to her, and her heart beat wildly. "You're clever, aren't you?" she asked him, stalking closer. "You can see through any politician's lies, but with me, you're utterly blind. Haven't you been paying attention? Have I been speaking in a foreign language all this time?"

"Tell me again, then." His voice was tight with something she couldn't name.

She was glad – glad that his carefully constructed walls were beginning to crack. They were far beyond mere performances now.

She reached up and gripped his chin, her stare hard as

flint. "Say the words, and I'm yours. I'll marry you and not him. You'd have my hand even if I had the world at my feet."

His sharp intake of breath and hesitation said more than words ever could.

Releasing him with a mirthless laugh, she said, "But as I mentioned when we first met, I don't expect you to abandon your precious life of debauchery and intrigue to rescue me."

Anne turned to leave, but he snagged her shoulder and yanked her back.

Somehow, his mouth found hers, a desperate need taking over as they kissed hard and wild, neither one willing nor able to break away from the other. Agony and pleasure entwined as he bit her lower lip, grazing her skin with his teeth before kissing her again.

Something guttural rumbled from Richard's chest, and his hand dived into the tangle of Anne's hair – tugging out pins – each jolt sending a spark of pain that made this real. Pain became her clarity; the gratification of his embrace was her source of power. His lips travelled down her neck, biting ever so softly beneath her collarbone, marking her as his own.

It would be a faint bruise by tomorrow, and by the time she left Ravenhill, it would be gone entirely – though part of her wanted a lasting reminder that this moment existed, that *he* existed.

Once they left this house, they would act as strangers – renew their performances.

He, the dissolute rake without a care in the world.

And she, the pretty little idiot.

Nothing had changed, yet everything had changed.

Anne pushed away, trying to gather herself. She had to repair her armour, reinforce the walls around her heart and return to reality. To the lies she was so adept at telling.

"I have to go. Granby will wonder where I am."

She was out the door before he could say another word.

∽ 22 ∽

Richard sat beside Anne at dinner, watching as she laughed with Granby, and felt like he was in the deepest corner of hell.

He'd honed his skills in the snakepits of politics; a deceiver, a schemer, a manipulator of the powerful. He'd thought himself the master of his domain – the grand architect of his destiny.

But then Anne entered his life, and everything came crashing down.

You'd have my hand even if I had the world at my feet, Anne had said.

Richard should have claimed her at that moment. Snatched her away and took her as his own, like a beast from some gothic fairytale.

But he hesitated, believing himself unworthy – and that mistake was ruinous.

Tonight, Anne was a vision in the crimson dress she'd

borrowed from Caroline, her fire-blessed hair illuminated by the chandelier light. All Richard wanted was to rip out her pins, one by one, and tangle his fingers into her locks as he kissed her. Tasted her. Possessed her completely.

But that would never be his right – not anymore.

Granby would be granted those intimacies in the future. He'd have Anne in bed each morning and pleasure her each night.

And Richard? Richard was left with nothing but gritted teeth and shallow pleasantries directed at the other woman beside him; he was an automaton parroting the same memorised lines he'd mastered for years. All the while, Granby stared at Anne with open admiration, seemingly oblivious to the misery in her expression as she rehearsed her own script of a cheerful lady who laughed at all the right moments.

Yes, this was hell – one of its deepest circles.

Then, just before Richard felt as if he'd lose his mind, Anne's palm brushed his beneath the table. She laced her fingers with his and squeezed gently. He closed his eyes briefly, then ran his thumb over her knuckles.

How long did he remain like that? Nodding along to the conversation, pretending he was listening, but all the while tuned out? He couldn't remember.

Anne must have sensed his detachment because she grasped his hand again and tipped her head slightly, a silent plea to stay focused.

"The debate around the Ballot Act is sure to cause uproar when Parliament's in session," Montgomery said, leaning back in his chair. "A lot of men are opposed to commoners having a say, let alone a secret ballot."

"And why shouldn't they?" Baron Camoys interjected; a young idiot still wet behind the ears. "Cowardly, if you ask me. A man should be brave enough to show where his loyalties lie."

"Yes," Montgomery said with a sharp smirk. "Honesty is easy for those who can keep a roof over their heads without fear of reprisal. Don't you think?"

Camoys' eyes narrowed. "Then perhaps they ought to vote as their landlords command. A cross in the right box is a small price for a home."

Montgomery's smile had a razor-like quality. "I'd argue the point, but I suppose you'd know more than me about votes being bought and paid for, Camoys?"

The other man blinked in shock, his mouth wide and unspeaking.

After a moment's silence, a few throats cleared, and some hushed murmurs resumed. "Surely we can discuss a more polite topic," said the debutante beside Montgomery with a laugh. "Why should we concern ourselves with commoners when there is a season to consider?"

"Perhaps," Miss Cecil said quietly, "it's because those men have a say in this country's future and should have the right to make it free of influence."

The other woman wrinkled her nose. "I almost asked how you know about such things, Miss Cecil, but I suppose you ought to have something to keep you occupied while sitting along the perimeter of the ballroom."

Miss Cecil's face pinkened, and the table went silent again. Anne and Richard opened their mouths to argue simultaneously – Richard was still crafting his searing put-down – but Montgomery spoke first, in his deep, honeyed voice. "My pardon," he said. "Lady Cornelia, isn't it? I couldn't help but notice we've never shared a dance."

A faint blush crept across Lady Cornelia's cheeks as she smiled coyly. "No. No, we haven't, my lord."

Montgomery nodded slowly and declared in a low tone full of steel, "Good. I intend to keep it that way."

Miss Cecil choked on her wine to stifle her laugh while Lady Cornelia shot her a poisonous glare.

Beside him, Richard saw Anne's face break into a smile just a moment before Granby said, "I say, that was uncalled for, Montgomery. This topic has no place at a table with gentlewomen present, especially not the daughter of one of our most esteemed MPs."

Anne's hand tightened in his. Her amusement disappeared, and her expression fell into a mask of panic. The words sent a burning rage through Richard, and he wished he could tear Sheffield apart for his lies.

Esteemed Member of Parliament?

The absurdity of Granby's statement was enough to make Richard choke on his tongue. Anne understood better than anyone the truth behind Sheffield's reputation.

"Ladies are perfectly capable of engaging in a conversation about politics," he growled, restraining his fury. "What do you think, Miss Sheffield?"

Speak, sweetheart, he willed her. *Speak. Let them know how brilliant you are.*

He watched her face transform as she gathered her thoughts, preparing to unleash them upon the room.

But before she could utter a word, Granby ruined it all with a dreadful chuckle. "Oh yes, I forgot," Granby said.

"Your sister has written several political essays, hasn't she, Mr Grey? I hear they're positively shocking."

The light faded from Anne's eyes. She was slipping back into her prison cell: Beauty, not brains.

"Often," Richard replied through gritted teeth, "those who appreciate Alexandra's work are the only ones with a modicum of intelligence."

"Well," Granby said, "I think it's good that Lady Alexandra can't vote in Parliament. We hardly need more radicals."

Montgomery looked close to murder. "And what, exactly, is the problem with women's suffrage?"

"Gentlemen." Caroline leaned forwards, though her glare was directed solely at Granby. "Let us change the topic, shall we?"

But Granby wasn't finished. "A wife's views don't differ from her husband's. His vote counts for them both, as Miss Sheffield's father brilliantly argued in *The Times*. Isn't that right, Miss Sheffield?"

Anne's hand clamped hard on Richard's, and all the fire she'd been about to unleash was gone. Her expression closed off again.

"He did," she muttered, her voice barely above a whisper. She cleared her throat and spoke into the silence. "If you don't mind, I find I have something of a headache. Would you all please excuse me?"

Under the table, she released Richard.

"Are you well, Miss Sheffield?" Granby said, all concern.

"Yes," she replied softly. "I'll be fine – carry on without me."

Richard watched her leave, but before he could rise,

Caroline halted him with a shake of her head. If he were to follow her out now, people would surely talk.

Caroline smiled warmly at her guests. "If you've all finished your repast, shall we move on to the drawing room? And if you'll pardon me, I will check on Miss Sheffield."

∾ 23 ∾

A chill permeated the night air as Anne sat in the garden beneath the sculpture of Venus emerging from the sea. The garden was still and quiet, save for the distant rustling of leaves. The Duchess of Hastings found her there, Caroline's brow knitted in concern.

"I'm sorry," she began, her voice barely audible.

"Don't." Anne couldn't bear any pity from the duchess. "Please don't apologise. Not you."

Anne couldn't help but envy Venus. Resplendent and self-assured, the goddess emerged from the ocean with a satisfied smirk that seemed to hold a thousand secrets.

"I've always hated her." Caroline gestured to the marble figure.

"Why?" Anne asked.

The duchess's reply was but a whisper, barely audible in the night's stillness. "She looks so free, doesn't she? So sure of herself. But even the goddess of love was desperate to flee a man determined to chain her down."

Had the other woman come there too? To that tranquil corner of the garden when the pain became unbearable? When it all grew too overwhelming, and her heart was at risk of shattering? Anne understood that hurt, having sought refuge there many times during her stay.

The memories made her cheeks heat and her throat feel dry and scratchy. How could she have been so foolish? Granby had revealed his true nature during dinner, but Anne should have seen it long before that. Every lesson or walk, he never asked for her opinion on anything, completely focused on his favourite topic of conversation.

Stupid girl, Anne scolded herself. He didn't care enough to ask.

But she knew. She was so desperate to escape her father she'd allowed danger to slip past unnoticed. And she had been distracted – by Richard.

Anne made a noise as if to express these thoughts aloud and then abandoned the impulse. What good would it do? "This is a lovely corner of the garden," she told Caroline instead. "Your smug goddess aside."

Caroline settled on the bench beside her. "You don't have to pretend with me. Speak freely. Venus is the only one to hear, and she is too busy lording it over us to care."

"I deserve her censure." Anne shook her head, releasing a brittle laugh.

"It's not your fault Granby's a lackwit," Caroline said. "I would never have put you two in each other's path if I'd known his views."

"He's not alone in that regard." Anne sighed. "Most men in Parliament think like him."

It took someone exceptional to see things differently –

like Richard or Montgomery. Anne had always thought politicians who fought against women's suffrage were shouting against the tide, willing it to stay put. There was a pointlessness in commanding the sea to bend to your will.

But even the currents had rhythms that ebbed and flowed. Progress could never succeed, it seemed, without backsliding along the way.

"Most men in Parliament are idiots," the duchess snapped, to Anne's surprise. "We're not property to be treated like furniture to come home to when convenient. We ought to have a say in our future, and we ought to—" Caroline inhaled sharply and glanced away. "I beg your pardon. I've said too much."

Anne felt her throat tighten. "I don't mean to pry about your husband not being here as host, but… did he leave you?"

Caroline stared at the trees, her voice soft but resolute. "He opened the door and never looked back. Hastings has many redeeming qualities, but being a good husband isn't one of them. No woman should be subjected to such a travesty in marriage if she can find another path." Her grip on Anne's hand was reassuring before letting go. "So ask yourself this: would you want to spend the remainder of days with a man who sees you as an inferior?"

"But what if I have no other choice?" she said, the thought of Richard's hesitation still lingering in her thoughts.

"Of course you do." She stood, her skirts rustling. "If I may be so bold: Scotland doesn't need special licences or permission for girls your age to wed. It also benefits from being out of your father's reach. For the vicar inquiry, tell him you've been living there for a month and have Richard make a generous tithe for his vicarage."

"But what if he—"

"If Richard refuses to wed you, I'll personally throttle him."

24

Once the house fell into a slumber, Anne stole through the halls. She slid her note beneath Richard's door with furtive, trembling hands, then vanished into the night, seeking refuge in the cottage.

It wasn't long before Anne heard his boots on the path, crunching over fallen leaves. The door creaked open. Richard stood there, his silhouette limned in silver by moonlight, framed by stonework. His blue eyes blazed with some feral emotion that seared through her, igniting a fire in the dark hollow she'd only just discovered deep inside herself.

"Hello," she greeted him softly.

"Granby is an imbecile who doesn't deserve you," he declared without preamble, his gaze fierce and possessive.

Anne laughed at his eagerness to defend her honour. "*Richard.*"

"I'm completely serious," Richard murmured as he prowled closer, slamming the door shut behind him. "I ought to have known anyone that obsessed with horses was an utter lackwit. And he has the stupidest damned hair I've ever laid eyes on."

Anne dissolved into laughter, winding her arms around Richard's neck as she leaned against his chest. "I adore you."

He growled softly into her ear. "Would you like me to hit him for you?"

Laughing again, Anne shook her head against his shoulder. "No."

"Maybe just... mangle him a bit?" he asked hopefully. "A little revenge for treating you so shabbily? I can destroy him. Run him out of London. Blackmail him into an early grave."

"Richard," she said as she brushed a lock of blond hair from his forehead. "No."

"Very well," he conceded with a sigh. "No mangling. No dismemberment. You don't care for him, do you?"

"Absolutely not." She gave a derisive snort, reflecting on the interminable prattle about racehorses that made her want to drown herself in the pond. "If we married, I would have strangled him in his sleep."

Richard quieted, holding her close as his thumb stroked circles over the nape of her neck. Anne's breath caught as Richard whispered in the softest voice imaginable, "You're not marrying him."

Somewhere within the chamber, a candle guttered. A window rattled gently in the breeze, and rain pattered in a steady rhythm against the panes.

Ever so slowly, Anne tilted her head and pressed her lips against Richard's throat. He loosed a shuddering exhale. She stepped closer, pressing against his body as desire coursed through her veins like wildfire.

"Is that your way of proposing?" she whispered.

Richard rumbled from low in his chest, a noise that spoke of need and craving. She realised then that there was power in this – a power so vast it could only be found and wielded in moments when hunger overrode propriety and even the powerful shuddered with yearning.

"Yes." A gasp of a sound.

Something primal and ravenous ignited deep within her as she grasped the magnitude of her control: she could make the most notorious rogue in London tremble with a mere touch.

"I think I deserve to be romanced," she said casually. "You've walked in here and demanded I break off an engagement for you. Earn me."

The look Richard gave her was pure sin incarnate. "You want me to earn you?" He made a soft noise. "How demanding you've become. Are your standards improving?"

"You're the one who taught me to make demands," she replied archly. "To not settle for less. To be b—What are you doing?"

A wicked grin spread across his face. "Unbuttoning your dress. I'm ready for round one of romancing."

25

Richard wanted to take it slow with Anne.

He could barely hold back, his need for her warring against honour that demanded he be gentle. Anne deserved more than a rushed consummation – more than his selfish wants.

There was time ahead of them. Years in which they'd learn each other's wants and desires. Discover what made the other moan, what drove them wild.

"You're sure?" Richard whispered, giving her one last chance to back out. To prove she could trust him, here and always. "I can be an unyielding bastard at times – extorting people and holding their secrets over their heads."

Anne arched an eyebrow. "What makes you think I'm any different? And I won't let you sleep in until noon."

He exhaled slowly. "You're a menace."

"Yes," she said with a sultry smile. "I am."

"A hellion and too clever by far."

"Those, too."

"God, I can't wait to marry you," Richard murmured as he swept her into his arms, practically hauling her into the cottage bedchamber.

Urgency surged through him as his lips pressed against hers, desire coursing through his veins.

Their kiss was a tempest. Like the clash of steel, her lips demanded his surrender. She grabbed tight, empowered by it, commanding more.

Richard tugged at her dress, and it cascaded from her body like spinning silk, pooling on the floor. His fingertips worked to remove her undergarments until she stood before him naked, and he rewarded each peeling layer with another kiss – featherlight nips that drove her to shuddering bliss. Every part of her was exquisite: smooth against his mouth like velvet, sweet as roses against his tongue.

His teeth grazed her throat. She shuddered in pleasure beneath him, a wordless assent as if entreating, *please more*.

"All these freckles," he whispered reverently. A smattering of constellations along her shoulders, arms, and even legs. "I'm in love with them."

"Are you?" She blushed. "I know they're not fashionable—"

"To hell with fashionable," he growled, mapping the delicate curves of her waist with his hands. "I plan to spend days kissing every last one of them."

"That would take a great deal of time, as there are so many."

"Yes. It's a hardship I'll have to endure. Starting now." His lips found her shoulder, brushing kisses there. "One. Two. Three, four, five. Six. Seven—"

Laughing, Anne pulled away. "Your clothes first. It's my turn."

Anne was not as gentle. Her hands moved with intent now, tearing off his coat and waistcoat in a single motion. The buttons of his shirt flew across the room as she ripped it open. Richard groaned when she reached for his trousers, tugging them down his hips to join the pile on the floor.

Anne's face blazed with a hunger he'd never seen before. An echoing need hummed through him – to feel her, touch her, worship her. To be inside her.

"Beautiful," she murmured against his chest, her tongue tracing a path to his throat. "You're so beautiful."

"That's my line. I'm supposed to be doing the romancing."

"Teach me more profanity," Anne whispered, her lips a lazy invitation. Her eyes smouldered with a heat Richard had only seen in the fires of a conflagration. "I want to know every filthy word you've ever heard or said."

He swept his hand through her hair, sending pins clattering to the floor like fallen stars. He wanted her wild, untethered and unleashed. "Shouldn't I be spouting sonnets and serenades? Etching sweet whispers into your heart?"

"I don't like sonnets, and I told you to earn me."

His chuckle was guttural and raw. "So it's obscenities you want?" He said, lips skating across hers in a scorching promise. "Then how about I set you down in that bed, lick your cunny until you scream my name, and fuck you until morning?"

She gasped, pleasure lacing the sound. "Yes."

Richard slowly slid down her body, savouring each inch as he went. When his mouth finally reached the apex of her thighs, he kissed her in an unholy invocation. The bed creaked beneath them like an altar of worship, and Richard found himself on his knees in silent reverence.

Her fingers twisted in his hair like a benediction, and when she shattered into rapture, it was with a gasp of something akin to surprise.

Soft laughter followed, and Richard looked up with an arched brow. "What?" he asked.

"Do that again," she said through dreamy eyes still glazed by pleasure.

His smile was slow and sharp as he rose between her thighs to position himself at her entrance. "Again and again," he promised her. "I'm going to bury my cock so deep inside you. Is that what you want?"

"Yes," she whispered, trying to draw him closer. Her knees gripped his hips. "Please."

Richard paused, a sudden gravity overtaking him. He wanted to make sure she knew what she was getting into – this was her first time, and he had no wish to betray her trust.

"Anne." He searched her gaze. "The first time isn't always—"

She cupped his cheek, stopping him mid-sentence. "I know. That's why I'm glad it's with you."

Richard shut his eyes and pressed his forehead against hers. "After we marry, I intend to show you all the ways a man should treat his wife. Always like this between us. No standards in the ground, understand?" He brushed his thumb over her jaw. "You deserve nothing less."

Anne's answer came without words, claiming his mouth with a desperate kiss before yanking him closer.

Richard slowly sank inside her. Anne gasped, then flinched at the sudden intrusion. He almost lifted his head to apologise – until she wrapped her legs around his hips, trapping him there.

Her solitary whisper burned into his flesh like liquid fire. "*Stay.*"

Stay. Richard would have stayed there forever if she had asked – contenting himself with soft kisses along her collarbones and shy explorations of the tender spot near her pulse. But then Anne moved beneath him, and a moan escaped those sweet lips – a plea.

More.

That summoned something dark and primal. An ache that seemed too bottomless ever to satisfy. Richard forged a steady rhythm, an act of devotion in that space between them. "You feel so damn good."

Anne's breath was like silk against his cheek, a lilting chorus of encouragements and prayer. *More.*

The pressure between them built until Richard was almost senseless with need. His forceful thrusts left her gasping, her nails digging into his buttocks in silent urging. Her heels dug into his thighs, and he knew she was as close as he was.

"Richard," she gasped as she twisted against him and cried out her climax.

He shuddered above her, pressing his forehead to her throat. They lay together until their breathing steadied again, tangled limbs heavy with exhaustion.

"Have I earned you yet?" he whispered at last. "Or am I romancing you again tonight?"

A mischievous smile curled her lips. "I think I'll need you to earn me *every* night."

Richard rolled her gently onto her back and kicked up a wicked grin. He'd be ready for romancing for round two. "I can do that." Then his voice dropped low as he let his gaze wander over her. "Now, about those freckles…"

26

Richard awoke, his body exhausted from hours of pleasure with Anne. He'd had her three times during the night and slept more soundly than he had in years. He smiled, intending to have her again before breakfast, but when he reached for her, she wasn't there.

She'd been absent long enough for the sheets to grow cold.

She must have returned to her room before the sun rose. He smirked at the thought of their scandalous rendezvous and the gossip it would stir.

Richard pulled on his clothes and strode back to the house. It was dead silent – no voices, no laughter, no footfalls – but Caroline's servants were well-trained; they prided themselves on being scarcely seen and certainly not heard. And as for the guests? Except for Anne and Granby, they rarely made it out of bed before noon.

And Richard had kept Anne very busy indeed.

A smirk tugged his lips as he trudged toward Caroline's study and knocked lightly on the door. Best to give the duchess the news that he and Anne would be leaving as soon as possible.

"Enter." Her voice was muffled behind the heavy oak barrier.

Richard stepped into the chamber that still bore traces of its former occupant – the duke – despite Caroline's efforts to feminise it with a vase of tulips on the edge of her desk. No matter what time of year, it seemed there were always tulips. Richard often wondered why.

His amusement died when he saw Caroline's blonde brows drawn together in a frown. "What's happened?"

She gave a sharp gesture towards the stack of papers folded neatly on the corner of her desk, with his name scrawled across them in familiar handwriting.

"Anne left you these and this note after breaking things off with Granby."

With a growl, Richard snatched up the letter.

Dear Richard,

I know how alarmed you must be right now; I am sorry for that. I had to leave Ravenhill in some haste.

My father sent a cable this morning. He sends notes when he requires my attention regarding a person he finds of immediate interest. The cable was about you. I cannot be selfish and prioritise my happiness and needs when he intends to harm you. You are more important to me than that.

I beg your forgiveness and have left you with the

remaining information on his allies, as promised. I will help
you the way you helped me.

Yours,

Anne

Richard crushed the letter in his fist, a low oath spilling from his lips. He dragged both hands through his hair like a man possessed. "You let her leave?"

"She's not a prisoner, Richard." Her gaze softened. "Are you going to read her papers or not?"

"Later." His laugh was mirthless and empty. "I have to go to London, find her, and shove her on the first bloody train to Scotland so I can marry her."

"I suggest you plan another course of action because short of kidnapping her, she won't come willingly. She cares too deeply for you."

Richard bared his teeth. "Then maybe I'll just strangle her father," he growled.

Caroline straightened with an incredulous look. "You can't be serious."

"Wasn't until I read that damn letter."

The duchess snatched his hands in hers, her voice a whip-crack of command. "Listen to me – the stupidest thing you could do right now is charge into Stanton Sheffield's house and drag his daughter away like some barbarian. She's not a sack of potatoes; she made it clear what she needs to do."

Richard raised an eyebrow. "So you're suggesting I shouldn't strangle him?"

Caroline held him fast. "You aren't listening! You're being a stupid, emotional, impulsive man – a terrible combination if there ever was one. *Listen*. Pay attention. Do you hear me?"

Richard didn't flinch beneath her grip, though he wondered if any bones were close to breaking. "Do I have a choice?"

"No." She gestured to the stack of documents with her chin. "Take what information she gave you and get your votes secured. Give her time to procure whatever else she needs, and then – when you've calmed down – make further plans. Understand?"

Good grief, she was downright terrifying when she put her mind to something. "I'm almost too afraid of what you'd do if I said no. I've never known you to be so fierce."

Caroline smiled brilliantly. "Good. Now pack your things and go to London."

27

Time was running out for Anne.

She knew it wouldn't be long before the whispers of the duchess's house party spread, and if her father caught wind of it, he'd cross-examine her like a criminal. Everyone had seen her with Lord Granby, and even though their extremely brief engagement hadn't been announced, rumours were sure to fly around soon enough.

When she entered her father's home in London, the butler informed her that Stanton wanted to speak to her. "Oh? When did he return from his trip?"

"Late yesterday evening, miss," Bates said.

Then Stanton must have ordered a cable sent when the telegraph office swung open its doors that morning. The Duchess of Hastings' butler had discreetly knocked on the cottage door while she was still abed with Richard. He'd been so exhausted that he didn't notice Anne hastily slip on her clothes and leave.

The cable had given her a sickening sense of dread.

Come home. R. Grey requiring immediate attention.

– SS

Immediate attention was her father's polite way of saying he intended to destroy a man.

Anne had watched him bring ruin to too many with his scheming, seen people she knew and respected crumble beneath his machinations. Families broken, futures sacrificed to line his pockets – and she'd helped him do it. When Sheffield set his sights on destroying someone, he usually succeeded.

She was complicit in their suffering – the black weight of guilt forever rooted deep in her heart. Not this time. She wouldn't allow him to do the same to Richard.

Anne came to the entry of her father's study and gave a soft tap.

"Don't trouble me unless you're my daughter," Sheffield bellowed from within.

"It's me," Anne replied quietly.

"Then enter."

Anne pushed open the thick oak door and stepped inside. Stanton Sheffield sat at his desk, surrounded by missives and proclamations, laws he expected others to obey while he ignored them himself.

He glanced up when she entered, pen frozen in mid-scratch. "Shut the door."

Anne did as he bade. "I trust your trip was successful."

Her father snorted. "We'll see if it yields fruit later." He made a sharp notation on a paper before him. "Now I have other matters that necessitate my attention."

"Richard Grey," Anne said, her tone unwavering.

Her father's lip curled in disdain. "That bastard has flipped five votes in three days with the help of that repellent criminal in Whitechapel."

Thorne. He was talking about Nicholas Thorne. It surprised Anne that he had never mentioned the other man before. In private, her father did not temper his words or vitriol – nor did he baulk from using his fists to make a point.

From the instant she closed the door, Anne became privy to the true Stanton Sheffield: the wolf beneath the sheepskin – the one who smiled only to show its teeth.

Anne had weathered his wrath for years. She'd learned how to retreat and stay hidden, so he assumed she was nothing more than the perfect student he'd carefully taught.

"I'm sorry," she said lightly. "Who are we discussing?"

Stanton's mouth was a tight line. "Nicholas Thorne, you bloody idiot."

Anne's jaw clenched, her fists quaking with a barely contained fury as she bowed her head in submission. "Your message mentioned Mr Grey."

"And they conspire together," Stanton snarled, his voice a slick blade of venom. "Try to keep up."

Anne feigned shame, tucking her nails into the soft flesh of her palms. "I apologise, Papa. Mr Grey is an utter wretch to manipulate Parliament."

Her voice was calm, serene, and detached from any hint of emotion.

"He'll seek to influence more," he muttered darkly. "Blackmailing the opposition is the only solution. I have to ensure Gladstone can't whip the votes to bring it to the floor."

Anne made a quiet noise of agreement.

Rage flashed across Stanton's face as his heavy fist crashed onto the desk. Anne jumped back in surprise. "I need this bill to fail, Anne." The demand was desperate and ruthless.

Anne kept her face neutral, masking the storm of emotions threatening her composure.

What was it about this bill?

"Do you?" she whispered. At Stanton's scowl, Anne averted her gaze. "It's only that you've lost votes before, and I don't like to see you so upset."

Stanton's expression sharpened with disdain. "Your gender debilitates your ability to understand anything beyond the season. If I'd had a son instead of a daughter with your memory, I wouldn't have to bother explaining."

Anne gritted her teeth and stayed quiet as rage bubbled beneath her skin. *Hold back. Show nothing.*

She thought of Richard then, what he'd say if he were here – probably profanity-laced and to the point. Oh, how she missed it already.

This is for him. Remember? This is for him.

A seething maelstrom of anger brewed within her, yet Anne kept her expression placid. "Forgive me for my lack of understanding. You're right – I don't grasp the complexities of politics."

"This isn't about politics." Stanton shoved aside the pile of papers he had been reading. "It's about money. I have landlords to whom I'm beholden – businessmen and lords who keep us in this lifestyle. Without them, we'd still be living in that shabby ruin with the leaking roof back in Dorset. Do you think they'll give me money when their tenants vote against their interests? When those Irish dogs use a secret ballot to vote in some independent party to force home rule?"

When she said nothing, he moved towards her as if to strike with his fist.

Anne recoiled, forcing her stare down. Her father was volatile with his fists, as if he delighted in keeping her guessing. She never knew what might tip the scale to violence – if he'd administer a hard knock that left her black and blue for days or simply meant to scare her into compliance. He'd go weeks without striking her. Months, even. Then…

But Stanton arrested the motion before it began. Instead, he gripped her chin, tugging her head up roughly. "Do you believe anyone will give a toss about you if things go sour? Not the duke, certainly. He never wanted you." His eyes narrowed. "Bribes aren't cheap, Anne. Neither is this house. Do you understand now?"

Anne pressed her lips together. *Calm.* "Yes, Papa."

But his grip only tightened. "If this vote passes, it's only a matter of time before the Irish get ideas. The Fenians may lack public sympathy after Clerkenwell, but it's been years. They won't need to slaughter people with a damn bomb if they can just vote in secret. Yes?"

"Yes, Papa," she repeated in a whisper.

Stanton stared at her with the condescension of an emperor. He strolled to the window and glared out. "Tell me everything you know about Richard Grey while I still have patience."

Anne knew what he was asking: give him precise details; no inflexion, opinion, or emotion allowed.

He always valued her for her capacity to remember facts and figures; it must have galled him to depend on a woman's memory when his own was so faltering. To Stanton, Anne was an insult to his manhood – a reminder of his ineptitude.

And he hated her for it.

It gave Anne a thrill to utilise the talent he'd exploited, a whip in his hands, and he'd drawn blood. It was hers now. She would reclaim it from the ashes of his scorn and use it as her ultimate weapon to topple him.

"Richard Grey is a liberal, though many would call him a radical. His first major contribution to politics was in bribes to pass the Second Reform Act, military reforms, civil service, and local government initiatives to aid the lower orders. At his sister's behest, he focuses on legislation affecting women and children, especially those in workhouses. He's engaged with MPs on how to meet the needs of workers. I can write a list of the laws he's taken a personal interest in, but specifically: the Cardwell Reforms, the Irish Land Act, the Education Act, Universities Tests Act, the—"

"Hurry it up, girl," Stanton spat. "You sound like you're advocating for the bastard."

Anne felt a chill ripple over her flesh. Her words were daggers as she continued. "Last year, Mr John Hardy got into a public row with Mr Grey's sister, Lady Alexandra, over his criticisms of her essays on women's suffrage.

Mr Hardy later voted against the whip on the Cardwell Reforms – possibly because of Mr Grey's interference. Grey's brother is the Earl of Kent, who—"

"Enough," her father said shortly.

The silence in the room was oppressive. Stanton tapped a finger against his desk as if counting each beat of her explanation and stared out at the silvery sky beyond the window.

"Put this information together, and what does it tell you?" he inquired quietly. "Give it a thought."

Anne struggled to hide the swell of emotion that coursed through her.

Richard's acts of charity and his influence in the Commons made her love him more. She vividly recalled her father's endless tirades about Grey's deeds and accomplishments; like some mythical beast requiring appeasement, his name had become a curse in their house.

Yet after learning the truth behind the dragon, Anne had found a flesh-and-blood man who could be her perfect match.

He belonged to her.

Anne fought to calm her thundering pulse as she injected feigned boredom into her voice. "I apologise again for my ignorance. You'll have to tell me."

Stanton barely appeared to be listening. He murmured, "Apart from being quite a bleeding heart for the needy, his family is rather a sensitive topic, isn't it? Especially the sister."

A chill crept up Anne's spine. She held her tongue, waiting for him to say more, but he stayed mute for a few minutes. Finally mustering her courage, Anne asked, "Is that all, Papa?"

His head snapped towards her, as if just remembering she was there. "Yes." Anne started to turn away, but his voice cut through the air again. "Wait. Send in your maid. I want an update."

The words landed like cold fingertips on Anne's skin. She paused, cursing herself for forgetting about Mary, who should have settled into her new position by now. How would she explain her absence?

Don't show alarm. Breathe.

Anne opted for a guise of ignorance and bewilderment. "Mary? I thought she came back here."

Stanton's eyes narrowed to slits of ice. "What do you mean?"

Anne frowned in feigned perplexity. "She wasn't on the train with me, Papa." She widened her stare, the picture of innocence as she leaned forward as if to impart a secret. "I think she has a beau. I've seen her sneak out at night after finishing her duties, and I distinctly recall her being especially fidgety the morning I left. Do you—"

"Enough," snapped Stanton. "I don't want to hear any details. God help that girl if she returns here with a bastard in tow." When it seemed as if he would send her away, Stanton scrutinised her once more. "Tell Bates to inform the cook that you'll be on bread and water for the foreseeable future. You know how the duke hates plump women."

Anne swallowed hard and tried to keep her face impassive. "Yes, Papa."

"Good." He motioned for her to go. "Now leave my sight."

She exited with preternatural grace and willpower. Her fingers flexed unconsciously, and when she noticed her nails had dug half-moons into her palms, she did not flinch. Not when far greater battles waited to be fought.

Vengeance brewed within her, a cauldron of anger reforged into exacting purpose.

She was going to destroy her father.

ᬬ 28 ᬭ

Upon arriving in London, Richard's first stop was his brother's residence in St James's.

The Earl of Kent's home at Pall Mall towered over the other buildings, an imposing example of Palazzo architecture with ornate columns and rows of tall windows set amid ornately decorated cornices.

It was a style that Richard found excessive and ostentatious, but it suited James's love of luxury.

James Grey was a socialite, the most sought-after bachelor in London's *beau monde*, always in demand at the most exclusive garden parties, balls, dinners, and soirees. He despised these events, yet he attended them all, masking his discomfort behind the veneer of a charming smile.

It was a stark contrast to Richard's preference for quiet and solitude. But since Richard couldn't very well show up on Anne's doorstep to inquire after her well-being, he resolved to do so covertly at the season's various gatherings.

Having one of Thorne's men staked outside her property wasn't enough; Richard had to see her himself.

God, he missed her already.

It had only been hours since she'd left, and his body felt like it had gone centuries without her.

Richard let himself into his brother's manor, much to Jeffries' dismay – the butler had long ago given up all hope of announcing him.

"Mr Grey, sir," said Jeffries from habit more than enthusiasm. "Welcome back."

"Good day, Jeffries. I haven't been here to keep you on your toes with my unexpected visits – I'll have to make it up to you now, won't I?"

Before Jeffries could respond, Richard heard a voice that could only belong to his sister, Alexandra. "*Finally*, you're home," she said. "It was growing dull around here."

Richard looked up as Alexandra sauntered down the stairs with an impish grin. He dismissed Jeffries and swept into an exaggerated bow. "Yes, the wayward scoundrel has returned."

Alexandra leaned forward to kiss his cheek. "I thought maybe you'd died. Where on earth have you been?"

Memories of laughter and whispered secrets rushed through his mind. Of skin touching skin and lips that tasted of paradise... and then losing it all in one morning.

Richard's expression turned rueful. "Through hell and back."

Alexandra rolled her eyes. "So dramatic."

"Did you miss me?"

She responded with a sly grin. "Only when I needed secrets to destroy a man."

Richard laughed. "So you've been up to your usual tricks, have you? How many men have you reduced to rubble in my absence?"

Whenever Richard saw Alexandra, he was floored by how much she had matured. Gone was the little girl who used to shadow him around the house. She had been replaced by a graceful woman with a devilish streak, never afraid to stir up trouble or ruffle some feathers with her outspoken essays on politics. While Alexandra was considered a great beauty – her features were a blessing they shared from their mother, with tussled golden locks and intense blue eyes – her daring mind made heads turn. Many people did not appreciate women who spoke publicly about government affairs, let alone one who earned money writing about it.

At twenty-three, Alexandra had been firmly tarnished with the label of spinsterhood. A badge she wore with fierce pride and a smirk – there was nothing so satisfying as having blokes hold you in contempt while secretly admiring your wit.

"Dozens," Alexandra murmured. "On my best days, I can annihilate two men by noon. So many essays to compose, scathing criticisms to express, protests to attend."

Richard's grin broadened. "My baby sister, a revolutionary. I couldn't be more proud."

"That's why you're my favourite brother." She winked. "For today, at least. James may steal the top spot this evening if he pays me the right compliments."

Which reminded him of his missing sibling.

Richard scanned the hallway for signs of James but found nothing, not even a glimmer of light under his study door. "Is he here?" he asked impatiently.

Alexandra raised an eyebrow at his tone. "No. Lately, he stays out half the night, if he comes home at all."

"Blast it." Richard ran his hands through his hair in agitation. "Where is he? At his club?"

"I'm not his nursemaid. He's a grown man, as far as I know."

"Damn," he said before he thought better of it. He generally tempered his language around Alexandra. She was his little sister, after all. "Fine. Send me a note when he gets back, will you?"

Richard turned on his heels, ready to depart. His sister's grip suddenly tightened on his coat sleeve. "Oh ho! I don't think so. You can't just prance in here with a smile and a wave only to skulk off like a wounded animal. Sit down and have tea before you go."

"No," he said curtly.

Alexandra's mouth fell open in shock. "What the devil? You've been away for weeks and won't even stay for tea?"

Richard shot her a stern look over his shoulder as he opened the door, the late afternoon sun casting a warm glow across St James's Square. "I'm busy. Don't you have some men to destroy? Get back to it."

But Alexandra trailed him outside into the bright sunlight, the early spring chill still lingering in the air. "You can't be serious! Are you trying to avoid me?"

"If I wanted to avoid you, I wouldn't have bothered coming around. I simply didn't expect you to follow me out onto the street like a stray dog," he said above the rattle of carriages passing by.

Their conversation had already caught the attention of a

few strolling ladies, and the buildings that surrounded them only seemed to amplify their voices.

"Stray dog? Stray dog? I'm your sister!"

"God damn it." Richard sighed deeply, his eyes flicking to the greenery of the square's gardens, seeking a quick escape from his sibling. "Go home."

"Not until you explain yourself."

He gritted his teeth. "There is nothing to explain. I have places I need to be," he said firmly.

"Oh, I see," Alexandra said with amusement as she finally caught up to him. "So it's a woman then."

Richard stopped and spun on her with such force she nearly lost her footing. "How did you suppose that?"

Her grin grew wider still. "Same way I'd identify a drunkard in an ale-house – it's written all over your face. A besotted male isn't hard to spot," she quipped. "Like seeing someone experience emotions for the first time. Makes you all look a bit constipated."

Richard glowered at her. "If I had another sister, you would be my least favourite by far."

She chuckled. "Let me guess: you're interested in a lady of the lower orders and need James's permission to marry her."

Richard resumed walking. He didn't have time for this nonsense. "No."

But her next words stopped him in his tracks. "You haven't got a woman with child, have you?"

He could scarcely breathe. "Absolutely not." Then, like a fool, added, "At least, I don't believe so."

The memory of Anne and their night together reared its head, but it brought a pleasant warmth that he couldn't deny, no matter how much he wanted to. Her body swelling with his child. *His*.

Oh, he was *beyond* besotted.

Alexandra's frown softened as she looked at him, her expression showing an unexpected perceptiveness. "Richard..."

He closed his eyes and took a deep breath. "I have work to do. I'll call on you later."

This time, she let him walk away without following.

29

It had been days since Richard had last saw Anne.

He checked in with Thorne's ruffian, Samuel, who had eyes on the Sheffield house. But while Stanton had come and gone, Anne had not. Nothing from his contacts throughout the city was any help, either.

Desperation clawed at Richard like a wild animal.

He'd made his way to Caroline's London residence, and the duchess didn't even flinch at the sight of him – bloodied, ragged, and sleep deprived from bending men to his will for the ballot vote.

Richard didn't resort to violence as a general rule – that was Thorne's approach – but Stanton Sheffield had redoubled his efforts to get men into line. The battle for that bill was growing brutal.

"Greetings, Duchess," Richard said, strolling into the studio after being announced. "I apologise for my unseemly appearance."

Caroline was at her easel, hard at work on her latest

piece – an awe-inspiring vista from the Cornish coastline. She had several hanging in the National Gallery, and by the glimpse of things, it was shaping to be another masterpiece.

"I find your unseemly appearance quite normal," Caroline mused, dragging a brush across the waves with delicate finesse. "Agitated, breathless, battered, lightly bloodied. Ah, yes, you've been out making threats with Mr Thorne again, haven't you?"

"How well you know me. Perhaps I ought to be alarmed by your lack of alarm. I look like hell."

A faint smirk crossed her lips. "No more than usual."

Ordinarily, Richard would've lauded Caroline's handiwork with effusive praises. Yet ever since Anne Sheffield came into his life, he'd been living his days in complete and utter chaos.

"Nice painting," he mumbled, wanting the floor to swallow him whole. "The...? The strokes are good."

Caroline's gaze snapped up from the canvas, pinning him with a stare that would have shamed Lucifer himself. "Say another word about the painting, and I'll have you thrown out," the duchess said, setting down her brush. "Just state your business."

"I'm a cad."

"At times," Caroline conceded.

"An absolute heel."

"That, too. Richard, do you really require my presence to flog yourself? Out with it – what do you want?"

The corners of Richard's lips lifted in a rueful smile. "I've asked too much of you lately. You must think me rude."

The duchess rescued him from dithering. She tossed her paintbrush into the pot of turpentine. "Stop it," she scolded gently. "I'm not a politician; I'm your friend. You don't have to grovel for favours."

Richard nodded in gratitude, feeling his muscles ease in relief. "I know that."

"Then tell me what you need – but if it involves Anne, I already said no—"

"Yes, yes, let her do what needs to be done. I got the message when you almost broke my hand expressing it."

"Then?"

A thick silence descended, broken only by Richard's shaky exhale. "It's been days since she left the house, and I'm worried," he said, voice fraying at the edges.

Caroline's face gentled as she understood. "Of course you are. You love her."

Richard paused, surprised by the insight. "I never—"

"You didn't have to," she said with a soft sigh.

The words hung in the air as Richard struggled within himself, unwilling to give them credence. In his experience, love was a snare for the gullible, and women only feigned that sentiment to extract something from him: money, baubles, gratification in bed.

Anne, however, sought none of those things from him; kindness and compassion were her standards because she had been deprived of them throughout her existence. Yet he loved her precisely because of her bravery.

The manner in which she defended herself – and him.

"I need to speak to her," Richard said hoarsely. "At least ensure she is safe."

Caroline glanced away thoughtfully. "What would you have me do? Short of abducting her, I'm afraid there is little I can offer."

"You've an established relationship." He paced about like a caged animal. "Her father approved of you seeing her before. Bring her to your house. Throw another of your fancy parties."

"No. Be clever about this." The duchess spoke sharply. "She just spent nearly a month at Ravenhill. Do you want him to get suspicious?"

"She's being forced to marry Kendal by the end of the season. The wedding announcement could come at any moment."

Caroline's brushwork had resumed its frenetic canvas scarring, as if a wild and unforgiving ocean was trying to wrest itself into life. After all these years, Richard understood the duchess better than anyone else – when her hands were busy, her mind was free to ponder.

"I know a way that won't raise any alarms," Caroline mused in a low voice. The sly cunning in her tone was reflected in the sparkle of her emerald gaze. "What about the Ashby's ball?"

Richard shook his head grimly. "I thought of it. But no. If Anne's locked away that tightly, she'll be accompanied by her father at all times."

"Stop thinking like a politician," said Caroline, rolling her eyes. "Think like a nobleman. You used to be good at both. Lord and Lady Ashby host the first ball of the season every year, and it would be advantageous for them to announce an engagement for a duke. They're close friends of mine – if I ask, they'll invite Anne under the guise of making an engagement to Kendal public. He's Hastings' cousin, after all."

"Forgive me for not thinking like a blasted nobleman,"

Richard grumbled. "But wasn't the entire point to avoid marrying him?"

"She has to pretend she's delighted to become a duchess, Richard. You want to speak to her? This is our only recourse. Without an engagement announcement, she won't be given any latitude while living in her father's household. At least with this approach, we can reassure her that we're here for her."

"Very well," Richard ground out from between clenched teeth. "Damn it. All right."

Caroline's look was sympathetic. "Don't worry. We'll find a way to fix this."

30

Anne hated pretending to be a dutiful daughter.

Her opulent home, a mausoleum of gilt and excess, suffocated her at each turn. It was as if her father was hell-bent on reminding her of his iron-fisted control, every room emblematic of his power.

And her father's desperation had been seeping through the lacquered wood for weeks.

Anne knew this. She could tell by the subtle shifts in his behaviour. He'd hold her captive, like a precious artefact, whenever he needed to bend someone to his will during a critical vote.

This vote was like all the rest – and yet so very different.

Stanton never shared his motives, only tossing her breadcrumbs of information in exchange for her silence. Names, addresses, payments – all leading to a final, spectacular immolation of evidence. Anne did her best to forget the lives she'd ruined, the people hurt, atrocities she'd abetted in the name of her father's machinations.

But this time? This time, Anne attempted to recognise the strategies behind Stanton's words.

It frustrated her that none of them had context. They were pieces of a mosaic, disparate and unconnected, without even a whisper of coherence to bind them together. She was only a tool in his grand scheme, a device to record and remember each puzzle piece.

It didn't help that Stanton had been relentless in his reminders of her obligations to the Duke of Kendal, urging her to renew their acquaintance before the wedding. The mere thought of Henry – his hands, his lips, his cruel remarks – made Anne's skin crawl with revulsion. But she couldn't hide from fate's harsh realities. Her father had sacrificed her in exchange for a fortune, and Anne was stuck in an unwanted arrangement.

Nothing more than a pretty, hollow vase bought by the duke for his mantelpiece.

Anne had been a bundle of nerves since pre-dawn. Kendal was due to arrive, and Anne had laid out his expectations to the new lady's maid with exacting precision. Hair bound primly in a chignon. Dresses buttoned up to the chin. No bold colours or anything that might draw attention.

Just like their marriage: unremarkable and dull.

"Tighter," she said on an exhale as the maid laced her corset, her voice barely audible beneath the ticking of the clock. Aileen gave her an odd look, but complied. "Tighter than that, Aileen."

Aileen worried over the laces. "Miss, if I cinch it any tighter, ye won't be able to breathe."

Anne shut her eyes briefly. "Yes," she murmured, as if to herself. "I believe that's rather the point."

Aileen looked appalled. "Miss?"

"Tighter," she said softly, with finality.

The maid let out a breath and did as Anne asked. The pressure was almost unbearable – but it was how he wanted her; slender and malleable like a blade of grass, bending in whatever wind blew past.

Hours later, she waited in the drawing room, dizzy from the tightness of the corset.

Stay calm. You've done this before. You'll do it again.

The silence grew oppressive. Her gaze drifted to the door as it opened, and in stepped Kendal. Anne rose with an insincere smile of welcome stretched across her lips.

No matter how impeccably dressed, Kendal was no gentleman. He had an air of elegance – tall and thin, with finely tailored clothes – but it was undercut by something sinister lurking in the depths of his icy blue eyes. And when he pressed an empty kiss to her cheek, she had to dig her nails into her palms not to draw blood.

"Anne." He made her name sound so formal. "It's been too long since I last saw you."

His stare raked up and down her figure, cloaked in the morning dress she chose for his benefit, the corset digging so hard into her ribs that she felt walls crushing around her fragile heart. His expression bore a smug satisfaction that ignited a furious flame in the pit of her stomach. She hated this – wearing the things he favoured, pretending that what she shared with Richard never happened.

"Are you well?" she asked lightly.

Kendal made a noise of approval deep in his throat, and Anne wanted to take a blade to him just for that sound alone. "Well enough."

The duke beckoned, his bony finger extended in invitation. Anne swallowed back terror, forcing herself to settle beside him on the settee. Close enough to smell the clove and whiskey that forever hung upon his breath like a halo of death. He liked it when she obeyed, and he expected obedience from his possessions.

Every muscle tensed as he settled a hand heavily on her thigh. "We've been invited to Lord and Lady Ashby's ball," Kendal said. He squeezed her leg harder, digging his fingers into her flesh until she winced.

"Have we?" she replied primly, though somewhere inside, rage bubbled and churned.

His blue eyes pierced her soul – as cold as her father's. Were they allies or adversaries? What power did Stanton wield over the duke to ensure his complete deference?

Anne had gone to Richard for help because Kendal would never relinquish her and free her of their betrothal – even if she was ruined.

Because Kendal had ruined her first.

He hadn't forced himself on her – he had considered her virginity a prize for later – but her father had granted him liberties no man should ever be permitted with a girl before she came of age to marry. He treated her as property he could touch before it bore its full value on their wedding night.

He said it was an incentive – a necessary trade.

Kendal had purchased her. For the privilege of owning her, he was allowed to grasp, test, and fondle her in all the ways he deemed fit.

"I hear you've become quite friendly with the Duchess of Hastings," Kendal said, barely looking at the tea she set before him.

"The duchess has been kind to me."

"What did she teach you?"

Anne was careful not to show any emotion. "Wifely duties. The same my mother would have taught me were she alive." As Kendal's piercing stare became too intense for her, Anne looked away and reached for a scone on the plate still laid out before them. "Here, why don't you have—"

He snagged her wrist, yanking her back into his lap.

"Duke—"

"Henry," he corrected gruffly, shifting his grip to the soft flesh of her upper arm. Painful enough to press a bruise on her delicate skin. "I gave you leave to use my Christian name."

"Yes, of course. My apologies."

But Kendal didn't seem to hear Anne. He seemed intent on her body now – the curves of flesh where the corset cut brutally deep – and she could only pray he wouldn't notice how much she trembled under his gaze.

"You fill out that dress," he said. "It's vulgar."

Anne struggled to keep her breathing even. "Yes."

She hated how he judged her body – as if some fatal flaw within it had been used to ensnare him.

"Yes? Is that all? Has the duchess undone all my teachings?"

"No. Henry—"

His lips came against hers like a branding iron, scalding her with his presumption of power and refusal to grant consent. His hand was brutal on her breast, and for one panicked moment, Anne remembered asking Richard if kisses hurt. This was pain, not pleasure, masquerading as romance.

Kissing is not meant to be painful. Ever.

Henry bit her lip so hard she couldn't suppress a flinch, and then said, "Did she tell you what happens on the wedding night?"

An icy resolve overcame Anne as she refused to show weakness or emotion. So she nodded.

Kendal's grip on her tightened. "Disregard it. I'll teach you the way I like it."

"Yes, Henry," Anne whispered.

"Good." Kendal shoved her off his lap and reached for his tea. "We'll make our announcement at the Ashby ball. We're to be married in a fortnight."

Anne felt like she was drowning beneath the waves of panic that threatened to consume her. "But—"

Kendal turned that hawkish gaze on her. "But what?"

A lifetime seemed to pass as she struggled for words before finally settling on something she hoped would keep his wrath at bay. "I had assumed it wouldn't be until the end of the season."

"Your father wants our alliance cemented before the Ballot Act comes up for vote, and I see no reason to wait. A fortnight." He grasped her chin and gave her one final bruising kiss. "Then you're mine to do with as I please."

Richard spotted Anne with Kendal the second they stepped inside the Ashby ball. A whisper of silk and a glimmer of jewels that stirred his pulse like some siren had beckoned to him on the wind.

He craved a smile from her, a secret communication that spoke of meetings later, light banter, and stolen kisses.

But these messages were gone now, erased by something far more sinister. Wariness replaced the sparkle in Anne's gaze, and pain lanced through Richard's chest at the sight.

Beside Richard, Alexandra made an exasperated noise. "Have you spoken to James? Look at him. Boredom is one thing, but he's moving about the ballroom with all the focus of an addled badger."

Richard glanced at their brother, waltzing with some debutante whose name escaped him. The poor bastard looked like an empty shell trailing through a crowd of strangers.

Before Richard left for Ravenhill, James had been

invited to the Masquerade – a club where men and women wore masks and slaked their darkest hunger in complete anonymity – and discovered someone beyond compare. A woman who inspired a devotion so deep it drove away reason itself.

Richard knew that feeling all too well.

"He has his reasons," Richard said shortly, focusing on Anne again.

Richard gritted his teeth, trying to swallow the fury that threatened to spill out. He forced himself to watch as Kendal took Anne's hand and led her into the crowd of dancers spinning in a waltz. Richard drank her in, every exquisite feature. But there was a chill air about her now, a false serenity born of a woman always watchful, knowing one misstep would invite Stanton or the duke's cruelty.

Kendal stood tall and proud, a false smile twisting his lips as he and Anne waltzed. Rage boiled in Richard's veins, coiling within his ribs and threatening to shatter his sanity.

He yearned to grip Kendal's throat, to crush the life out of him.

Alexandra stepped beside him. He fought to remain still as granite, gritting his teeth until his jaw ached.

"What is that look?" Alexandra asked. "Like you want to maul someone with your bare hands, but I can't tell who."

Richard closed his eyes briefly, then exhaled slowly before turning to meet her gaze. "It's nothing."

"Liar," she shot back. Her honey-gold hair tickled his nose as she leaned closer to survey the crowd. "Come now, give me details. Whisper your victim in my ear if you must."

"I won't gossip with you, Alexandra. Go dance with someone."

"My dance card is empty," Alexandra said brightly. "Every man here is scared of me – except you and James, of course."

"Oh, we're *terrified* of you. We just have a healthy appreciation of fierce women."

The swirl of Anne's skirts returned his attention to the waltz. It was an understated gown, designed to be unremarkable – but for him, it only made her shine brighter.

"You dance with me, then," Alexandra said.

"Not interested," Richard said curtly.

"What are you staring at? Or, should I ask, who?"

Anne's gaze clashed with his. Richard felt the breath expel from his lungs, the world fall away. All thoughts vanished except the desire coursing through him – the compulsion to keep her safe and close.

She shook her head ever so faintly.

To hell with it. He angled his chin towards the terrace doors, a silent command: *Meet me; we have to talk.*

With deliberate measure, Anne turned her back. She was refusing him.

Blast it.

"*Richard,*" Alexandra snapped.

He ground his teeth together. "Excuse me. I need to be somewhere."

Alexandra gaped as he stepped away, weaving through the dancers until he could be alone with Anne. Her father's plans be damned. Richard needed to ensure she was well. He yearned to kiss and comfort her, to let her know he would always be there whenever she needed him.

Thus began an hour of Anne slipping from one group of guests to the next, dancing with anyone but Richard. Even when Kendal retired to play cards in the salon, Anne kept herself surrounded by others.

Another partner.

Another dance.

Richard would wait for her all bloody night if he had to.

He prowled towards Alexandra and James, who loitered near the refreshments table. "I need something stronger than punch," Richard growled. "Where is that damned waiter?"

Alexandra had been in the midst of giving their brother a thorough tongue-lashing when he'd interrupted her. She shot him a poisonous look. "And you. You have been surly since returning from that house party. For goodness' sake, I'm being raked over the coals by gossip about me appearing as Satan himself in a newspaper illustration, yet you don't see me brooding."

Enough of this. Richard was not in the mood for another of his sister's reprimands.

"Shut it, Alexandra," he snarled, swiping a champagne flute out of James's grip and downing its contents in a gulp. "For once in your life, stop talking. You're not the only one with problems."

He spotted Anne across his sister's shoulder, alone this time – though his mounting rage barely registered it.

James and Alexandra followed his gaze to where Anne stood. When she realised they were watching her, she flushed and hastened out of the ballroom.

"Miss Sheffield," Alexandra said in interest. "It's rare to see her away from home these days; I heard a while back her father promised her to an old duke or something."

"Kendal is thirty years her senior," Richard spat. "I know all about it."

James – not exactly slow on the uptake – stepped closer and murmured, "If you've compromised Stanton Sheffield's daughter, I'll punch you in the throat."

Fury coursed like molten iron through Richard's veins.

"Oh, shove off Kent," he snarled. "For once in your miserable existence, just mind your sodding business."

He thrust his empty champagne flute into a baffled waiter's hands before hurrying after Anne.

She strode through the corridor with resolve, her brows furrowed in concentration. He tracked her every move until she slipped into a chamber at the end of the corridor. Richard followed, closing the door with a soft click. The gaslights hissed as he turned them up to their brightest setting.

Anne spun on her heel. "Richard," she said breathlessly. Her gaze swept behind him. "Anyone could come in here."

He turned the key in the lock and faced her once more. They were in Lord Ashby's private library, a cosy little room of leather-bound books, lush furniture, and smoky cigars. It was an undeniably masculine space – but Anne stood out like a snowdrop in winter, pristine and pale with an expression that might as well have been carved from marble for all its emotionless composure.

He had to get through to her, to quell the icy exterior that encased her heart like some frigid tomb. She wasn't a statue; she was flesh and blood.

"You're avoiding me," Richard said, leaning back against the door.

A sigh from Anne, and there it was – a crack in her armour. Sweet, tranquil on the outside. No one ever knew the suffering she carried with her as she walked this world like a ghost.

"Yes," she murmured after a few seconds of tense silence. "It's... easier that way."

"Easier for whom?" Richard raked his fingers through his hair. Anxiety twisted his guts into knots. "Do you have any idea how worried I've been?"

Anne came forward. "I had to. I'm so sorry, but I had to."

He couldn't resist. Drawing her near, Richard buried his face in the fragrant waves of her hair, as if his embrace alone could ward off the trials that beset her. All he wanted was to steal her from the burdens that plagued her, to shield her from the harsh realities that shadowed her steps.

A choked sound escaped Anne, her body quaking as she clung to him with all her might, as if afraid he'd slip away like sand through her fingers. It was no wonder she kept so much hidden behind that impenetrable façade. It was how she found the will to endure.

"It's all right," Richard murmured, his voice a soft balm against her ear.

Anne shook her head. "I can't make sense of his information," she said into his chest, barely audible above the roaring tumult in his mind. "Addresses, sums of money... I can't tell what he's searching for on you."

"It doesn't matter," he said. But Anne was digging her fingernails into his tailcoat, her hands making some frantic exploration of his body as if to assure herself that he was still there. He grabbed her wrists and gently held on. "Anne, stop. It's not important."

"It matters to me," she whispered. "Do you have any

idea how many men my father has destroyed? I helped ruin their families, their lives… I—"

"Look at me." Ever so slowly, she raised her gaze to meet his, and he felt as if he'd been struck. Her eyes were wet with tears; the marble façade had shattered completely.

"God help me. I can't stand to see you cry," he rasped out before brushing each droplet with his lips, catching them on his tongue. He kissed away all the sorrow until she finally loosened her grip on him. Only then did Richard murmur, "I don't have any secrets he can use. I promise you."

She shuddered out a breath at the last press of lips to damp skin. "What about your family? Your sister?"

Richard went still. Could Alexandra be sitting on something so damning that even Stanton would take note? She was ornery enough with no invitation to temptation.

"I don't think so."

"Be sure, Richard," Anne said. "He's close to something."

The thought troubled him – while Alexandra shared her political beliefs readily, he could not be present at her side every moment of the day. What if she had become embroiled in something beyond his sight? His clandestine activities were too numerous to be well known by either of his siblings.

As if Anne read the trepidation in his expression, she pressed her hands against his chest. "You see now why I must stay."

"I hate this," he muttered, somewhere between a whisper and a sigh.

"So do I. But there's something else."

"What is it?"

She took a deep breath, like she was trying to steel

herself for what came next. "My engagement to Kendal will be announced tonight. But my father has forced him into advancing the wedding date. We'll be married within a fortnight."

A shiver ran through him at those words. "Forced how?"

Her mouth curled, and a filthy oath left her lips, a word he had taught her himself. At any other moment, he might have grinned and praised her for being such an eager pupil. But not now. Not here.

"I don't suppose I ever told you, but Father's blackmailed Kendal for years. It's why he agreed to the marriage contract."

Richard trailed his fingers down her neck as he processed her story, considering all angles he could. Of course Sheffield would have been willing to stoop to blackmail to get a man as influential as the Duke of Kendal to marry Anne. Sheffield must have been desperate to sell off his only daughter at such a young age.

"Problems with finances?" Richard asked.

It felt so natural to touch her. She was an intoxicant like no other – beckoning him and daring him to give in to her spell.

"Yes." Anne's head dipped forward almost imperceptibly, granting him access to the back of her gown. As his nimble fingers relearned each button unhurriedly, she added simply, "Among other things."

"Such as?" Richard's attention could not stray far enough away from her skin – beautiful and smooth like porcelain.

Another button. Another.

Anne pressed closer. "He squandered my mother's fortune

in his rise to power. I believe he now owes a number of men a great deal of money."

Beneath her gaze, Richard inched the neckline of her dress down so he could press a kiss into the curve of her throat. "Is Kendal supplying it?" he murmured against her skin, dragging his tongue over her pulse until her breath was an audible gasp.

"I can't be sure. But I think so."

Richard eased away, brushing a thumb across her lower lip before whispering, "You keep at work on your father, and I'll see what I can uncover on Kendal. Yes?"

Anne looked up at Richard with burning eyes, and at that moment, he felt like he was falling through starlit galaxies and crashing into the depths of an infinite sea.

All without speaking a single word.

Words are unnecessary, he thought, as she pressed her lips against his.

Anne's kiss spoke volumes, a language beyond words, conveying everything he needed to know. Her body shifted towards him with a magnetic pull, a force that defied explanation. He murmured her name like a prayer, fingers deftly undoing each button of her dress until it hung open on her shoulders.

He gazed upon her creamy complexion and curves before him, almost reverently. He leaned in, tasting her scent on his tongue. Then he saw them, defiant splashes of colour against the flawless canvas of her skin – bruises in the shape of fingerprints, branding her shoulder.

"What are these?" he growled, his voice throbbing with rage.

Anne pulled away, refusing to meet his gaze. "Kendal isn't gentle with me," she said quietly.

Something inside Richard snapped like an overstretched wire. The words caught in his throat like jagged stones, but he dragged them out anyway. "Did he... did he force himself on you?"

"No," Anne said. "Not that. He tells me he's preparing me for our wedding night."

The urge to find the duke and pummel him senseless surged through Richard's veins.

"Good God," Richard breathed, pulling her close against him. "I'll kill that bastard – I'm going to—"

Again, Anne shook her head, pressing a hand against his chest. "Please," she implored in a soft murmur, "help me forget. Just for this moment."

Richard thought about resisting. He wanted to take her somewhere safe, but he knew she would refuse such comfort if it were offered by guile or compulsion. He could not be like every other man who sought only to bend her will to his own ends.

So instead, he showed her his love and honour with each touch and caress, treating her as she deserved to be treated from the start – with respect, kindness, and tenderness. He banished the darkness that threatened to swallow her, burying it beneath a firmament of light as he explored every inch of her with his lips and hands.

Richard pushed Anne back against the door, trying to assert some control over the situation, but she refused to be contained. Her fervent need drove her to claw and rip at his shirt with urgent movements.

He yielded to her, giving himself over to her as she sought

her pleasure. As their frenzied dance of desire unfolded, a flame was ignited in him, too, consuming him in a fiery embrace.

This was not soft – not here. Not now.

He yearned.

She hungered.

"Please," she whispered, undoing the buttons of his trousers to free him. "Please."

No, she would not need to beg. Richard craved this. The smell of her, the taste of her – all of her – and his hands roamed hungrily over the carefully concealed curves hidden beneath her layers of fabric and finery. The corset, the petticoats... it seemed a crime to hide such perfection. He longed to bare every inch of her against him – nothing but naked skin between them.

But he'd take whatever he could get.

He'd take everything.

He grabbed Anne's skirts – raising layer after layer – until he reached the split in her drawers. She shuddered as he slipped his finger into her.

Christ, yes, she was so ready.

"Hold on to me," Richard rasped, his breathing harsh.

Anne grasped his shoulders as he swung her up and used his body to pin her against the door.

With one desperate motion, he pushed inside her.

Richard thrust into Anne with unbridled passion, each jerk of his hips more forceful than the last. He moved against her with a primal intensity devoid of finesse or restraint, driven only by his burning desire. Not a word escaped Anne until a sharp gasp slipped out.

"*Yes*," she hissed against his neck, her back arched in ecstasy. "Yes, just like that. Please, don't stop."

Rippling fire coursed through Richard's veins, urging him faster and harder. He felt Anne's thighs squeeze tight around him, her hips lifting to accept his onslaught. Her breath scorched his throat, each kiss branding his skin. Soft cries of pleasure tumbled from her lips.

This was torment. This was heaven. Too many sensations swirled within him, an unquenchable thirst he could never quite satisfy. In these moments, Richard lost himself, body and soul devoured by physicality as they moved together – hot skin on burning skin, clothes gripped by savage hands, bodies writhing in unison, her name whispered like a prayer.

Some sound escaped her as she threw her head back. She repeated his name as she came. In wonder, revelation – or perhaps in agony, too. For this was agony – their time was not enough.

Anne gently bit his neck, drawing a low groan from Richard as he climaxed, waves of shuddering bliss rolling over him. She held him tight, understanding the desire for quiet – or maybe she needed to hold him, too.

Finally, they disentangled, and Richard stepped back from the door. He guided her down to the ground, fabric rustling in the silence that followed their joining.

Their breathing had yet to come down. It seemed to roar in that small space – a betrayal of their secret coupling.

"I have to go," she whispered, pressing a hand to her chest as if to gather herself. "Before Kendal wonders where I've gone."

Richard tightened his grasp, only for a moment, before releasing her. He helped smooth her skirts and button her up, covering up all those beautiful freckles like he was helping her don armour.

Her gaze in the library's gilt mirror was almost cold as she straightened some loose curls – erasing every trace of what they'd done.

Richard couldn't resist stealing one last kiss from her lips. She turned away, jaw clenched. "I have to go," she forced out again.

"Anne, I—"

She silenced him with a finger pressed against his mouth. "I know."

Her departure left an ache in his chest that felt like it might swallow him whole.

∽ 32 ∽

The days following the engagement announcement were a nightmare for Anne. She endured constant scrutiny and measurement as she was fitted for her wedding dress, her body examined for any imperfections. There was no thought given to her desires or needs, only a cold understanding of what was expected of her. Kendal's title demanded obedience.

Her dressmakers were elated to serve a future duchess. Her intended was almost as good as royalty. Wasn't she thrilled to wed him? Never mind his age... it made no difference when one married a man of status.

Anne had become little more than a rich man's bauble, crafted merely to amuse him while he frittered away his days in luxury. But she persevered, if only for survival. And then there was Richard. That flicker of hope that perhaps, when all was done and said, they could still make something of their lives together. That she could finally show the world who she truly was.

"Aileen," Anne said as the maid gamely wound her hair into a neat plait. "You had the pleasure of serving the late Dowager Duchess of Worth prior, correct?"

"Yes, miss," came her reply.

"Was she... happy?"

The girl seemed confused. "Miss?"

"No matter. On with your task, please." As with all her father's servants, she had to remind herself that this girl could not be trusted. She had no one with whom she could freely speak.

Aileen remained hushed as she looped another plait around the crown of her head. "Yes, miss, she was happy," the maid said quietly. "After His Grace's sudden passing."

"And before that?" Anne pressed. "Did she confide in you?"

A silence hung between them as Aileen went about with her work. "All the time, miss," she murmured, pinning Anne's locks into place. "He wasn't kind to her. Much like yer duke and yer father, if ye don't mind me sayin' so."

The risk Anne was taking was monumental – her father paid this maid, after all. But trusting someone had been something Richard had taught her, and it was a comfort not to be alone.

Anne's trembling fingers locked with the other woman's. "If I'm ever in need of your help," she said quietly, "will you provide it? I fear I may require it one day."

The silence hung heavy as Aileen considered Anne's words. Dear God, had she made a mistake?

But then came a whisper. "Should you ever require it."

Before Anne could say more, Stanton stormed into the chamber like a caged animal. He pointed a finger at Aileen.

"Out," he snarled. "My daughter and I have matters to discuss." The maid curtsied and hastily left.

Anne's heart pounded hard against her chest. Had he heard their conversation? Was he aware of Richard or Granby? Could he have got wind of what had transpired between them? Her breath caught in her throat—

"Addresses," he said, producing scraps of paper. "Times." He held up more papers. "Map." He put down a cartograph on the table. "Get to work."

Dread seeped through Anne's veins as Stanton placed the objects before her. Whatever he was hunting for must be important – did it have something to do with Richard? She opened her mouth to speak.

"I didn't come here to answer questions," Stanton hissed, cutting Anne off. "I came here to use that freak mind of yours."

Anne's lips tightened as she scanned the pages. There was no point in providing her with all this geographical detail. She already had it memorised. Every street, every turn, 975 turns in this area, to be precise. She knew them better than anyone living or dead – especially now that she'd corrected and honed her mental map of the city, understanding the ebb and flow of people who moved like a flock of starlings through the urban landscape.

She understood what he wanted. A location, some clandestine meeting place his spies had uncovered in the chaos of night and shadows. Whoever put this together was clever – the clues were maddeningly disjointed – but Anne had a knack for recognising patterns.

Such a beautiful gift, so dangerous in the wrong grasp.

With an inward sigh, she pointed to two addresses.

"There," then again with more authority, "and there." All these movements led between those points.

He snatched up the papers so eagerly that his fingers trembled. "Good work. Good work," he muttered distractedly before striding towards the door.

It took Anne a moment to realise something was off: her father had never complimented her on anything – ever. "Father?" she called after him as he reached for the knob, body tense and uncertain. Suspicion would only add fuel to his fire. So instead, she smiled brightly and said in a voice far lighter than how she felt inside, "My hats are all from last season. I thought I could buy some new ones for my trousseau. Kendal seems to love them – perhaps some dresses? For after the wedding?"

He waved a dismissive hand and didn't bother turning around. "Buy as many as you want," he spat over his shoulder. "I don't give a damn." He stepped out into the hall and made a hasty retreat.

Anne gazed after him in disbelief. Buy as many as she wanted? Something was amiss. Acting without hesitation, she sprinted for the bell pull and yanked it hard, summoning Aileen. She needed to go out.

She had to warn Richard.

R ichard went to bed every night thinking about Anne's
bruises.

He wanted to march into the duke's home and drag
Kendal out by his throat, tear that bastard limb from limb
for the hurt he'd caused her.

But Richard was too much of a pragmatist to hang for
murder – Anne deserved better than that.

No, he would do it right. Bring down Kendal wholly and
utterly – obliterate his name until there was nothing left
but ash and dust. After years of playing politics, Richard
had destroyed more than one man in his darkest days –
and he would ensure Kendal felt the full force of the pain
he'd inflicted on Anne.

So Richard visited his brother; James was an active
member of the House of Lords who had sparred with
Kendal more than once. With knowledge came power, and
Richard would exploit it to uncover every vulnerability
and strength in the duke's arsenal.

But when he strode into James's abode on Pall Mall, something felt off. The butler stood there with concern etched into his face. "The earl is in his study, sir," said Jeffries, "but I'm not sure wishes to be disturbed just now."

"Oh?" Richard raised both brows. "Don't tell me he's got a woman in there."

The man frowned. "Not a woman, sir. He... may be feeling under the weather."

"In that case" – he gave Jeffries a devilish grin – "all the more reason to check up on him."

"But, sir—"

"Don't mind me," Richard said, brushing past the butler. "You know he always blames me for escaping from you."

Richard strolled down the hallway to his brother's study and lingered at the doorframe. James swigged from a bottle, mumbling curses about damnable women.

The *ton* often mistook them for twins – same blond hair, same blue eyes, same height, same physique. But one look at their mannerisms told a different story. Richard was wildness personified, while James embodied practicality... until today.

Here was the perfect image of wretchedness, looking like hell had chewed him up and spat him back out.

Ah. Now his muttered rantings made sense.

"So you've found solace in spirits?" Richard murmured from the doorway, nostrils flaring with the reek of stale alcohol. "No wonder your butler looked so concerned when I came in. Do you know what this place smells like?"

James squinted at him and groaned, grasping the nearest bottle as though he'd seen something unpleasant, like a small rodent or a bug in his food. Richard had a habit of interrupting James at inopportune times, so he couldn't blame his brother. Only this time, he needed his brother to be practical, and here he was, wallowing in misery.

"If you've nothing useful to say," James said, sounding – and, frankly, looking – as if he'd just crawled out of the devil's backside, "then get out."

"I thought that was useful information," Richard countered. "When did you last wash? When did you last change your clothes?"

James shrugged and finished the bottle. Good grief, what trouble prompted this mess? "Don't you have something else to keep you busy, Richard? A new lover to entertain?"

James was one to bloody talk, considering he was sitting there drinking in the middle of the afternoon and whinging over some woman.

"I don't care to discuss it," Richard said.

"Ah. It's to do with Miss Sheffield, then. Did you bed her?"

Richard set his jaw, clenching hard at his brother's audacity to reduce Anne to nothing more than a conquest. He understood why James would believe it; he had played the part of a carefree rake for far too long, seducing any willing woman that crossed his path.

But Anne was different. She was the love of his life, and he intended to marry her someday. Richard couldn't tolerate his drunken brother's disrespect towards her.

Richard strode forward and snatched the glass out of James's hand. The stench of cheap gin curled up his nostrils like a deranged snake.

"Bloody hell, James. Gin? Where did you scrounge this up?"

"A gin palace in Spitalfields. Better than opium."

The corner of Richard's mouth twisted in disdain. Opium, gin – what was the difference? Both were only distractions to dull the pain and avoid reality. "Am I supposed to be relieved? No wonder you're such foul company. Have you seen yourself lately?"

James looked away, unable or unwilling to meet his brother's gaze. "If I wanted to hear a sermon, I'd attend church." He grasped the bottle with surprising speed for someone so soused. "Go home."

Richard stared at his brother. What the bloody hell had happened in his absence? He didn't seem this much of a mess at the Ashby ball. Good Lord, it had only been days since, and now James was boozed up and useless just when Richard needed his help most.

Certainly, political information could be garnered quickly from a drunk. Richard had done that numerous times, but he had no stomach for manipulating his brother – his morals might be loose, but they weren't nonexistent.

Richard exhaled a weary sigh. "I assume your plight to self-destruction hasn't sprung from nothing. What happened with your masked woman?"

James's blue eyes were empty and suddenly very, very sober. "She lied to me and didn't care for honesty. So we went our separate ways."

Richard snorted. The Masquerade was all about lies and seduction, and things better left unsaid. Rules regarding identity disclosure were strictly enforced.

"It's the Masquerade, James. It's all a game of masks and half-truths."

"I know that," James spat back, his voice taut with bitterness.

Something in his tone caused Richard's smile to disappear. "You let her see you without your mask."

"Worse," James replied with disgust. "Made a fool of myself."

Ah, blast it. "You offered to *marry* her?" When James didn't reply, Richard ran a hand through his hair. "Good Lord. What did she say?"

Oh, no – his brother was reaching for the brandy in his desk drawer. So it had come to this. His brother, pouring himself an obscenely large serving of liquor, like some callow youth attempting to drown his sorrows.

"I've been drinking the foulest liquor in London for three days, Richard. What do you think she said?"

Richard let out a breath. As pathetic as his brother was in his current state, Richard could still identify with him. After all, hadn't he been an absolute wreck while Anne had been away? He'd spent hours worrying over her, remembering those bruises on her shoulder and entertaining violent fantasies involving the murder of a duke.

But getting foxed helped no one. All it got you was more trouble and the misery of a pounding headache.

His expression softened. "James, a man doesn't turn to drink – especially something as revolting as gin – just because a woman rejected him." His brother gazed sharply at him, as if daring him for more. "No," Richard continued gently. "A man does not do such things unless he loves her."

James stared into his drink again. "That would be foolish," he mused.

"Ah, and yet here you are." Richard's voice remained steady and sympathetic. "Drunkenness, foul smell, an excess of ridiculous emotions – all hallmarks of genuine affection."

A sharp bark of laughter escaped James's lips. "Then no wonder I'm such a wreck," he muttered to himself. "Love does unspeakable things to people."

"Not everyone. You're thinking of Mother, and she's not an ideal example," Richard said. "She was unwell."

James shook his head. "You were too young to remember. During the months between Father's visits, Mother refused food from the servants while she was pregnant with Alexandra. Our governess made sure you were occupied in the nursery."

"I recall some things," he replied ruefully. His few memories were enough; the countess had paid no mind to her second son; he did not matter to her. "Like how she was always in bed."

James nodded. "Mother would only accept meals if I brought them up myself. The doctor warned me that the pregnancy might kill her if I didn't remain vigilant – so I did." He closed his eyes before adding, "She was unhappy."

"Unhappy?" Richard repeated, incredulous. "She was a countess, living in luxury. What could she possibly be unhappy about?"

"Why do you think?" His brother let out a dry laugh and downed a little more liquid destruction. "She was *in love*. And she hoped if she kept herself ill enough and Father heard of it, he'd tear himself away from his dalliances and come home. Love is a sickness, Richard. It clouds all reason."

"Is it?" He thought of Anne and realised it was the furthest thing from true. His thoughts had never been clearer than now. "I don't believe that."

Because it was a rotgut of nonsense.

Utter bloody lies.

Richard remembered two indelible moments that told him everything he needed to know about his parents: After he'd stumbled into his mother's chamber in the throes of a nightmare, she had shooed him away like a bothersome pest – a nuisance. And when their father did visit... well, she had cooed and fawned over Richard before becoming distant the moment the old earl departed; he was only a piece in her game of vengeance.

There was no love there – only spite – no matter how sweetly worded it may have been.

"That's because you don't know anything," James said sharply.

Richard scowled. If James's woman loved him, she had her reasons for turning down his proposal. Women didn't chance their reputation for nothing. Yet here was Richard's brother, blundering around his study and guzzling one bottle after another, refusing to contemplate the cost of such sacrifice.

Anne taught Richard just how high that price was.

"Calling me ignorant is a convenient excuse," Richard said in disgust. "Here's the truth: Mother cared more about punishing Father than damn well taking care of her children. She made that perfectly clear. And if an unmarried woman is risking ruin for nothing more than a dalliance?" Here, he paused, an eyebrow raised. "I suggest you ask yourself why that might be. Here's a tip: it would require tearing yourself away from that bottle for longer than five seconds."

He spun on his heel and strode out of the room, slamming the door with vicious finality.

Yes, there would be no help here.

⌒ 34 ⌒

"I need you to tell me about the Duke of Kendal," Richard said, striding into Caroline's studio. "Everything. Leave nothing out."

Caroline was absorbed in her painting, a ritual that comforted her when the world became too much to bear. Her brush moved with practised grace across the canvas, creating a masterpiece inch by inch. Richard felt guilty invading her refuge like this, but he had no choice. He needed her help – again.

"I've only ever met him a few times," she muttered, nose wrinkled in concentration as she inspected her work. "Hastings would know more than me. Have you tried asking your brother? Kent and the duke have quite a rivalry in the Lords, don't they?"

"One careless word from a brawl, you mean?"

Her lip curled in a smile. "If you like."

Richard shook his head. "James is a complete and utter wreck right now. I dropped by this morning to find him reeking of gin and going on about that age-old quandary."

"The answer to the universe and everything?"

"Lord, no. Nothing so dramatic – although the way he's carrying on, you'd think he was in the middle of some life or death crisis. It's about if he's in love."

Caroline stilled, her gaze fixed somewhere beyond the painting. "Ah," she said softly. "That eternal question."

Something about her tone made Richard frown. "What is it?"

Richard stepped around the easel and saw the portrait of her husband there – the Duke of Hastings with those sharp cheekbones, a hint of mystery on his lips that hinted at a knowing smile. She'd captured him in a moment of surprise, as if both duke and viewer had spotted each other across a ballroom and silently shared an understanding. The painting was a masterpiece of precision, every brushstroke infused with delicate detail.

"You're staring," Caroline said. She cleared her throat. "Do you hate it so much?"

If he were being honest, he'd tell her this was her finest effort yet. But such a compliment would come with a barb so cruel he could not bring himself to speak it aloud. He refused to hurt her with his words.

"I find your work truly lovely," Richard said at last. "This piece is no exception. I wasn't aware the duke was such an accomplished model."

"Yes," she said quietly. "My first. When we were friends, Hastings used to sit for me for hours in secret, with clothes and without them. But now I wish I had never asked, to tell the truth."

Richard stared down at the duchess. In moments like this, when she wasn't charming a crowd, he thought her the loneliest person he knew. And that broke his heart. "Why?"

Caroline shook her head. "I fell in love with him each time."

At those words, Richard could see what he hadn't before – a longing that permeated every brushstroke, a moment captured forever in paint. What had happened between them to make it impossible for a woman this beautiful and kind to reconcile?

He placed a gentle hand on her shoulder, feeling the weight of her sadness. "You miss him. It's there in your portrait."

"Sometimes I do. Other times I'm so *furious* with him—" She let out a breath and grabbed the corners of the frame to lift it. "You're a liar, Richard – it's a terrible piece of work. I ought to have burned it years ago."

She moved as if to throw the painting in the fireplace, but he apprehended her forearm like stone, whispering gruffly, "Don't you dare. That was no lie, as you well know."

"Fine," she said. "No lie. Then what about this? It's been seven bloody years since he left. If he'd gone off to battle, that would be long enough for the war office to declare him dead. Why can't I just let go of a man who doesn't want me? This portrait is evidence; why keep it?"

"Because you still love him." At her start, he said softly, "I only wonder if he deserves you."

Her eyelids fluttered, and her expression twisted with pain. "Yes," she murmured, slipping from his grasp. Caroline delicately placed the portrait back on the easel, her fingertips lingering on its surface like phantoms. "But he loved someone else."

"Who?" Richard asked, sensing her unspoken hurt.

"Our friend Grace," Caroline replied, her voice barely above a whisper. "His feelings were unrequited. She died of scarlet fever after we wed. I don't think Hastings has ever forgiven me for trapping him into marriage."

A slight sound escaped Richard's lips. "You didn't trap—"

"Not intentionally," Caroline interrupted, averting her gaze. "Grace believed Hastings loved me and not her, so I kissed him in the gardens at a ball – a mistake. We were seen." She smiled bitterly. "I can't blame him for loving Grace. She was wonderful; the best person I knew." After a pause, she looked up at Richard and waved a hand towards the painting. "Hastings rescued her from Kendal once, come to think of it."

Richard frowned. "Rescued her how?"

"Grace was uncommonly beautiful. She was uneasy with the amount of attention she received. Men took… unwanted interest in her."

Richard swallowed, his throat like sandpaper. "Go on."

"Kendal visited Ravenhill when Grace and I were both thirteen, far too young for him. He made her feel uncomfortable from the start. Hastings found Kendal in the gallery being rough with Grace, and he hit Kendal over the head with a Ming vase. Hastings was only sixteen then, still rangy and awkward, but he thrashed the duke enough to leave him bleeding." She forced a dry laugh. "The only time I ever saw Kendal again was when he offered to become a patron for my orphanage, if you can believe it. I turned him down."

Something coiled in Richard's gut, anger and rage and instincts honed from years of secrets and wielding them against men like blades. He gritted his teeth. "What reason did he give for wanting to become a patron?"

Caroline's face hardened into stone. "He said, and I'm quoting directly, that he had quite an affection for children. He made my skin crawl."

⌒ 35 ⌒

Anne was being followed.

The milliner. The teashop. The modiste. Richard had assigned this man to tail her, of that much she was certain.

The man following her probably thought himself a phantom, but Anne knew better. Clothes, faces, movements – they all gave him away. Every break in the usual flow of the surrounding patterns alerted her senses.

And yet, for once, there existed a comfort in the situation – a sense of safety born from the knowledge that she wasn't alone. She could find no emotion deep enough within herself – except perhaps gratitude. Gratitude that help was possible, that freedom wasn't just an illusion crafted by manipulative men who wanted something from her.

Anne had to be careful. Stanton had hired a new bodyguard under the guise of protecting her, but she knew better. The man was a hawk, vigilant to her every action, never granting her a moment's respite.

Stanton professed concern that Thorne's rogues might

ensnare Anne, coercing him to abandon his machinations over the Ballot Act. Little did he know that Anne and Thorne's men were on the same side. She was playing a dangerous game, and every move she made had to be calculated.

So she watched Richard's agent, memorised his movements, and waited for her chance.

"I'd like to visit the bookshop," Anne informed her bodyguard as they strolled along the bustling streets of Mayfair.

The sun shone high, casting elongated shadows on the cobblestone pavement as carriages rattled by. The scent of blooming flowers from nearby gardens intermingled with the smoky aroma of chimneys.

Anne kept her gaze down, feigning interest in the displays of the various shops and businesses lining the avenue.

Richard's agent would pass by soon enough.

"Your father requested ye return before mid-afternoon," Owens told her.

"It won't take long, Owens," she said firmly. "It's just up the – oof!" She hadn't taken more than a few steps when she ploughed into a solid wall of man – right on cue. "My goodness." She put on a good show of appearing contrite. "I'm so sorry, sir."

"Ho there!" Owens called out, his footsteps quick as he caught up with Anne. "Are ye all right, Miss Sheffield?"

"I'm perfectly all right," she replied, her voice calm and collected. Anne's calculating gaze focused on the stranger who had collided with her, and she smiled sweetly. "And you?"

The stranger's smile was swift, a hint of deference that

indicated he had been instructed to blend in with the shadows. "I'm fine, madam."

"Good. If you'll excuse me." As she passed him, she dropped a small piece of paper on the ground, knowing he'd pick it up, and resumed her walk to the bookstore.

Anne lingered in the aisles, trailing her fingertips across the book spines. Owens' frustration was palpable – they'd been in the bookshop an hour already.

She was burning with impatience. Had Richard received her message? What if her mysterious pursuer hadn't seen her drop it? Every possibility seemed to forebode failure.

Then, as she reached for a book, the bell over the door jangled.

Anne let out a sigh of relief as Richard stalked in, her eyes drifting over him. Dear God, he should be banned from public places. For he was beautiful – a wickedness crafted to beguile mortal women, with those sharp cheekbones and eyes bluer than July skies. When he smiled, it almost felt like an invitation to sin.

Richard's hands were buried in his pockets as he greeted the shopkeeper and sauntered toward the shelves. A regal sight: dark grey overcoat, tailored trousers skimming the contours of his body, boots shined to a mirror finish. The only imperfection was his wind-swept hair – he must have bolted there at the first sign of trouble.

Richard's gaze collided with Anne's, and she gave her head an imperceptible shake. Owens loomed by the entrance, ever-present and sure to report any inappropriate contact between a gentleman and his charge.

Anne pressed her lips into a firm line and opened her volume, pretending to read.

Richard, for his part, tried to look as if he were browsing. When he passed her, his fingertips brushed hers.

Electricity arced between them, a heat that made Anne shiver. Would his touch ever cease to do this? As he wandered further down the aisle, the sensation still lingered.

She cleared her throat and approached her bodyguard. "Owens," she said with false patience, "I'm so sorry, but I'll need more time to decide." She tapped the book. "I'd like to read more of this."

The man sighed heavily. "Very well, miss."

"I imagine this isn't enjoyable for you: stuck here doing nothing while I meander around. Why don't you go down the street to the teashop and get something to eat while I finish?"

Owens hesitated, clearly unsure about leaving Anne alone. "Miss, the boss wouldn't want me to leave ye by yerself. If somethin' were to happen—"

Anne cut him off, her voice firm. "It's not as if someone will kidnap or assault me in broad daylight. Certainly not in the few minutes it would take to purchase a cake."

Despite her reassurances, Owens still seemed uncertain. "I reckon not."

"Go on, then. By the time you get back, I'll be ready."

When Owens had slithered out of sight, Anne spun and silently beckoned Richard deeper into the bookshelves.

The sounds of the street faded as they stepped into a shadowed corner of the stacks, and suddenly there was no one but them in this world. She seized his lapel and tugged him close, her lips hungrily claiming his.

A low growl worked its way from Richard's throat as he slammed her against the bookcase with a force that stole her breath. His hands lashed into her hair, kissing her in a blaze of heat that stoked her own, and it made her remember what it was to be alive. This fire – the press of his lips against hers – was a stark reminder that she wasn't some tame creature shrunken by the shadow of others' expectations. No, she was wildness and flame. There'd be no tempering her now.

With feverish desire pulsing through her veins, drawing them irresistibly closer – his fingers upon her hips, the unyielding ardour of his kiss – reality threatened to overwhelm her. It was all too intense, too visceral.

"I've missed you," he murmured. "When I received your note…"

She wanted to savour every second, cling to these moments while they still existed between them, but they had no time. The ticking clock reminded her that Owens would soon return, and if he found them like this, it wouldn't end well for either of them.

Anne reluctantly pulled back, her heart aching with longing.

"Time's running short," she said in a low voice. "Owens will be back."

He chuckled, his lazy smile giving her more than one idea. "So you're telling me all this trouble wasn't for clandestine kissing in a bookshop? I'm disappointed."

Anne rolled her eyes, laughing despite herself. "You're such a—"

"Rake?" The wicked gleam in his eye told her he quite liked the title. He leaned close and spoke against the sensitive skin behind her ear. "Want to know the best part about marrying a rake?" A slow grin spread across his face. "I have no qualms about lifting your skirts and taking you hard and fast against a bookcase."

Her lips twitched. She'd missed that – his confidence, the way he made heat pool between her legs. "Any bookcase? Even in public?"

He placed a palm against the wooden shelf beside them. "This one seems sturdy enough." He raised an eyebrow. "What do you say? This one?"

But then she remembered – and her good mood dissipated like smoke on the wind. "We're pressed for time."

"Aren't we always?" His sigh was heavy as he nuzzled her cheek. "Very well. What was so urgent?"

Anne read back an address on the list her father had given her. "Do you know it?"

Richard seemed to cease breathing for a moment. "My brother's house. The others?"

"They pointed to a precise location in Whitechapel, but I'm not familiar enough with that area."

When she told him, he swore softly. "The Brimstone – Thorne's club. A place where men go only when they want to play deep and bury themselves in drink and disgrace."

"Then he must be following Mr Thorne, yes?"

Richard frowned thoughtfully. "That doesn't explain why my brother's address was on your father's map. I don't live there, and Thorne would certainly have no reason to show up on Kent's doorstep."

"Perhaps the earl...?"

"No. James is enough of a mess right now without any help from the Brimstone." He saw Anne's concern and brought his hand to her cheek, caressing it softly. "I'll figure it out. You're not to worry, promise me?"

"You ask for the impossible."

"I know it, love."

She kissed his palm, braver with each passing second in his company. "Just be careful, won't you? I couldn't bear it if something happened to you. I'm quite fond of you."

Richard's lips curved into a smile. "Brilliant girl," he whispered affectionately before continuing in a more serious tone. "We'll have to discuss my feelings when time allows us more than a moment together," he said softly, dipping his head towards her. "I'm far more than *fond*, as it happens."

His words ignited a hunger inside Anne that she had never felt before, and it terrified her even as it left her craving more.

It was little wonder her father feared him. Richard was a radical, a revolutionary. An agent of change and disruption. He was worth more than money, more than power. He was freedom itself, and he belonged to her.

But this wasn't the place for declarations of love. Time was too precious in this moment they'd stolen from fate and circumstance. Instead, she settled for a soft kiss, and then another, until neither could summon the will to break apart.

But then a thought occurred to him, and Richard pulled back sharply. "Does Kendal have another close ally? Anyone I can leverage for information?"

"Lord St Vincent," she replied in a whisper. "My father uses him as an informant on whether a bill looks likely to pass in the Lords." She looked around quickly to ensure no one was about and leaned in. "He's a bigamist."

Richard's eyebrows shot up. "The viscount?" He seemed to ponder that for a moment. "I suppose that makes sense."

"Why is that?"

"No particular reason. I just hate him."

Before she could stop herself, Anne uttered a laugh that bordered on being too loud for the environment.

Then Richard lifted his hand and placed a calloused finger beneath her chin, his gaze suddenly full of something Anne hadn't seen in days – warmth, longing… love?

"There's that smile, dimple and all. I've missed it."

I love you, she wanted to say. *I love you.*

The bell over the shop door tolled again. Owens was back – the timing was precisely right.

"Be careful, Richard," Anne whispered.

"Always am, sweetheart."

She pressed one last, soft kiss to Richard's lips and left him among the stacks.

36

The Brimstone was the most opulent club in London. A glittering jewel in a city of grime, its reputation stretched far beyond the ferrous fog of the smog-choked East End. It was a chasm of debauchery, where the noxious scents of alcohol and sweat combined with a heady blend of avarice and self-importance.

Exclusivity meant nothing at the Brimstone, no matter your standing on the societal ladder; here, rich men gambled with commoners, and businessmen mingled with dukes.

Nicholas Thorne had made a fortune from his humble roots by ruthlessly capitalising on the chaos of the East End, controlling three councils that spanned from the banks of the Thames to the streets of residents barely clinging to life.

He was often at the heart of it all, surrounded by gentlemen and merchants alike, gambling away their fortunes while attempting to curry favour with the mysterious owner. But tonight, Richard found his presence elusive; somewhere in London, Nicholas Thorne went about his business unfettered by prying eyes.

Thorne had spared no expense in creating his pocket of sin. The Brimstone was a palace of excess – teardrop chandeliers, frescoed ceilings, and lush red carpets made to comfort the affluent. Delicacies from France and East End oysters were served together on platters of silver, a lavish mingling of different tastes that Thorne had masterminded with surgical precision.

The gaming tables were alive with men slamming cards, smoking cigars, and bellowing curses at their misfortune. It was an unceasing chorus of sound and fury that filled the room until late into the night.

Leo O'Sullivan, Thorne's right-hand man, marked Richard's arrival with a nod of recognition. The ex-pugilist had the massive body of a bruiser with the face of an angel. He wore thin wire-framed spectacles that further softened his appearance, but it was an illusion. Leo could brawl like no one Richard had ever seen.

"Grey," he said in greeting. "Thorne's out at the moment. Unless you came to play a bit of hazard."

Richard surveyed the tables. "Here on different business. I heard Lord St Vincent's been visiting often. Care to confirm?"

The Irishman examined him with shrewd eyes. "Yeah. What of it?"

"Take me to him. I've got a few things to ask. I'm going to need you to clear a room."

Leo sighed. "Don't start a fight in my club, Grey."

"But it's Thorne's club, isn't it?"

"Tonight it's mine," Leo said darkly. "Know what I mean?"

At Richard's nod, Leo beckoned and led him to one of the salons reserved for high-stakes games.

Lord St Vincent was lost in a swirling sea of drunkenness and distraction, surrounded by cards, bottles, and half-dressed women. The viscount sat engaged in a game of *vingt-et-un* with a prostitute draped over his lap – further dwindling his already limited funds.

Leo discreetly tapped the other two players on the shoulder. They folded and quit the room, no questions asked. There weren't many men who risked angering Leo, and those who did came to regret it.

St Vincent, the imbecilic sot, was too far into his cups to notice.

"St Vincent," Richard said in greeting.

He settled into one of the empty chairs. Leo sent out the dealer and took over, shuffling the cards before dealing Richard in. He was probably sticking around to keep an eye on things.

"Grey," the viscount said, staring down at his cards. "Wasn't aware you came down to the Brimstone."

Richard glanced at St Vincent's companion, her posterior brazenly perched on the viscount's lap. "When I have certain matters to discuss," Richard murmured. "I believe you might be able to help me with a few."

St Vincent's visage darkened. "Grey, does she look like business to you?" He grabbed the prostitute's buttocks as he adjusted her position.

She giggled, but Richard noticed she rolled her eyes as she leaned back. The woman didn't want to be there any more than Richard did. He could not fault her; St Vincent was a debauched, inebriated wretch, his talon-like fingers far from inviting. Even for a seasoned lady of the night, this would prove a daunting task, and she seemed no older than Anne.

Ignoring the question, Richard bent forward in his seat and fixed the woman with what he hoped was a charming look. "What's your name, sweetheart?"

"Millie."

"Millie," he repeated, donning his most debonair smirk. "A beautiful name for a captivating creature."

St Vincent spat out an oath. "Bugger off, Grey. She's mine."

Richard raised an eyebrow. "I doubt she'll be going anywhere with you."

"What the hell are you talking about?"

He made a sharp click of his tongue against his teeth, studying his cards. "All in good time. Before that, tell me about the Duke of Kendal. He's a friend of yours, isn't he?"

"I told you," St Vincent said, downing his brandy in one gulp. "I'm not here on business."

Richard gave Millie another lazy grin before meeting St Vincent's glare again. "That's a bit of a problem, because I am. And I want to know about Kendal." He gestured for the woman to leave with a sly wink. "Could you give us some space, darling? I'm afraid I need to borrow him. I promise I'll make it worth your while."

The woman ignored the older man's spluttering and clambered away from the viscount's grasp. She stood next to Leo, her expression betraying her immense relief.

"Damn you, Grey. I don't have to tolerate your boorish behaviour."

St Vincent rose indignantly – reaching for Millie – but

Richard was faster. With brute force, he shoved the viscount down once more.

"I'm not finished with you yet." Richard's voice brimmed with an icy authority that could cut glass. "Sit."

The viscount blinked in shock. "What is the meaning of this?"

"I need information, and you'll provide it. No questions asked," Richard said firmly.

St Vincent's nostrils flared in outrage. "I've no obligation to give you anything, Grey."

A sly grin split Richard's face. "Oh, I think you may reconsider that stance after hearing my proposal. But first, a query: I've heard Kendal fancies girls on the young side," Richard said casually. "On the *very* young side." It was a lie, but he went on instinct. So many men of standing had revolting predilections, and nothing shocked him anymore. "You wouldn't know about that, would you?"

St Vincent shunted his gaze away. "No, of course not. Now would—"

"Do you fancy risking your family's fortune on that?"

The viscount seemed even more uneasy. "I don't understand what you mean."

"Oh, I think you do. The question is, which family? The one here in London, or the one at that nice little country cottage in Alnwick?"

St Vincent lost his grip on himself. He staggered from the seat and rushed to the door, but Richard got there first. He seized the viscount by the collar and slammed him against the hazard table.

"Grey," Leo snapped.

"I haven't hit him yet, Leo," Richard said in a low voice,

staring down at the man fighting his hold like a flapping fish. "But here's my proposal: you tell me everything I need to know, and I won't break your bloody nose and inform everyone the Viscount of St Vincent is a bigamist. What do you say?"

"All right, *all right*," the viscount said, his expression placating. "For God's sake, just—"

Richard yanked him forward, letting the full weight of his anger fuel the words. "Don't make demands. Start talking. Now."

"I may have accompanied the duke to a few places in Whitechapel that specialise in certain... unique preferences."

Rage roiled in Richard's veins, electric and alive. "Continue."

"He was barred from them after his habit of, er, damaging the merchandise, as it were," St Vincent stammered. "He moved on to different establishments after that."

Crimson blurred Richard's vision; speech seemed a distant impossibility. His hold on the viscount tightened, eliciting a pitiful whine. Fortune favoured St Vincent; were Richard a man akin to Thorne, the wretch would have met his demise in that very instant.

"Where did he go?"

The viscount whimpered again, and Richard slammed him back into the gambling table with enough force to rattle it to its foundations for good measure. "Tell me, or I swear I will break you here and now. *Where?*"

The man shivered, eyes wide with terror.

"I don't know. I only witnessed him pay a mongrel from the Nichol. Malloy, I believe he called him. That's all I saw."

And Richard believed him. He released St Vincent and stepped away, breathing hard as he fought to master the beast within his chest. "Leo," he said at last, voice deceptively tranquil despite his rage, "when I leave here, you're to speak with your contact at *The Times*. Tell him about the man sitting in the House of Lords who preaches the rule of law while committing bigamy."

St Vincent gaped at him for a long moment, the sap too dumbstruck to process what was happening. "B-but... but you promised—"

"I lied. Consider yourself lucky I'm giving you fair warning." He nodded to the door. "Now get the hell out."

The viscount's expression blazed with seething fury as he adjusted his coat. "You're nothing but a common thug," St Vincent spat, spittle flying from his lips. "Thorne may be your ally, but he'll never be one of us, no matter how often he slinks about St James's playing at being a gentleman. That's right, don't think I haven't noticed him skulking around your brother's home. Mark my words, Grey, I'll destroy both of you. I'm going to—"

Richard smashed his fist into St Vincent's face. A devastating left hook sent St Vincent tumbling onto the carpet, out cold and oozing blood, his nose bent at an unappealing angle.

Leo sighed. "Damn it, Grey."

Richard shrugged indifferently. "He wouldn't leave. Do you know the man he spoke of? Malloy?"

Leo shook his head. "I'll make some inquiries."

"Don't tell Thorne yet. I'll break the news when the time is right." Richard's eyes flickered to the pathetic aristocrat on the floor. "What did he mean about Thorne outside my brother's home?" he asked, thinking of what Anne said in the bookshop. What business could Thorne have in St James's?

Leo shifted uneasily and averted his gaze. "Not my place to say."

"Leo—"

"Not. My. Business." He scowled and crouched near St Vincent, busy with his own tasks. "Now, if you'll excuse me, I've got a wretch to dispose of."

Richard finally noticed Millie still standing in the corner, watching the entire show with a great deal of amusement. He dug into his pocket and drew out a thick wad of notes, face rueful. "What was he offering for the night, sweetheart?"

Millie smiled. "Ten quid."

"Lies and damned lies," he drawled, adding more money to the stack with an amused smirk. "But I admire your savvy. Here's triple."

Millie gawked at him before regaining her composure, her gaze sweeping over his body as she purred, "You lookin' for company tonight?"

"I'm taken," he said softly and sincerely, "and very much in love."

Millie exhaled in disappointment. "Lucky girl."

∽ 37 ∽

The Sheffields' house had finally gone quiet.

Anne had waited all morning for her father to depart for his scheduled meetings. He was in an apoplectic mood; his bellows of rage echoed through the house's corridors. Blessedly, the slam of the front door heralded his departure.

She had ten minutes before the staff began their cleaning routine – enough time to search Stanton's bedchamber for the key to his study.

She hurried down the hall and slipped quietly into his room. The sheets were thrown carelessly about the bed, evidence of how fitful his slumber must have been these past few days. With a vote looming on the Ballot Act, unease was a living thing between the walls of this house.

Her gaze moved to the dressing table across the room, and Anne drew a breath. "Key... where would he keep it?"

Stanton had many secrets, none more carefully guarded than what remained inside his study. The servants were never allowed near it – her father was suspicious by nature, always wary that information might leak.

But no matter how shrewd Stanton Sheffield was, his memory lacked consistency. Making sense of legal documents or long-standing agreements was beyond him; instead, he relied on rhetoric and charm to woo his audience in Parliament. He'd talk circles around any opposition until they felt foolish.

Despite his grandstanding in the Commons, Stanton forgot details like bribes or money. He depended on Anne for that.

Stanton's forgetfulness had one unexpected blessing: his key to the study remained in the same place. He railed for days when he once misplaced it.

Anne rummaged through several drawers but found nothing of use. Grunting in frustration, she stole towards the bureau. A relic of antiquity, with plenty of nooks and crannies. She twisted a knob, and a compartment fell open.

Aha! There it was.

Anne snatched the key, hurried out of the room and down the stairs. On the way, she passed the maids who were just going up to clean.

Too close.

"Quickly," she told herself as she unlocked the door to the study. "Quickly."

The desk yielded a few dull papers on bills, constituents, and property – likewise, his many ledgers detailing all expenses. The hidden compartments were equally fruitless. Not even a scrap of paper in the wastebasket, save for reminders that he didn't need anymore: *meeting at 8:15, dinner after next week's session...*

And then one that knotted her stomach.

Grey & Thorne – Gretna. 4 September 1867.

Richard and Thorne? What had they done in Gretna?

Anne's blood froze as an icy voice echoed from the hall. "Well, where the bloody hell is she? Her father assured me she would be at home."

Bates answered weakly, "I'm dreadfully sorry, sir. She was in her chambers—"

Anne didn't hear the rest as she desperately chucked the crumpled papers into the rubbish and made for the door. On her way, she nabbed a book off the nearest shelf and began humming loud enough to cover her escape.

Nothing to see, she thought. *I am only reading this book on... cattle farming. Compelling literature, this.*

"Ah, here she is," Bates muttered in relief. "Miss Sheffield, His Grace has been—"

"Been left waiting," Kendal interrupted as he scanned Anne up and down. "And I don't like to wait. We've discussed the matter, haven't we?"

Anne shut the volume softly and bowed her head in submission. "My apologies, Duke. I was in the library and didn't hear your arrival." She nodded to the butler. "Tea for His Grace, please."

Kendal snorted in derision and flicked his finger at her. "Don't bother. Come to the sitting room with me now."

He strode off without another word, leaving her standing there with Bates.

Anne lingered for a moment longer in the foyer with the butler. "I know this breaches protocol," she whispered, her voice trembling. "But if I don't leave there within ten minutes, bring Owens and call me away on some emergency. Understand?"

The butler's face was etched with worry, but he nodded. "Yes, miss."

They all knew what was going on here, what kind of cruelty the duke showed her in private, how he'd break her spirit, carve away at it until it yielded the shape of his ideal woman.

And yet they could do nothing – just the smallest acts of kindness to remind Anne that not everyone in the house hated her.

Gripping her skirts in one white-knuckled fist, Anne entered the sitting room to find Kendal lounging on the chaise with a frigid blue gaze that bordered on contemptuous.

"Close the door behind you," he said without rising. "We don't need to be disturbed."

Anne obeyed with fingers stiff from fear. She'd been here before; she knew what these lessons entailed – humiliation after humiliation until she fit neatly into his idea of perfection.

Anne forced her lips into a facsimile of a smile. "What did you wish to speak of?"

Kendal leaned back and regarded her with those icy eyes. Even the most beautiful blues were cold when they looked at her like this. He reminded her of the winter seas, endless and unforgiving.

"I convened with your father at our club yesterday," he said, oblivious to her discomfort. "He spoke of a change in your behaviour since returning from the Duchess of Hastings' estate. I could scarcely believe it – you seemed quite tamed at the Ashby ball. But today, I was left waiting."

Tamed? Was she an animal trained to obey orders or a

wild beast broken by its master and kept as a pet? That was all she was to him and her father; something to be managed and owned, but never someone with thoughts or feelings of her own.

"I didn't mean to—"

"Not yet," he growled, cutting her off. "Come here."

Anne ventured forward silently, each step echoing in the cavernous room.

Don't show weakness. Show nothing. He will get nothing from you.

"You're not so simple-minded that you don't know I've always loathed you," the duke continued, placing his hand on her waist as Anne stood before him. "I didn't want you and didn't take well to being bribed. But now may be a good time to face facts: we're marrying. But you should do whatever it takes to please me before then, shouldn't you?"

"Yes, Henry," she whispered.

"Good. Then take off your dress."

You are stone. Stone does not yield. It can sharpen a blade. Your mind is that blade. Your mind is a weapon.

With trembling hands, she reached behind her and began undoing the hidden hooks of her day dress.

You can endure this. You will survive this.

"Your corset closes in front, I see. Take it off. Underthings, as well," he said when she had finished.

Don't you understand how strong you are? You've survived all this time. You saved yourself. You'll save yourself again.

Anne felt an icy violation as her garments slipped to the floor, bile rising in her throat at the invasion of her privacy. She met Kendal's gaze with steely defiance, refusing to show weakness. Not now. Not like this.

"There we go," he murmured when she was naked. His fingertips grazed her bare waist. "Let me look."

He cannot break you. He cannot break you. He cannot break you.

"Good Lord." Kendal laughed. "All these wretched freckles."

The ghost of Richard's voice whispered in her mind: *All these freckles. I'm in love with them.*

Anne held her tongue and kept her eyes forward, determined not to remember Richard at this moment.

This is your body. Your power. Yours alone, and no one else can take it away from you.

"Your breasts are too large, Anne," he muttered, disgust clear in his voice. "I hope you don't intend to eat this much once we're married." His hand moved further down, clasping her bottom firmly. "But this is nicely shaped. Come sit on my lap. I'd like to have you to myself for—"

An insistent knock sounded at the door, jarring her from Kendal's grip like an electric shock. "Miss Sheffield!" Bates. Lord in heaven, she could kiss the man. "Miss Sheffield, I'm afraid something requires your urgent attention."

Kendal answered before Anne had a chance. "Can't it wait?"

"No, Yer Grace," Owens' gruff tones interjected. "Miss Sheffield must attend to it at once."

Kendal made a noise of displeasure and shoved Anne aside. "Go," he said, rising to his feet. "Handle the matter with your servants. I'll take my leave."

"Yes, Henry."

"And Anne?" Kendal paused. "There won't be any servants to save you from my bed."

He threw open the door and left.

Anne clutched her clothes in front of her, shaking so badly that she stood frozen in place.

Bates and Owens entered the room without so much as batting an eyelid towards her undressed state. Numb relief flooded her veins, and she felt grateful for their presence. If she could move, she'd have hugged both of them on the spot.

"Thank you," she whispered against the muslin of her dress that barely clung to her frame. Then, regaining some semblance of composure: "Bates, summon Aileen to me; I think I may need assistance."

"Yes, miss."

"Owens," she added quietly, trying to quell the tremble in her voice, "please ask the cook to make tea. I think I need some."

"Happy to, miss," the bodyguard replied.

Both men bowed their way out of the drawing room – leaving Anne alone, clutching desperately onto what little shreds of dignity she had remaining. She stood tall, refusing to give in to the urge to collapse into a heap on the floor.

She would not be broken.

∽ 38 ∽

Richard found himself holed up in a hotel room instead of his comfortable Belgravia townhouse. Everything was unfamiliar, from the silk sheets to the faint smell of lemon cleaning solution. He was in the middle of a restless doze when a sharp rap sounded at the door.

He groaned, got up, and flung it open to find Leo standing there with his hands in his pockets.

"Nice place," Leo drawled, pushing his way inside without invitation. "I stopped by your house and stumbled on a pretty little thing during tea time. Looked like she was miserable. Had a row with your lover?"

"She's my brother's lover," Richard corrected distractedly, shutting the door.

Leo wrinkled his nose in disgust. "You share your brother's women? You aristos are—"

"No, no." Good Lord, he needed sleep. "James is a fool who won't admit he's in love with her, so she's staying at my home until he comes to his senses."

The revelation that his brother's elusive masked paramour was actually a servant in Kent's household had thrown a new wrench into the already tangled gears of Richard's life. And now he was stuck in a strange hotel, forced to navigate unfamiliar surroundings all because James was too bloody daft to realise he should just marry the woman already. Imbecile.

Leo cocked an eyebrow, as though acts of decency from aristocrats were rarer than hen's teeth. "And you're staying here because…?"

Richard's composure cracked, fatigue gnawing through the well-crafted mask. "Because James is a bloody disaster and I needed some space," Richard snapped. "Do you have information on Malloy, or not?"

The Irishman smiled, a sparkle of mischief in his gaze that suggested Richard's fraying nerves delighted him to no end. Under normal circumstances, he'd indulge in Leo's antics, but with Anne's well-being hanging by a thread, there was no time for games.

"Of course I do," Leo said, as he helped himself to some of Richard's brandy without invitation. He slammed down the glass too hard and continued. "I'm good at my job. He fancies a tipple at the Seven Bells in Spitalfields. Know it?"

"Heard of it."

"Then you'd best speak to Malloy tonight because he'll bounce once he hears I've been looking for him."

"And why would that be?"

"Because men I'm looking for tend to be found floating in the Thames." At Richard's scowl, Leo's lips curved into a grin. Behind those spectacles, his eyes flashed with darkness. "But you were already aware of that."

"Yes," Richard said through gritted teeth. "I just don't particularly approve."

Leo shrugged and moved to the door. "Are you coming?"

"I'll come." He grabbed his coat. "But we're playing by my rules tonight."

"This once," Leo conceded. "After that, I make no promises." Then, eyeing Richard's wardrobe: "And unless you want your pocket picked, you better change those clothes before we get there."

The Seven Bells cast a baleful light into the London evening. It was a place to drown your sorrows or find fresh ones.

To those with wealth, it might have been a slum – but the people of the East End had no other luxury. For them, the Seven Bells was a reprieve from life's miseries, where broken souls congregated and spent their last coins on drink and company.

Richard sensed the chaotic energy in the air. He heard laughter, glass breaking, and screams echoing from far away. It seemed almost as if Spitalfields had become some part of hell – where coal-blackened skies smothered them all beneath its oppressive mantle.

He passed an unconscious man lying in the gutter, a bottle still clutched in his hand, then watched as a woman was taken against one of the alley walls. A drunken figure emerged from the double doors of the Seven Bells just before they arrived, tumbling unceremoniously into the filth of the street.

The two men stepped inside the Seven Bells, and its atmosphere only added to its casualness. A man in a corner wailed on a fiddle while patrons stomped their boots to the rhythm. Drunken, bawdy lyrics emanated through the room as mugs of ale clanked against each other before mistakenly crashing onto the hardwood floor – like an ode to intoxication.

Serving girls weaved between tables. Leo flagged down one before murmuring something into her ear. She pointed to a table where an emaciated young man sat, nursing a tankard of ale.

Malloy, obviously malnourished and trembling in fear, was younger than Richard had expected – the hardships of living on this side of town ageing him beyond his years. Stringy black hair framed malnutrition-ravaged features, while childhood diseases left pale scars on his wan face.

"Malloy, yes?" Richard inquired calmly, though his wave summoned the serving girl at a pace that spoke of hidden threats. He raised two fingers in a silent demand for ale and returned his attention to the man before him.

The other man's eyes narrowed in suspicion as he glanced between Richard and Leo. "Who's askin'?"

"I'm Richard Grey, and this would be Leo O'Sullivan. I'd wager you've heard of him."

O'Sullivan flashed a smile like a viper about to strike. "Yeah, he has."

Terror swam in Malloy's expression. He tried to stand, but Richard seized his hand before he could rise and, with a sharp bend of his finger backwards, had him screaming in pain within seconds. The wail was lost amid the raucous fiddle music.

"Sit your arse down," Richard snarled. "Or I'll break it off."

Malloy complied promptly, eyes wide and chest heaving beneath his coat like a hunted creature ready to bolt. "What do ye want?"

Richard smiled at the serving girl as she placed tankards of ale upon their table with nary a blink at the ongoing torture between them.

"Thank you, darling," he murmured, returning his attention to Malloy. "First, let me establish rules."

Malloy flinched as Richard shoved his finger back farther. "Please don't—"

"Quiet," Richard rumbled darkly. "Leo here certainly doesn't appreciate rules. Do you, Leo?"

"Nope." Leo chuckled. "Can't say I can abide 'em."

"See? So it's best to listen to me, or you'll have to deal with O'Sullivan here, and he's not nearly as pleasant as I am. Understood?"

Malloy trembled, sweat beginning to bead along his upper lip, but he managed a desperate nod.

"I thought so. Now then, rule one: every time you try to run, I break a finger. Got it?"

"Aye. Jesus, all right."

"Rule two: you'll answer every question I ask without complaint, or I break a finger. Nod," Richard continued sternly. Malloy swallowed, suppressing a whimper as he nodded once more. "Good. Rule three: if I reach four broken fingers on this hand" – Richard waved the offending appendage with a faint smirk – "you get to deal with Leo here. Your thumb will remain intact because I'm feeling generous, and all five remaining digits, too, because no man should suffer through lonely nights with both hands maimed beyond all hope of pleasure." He trailed off, leaving an expectant silence punctuated by Leo's throaty laughter. "I doubt Leo will let you off so easily. Will you, Leo?"

"No." Leo's eyes glinted behind his spectacles. "I won't."

"Agreed, Malloy?"

Malloy's eyes darted to Leo, then to where Richard held his finger back. He must have sensed the futility of resistance because he muttered, "Bugger it. Aye."

Richard smiled. "Good. Now tell me about the Duke of Kendal."

Malloy made some noise like a frightened animal and shoved away from the bench. Richard was faster. With a swift jerk, he broke Malloy's forefinger and grasped the next. The other man's sharp cry caused more than one head to turn in their direction, but after a quick assessment, the other patrons looked away.

This was life in Spitalfields; no one saved you from your stupidity. They were all immune from the horror of crime, intimidation, and bribery. This was their normality, not a sight to gawp at. They minded their business.

"Take a seat, or I'll break another finger." Richard had never used such a tone – never had the need. This was brought on by the knowledge that he was about to uncover an atrocity to shake the very foundations of the British government.

And Anne was caught in the middle of it.

Malloy sat back down, his breath coming rough. "Please – please don't – he'll have me murdered."

Richard's voice was a whip crack of ice. "And do you think O'Sullivan will let you walk away from this? Make your choice, Malloy. Tell me about Kendal, or I'll start breaking the bones in this pretty little hand of yours."

Malloy's shoulders were hunched in an attempt to diminish himself. "Just some toff, comes 'round every now and then."

Richard's lips curled into a chilling smile. "Do you take me for a fool? Try again."

Malloy glanced between Leo and Richard, his eyes wide with fear. "Uhhh… He pays for 'em, but I don't know what he does with 'em. Honest! Please don't hurt me. I—"

But Richard kept squeezing tighter, and Malloy's whimper echoed through the room. "Pays for whom?" His voice took on an edge of menace when Malloy hesitated too long before answering. "Talk. Or so help me God, I'll crush this hand to dust."

"Them kids," he whispered, looking around nervously. "The ones that come from orphanages? He tells me which he wants, and I pick 'em up and deliver 'em."

Richard watched Leo, who was staring at Malloy with undisguised rage. The Viscount of St Vincent had already revealed the duke's moral bankruptcy – only a fool couldn't connect the rest of the dots.

"How many?" Richard bit off.

"Dunno." He nibbled his lip. "Coupla dozen, maybe, over th' years."

Leo let out an enraged hiss. "Dear God," he whispered.

God help them if it wasn't faith alone keeping O'Sullivan from leaping across the table and smashing Malloy's face in.

"How much does he pay you?" Richard inquired, desperate to finish this conversation before things got bloody.

"A dragon each kid," Malloy said in a low voice. At Leo's sharp intake of breath, he said defensively, "What? He asked!"

"You sold children for a fucking sovereign," Leo snarled.

Malloy snapped back, "Got a life o' me own, don't I? Need coin to pay me landlord, right?"

"And it doesn't matter to you what happens to them?" Leo's chest heaved. "Does it, Malloy?"

"Leo—"

Richard was too distracted by Leo's sudden anger. He made the mistake of looking away from the man in his grip.

Malloy finally took his chance.

He yanked free of Richard and knocked over a tankard of ale as he fled. Liquid spilled all over the floor. A man shouted a foul curse at Malloy as he staggered into a serving girl. Spinning, he scampered through a crowd of patrons and darted out of the door of the Bells.

Leo lunged forwards with the intent to give chase, but Richard put out a hand in warning. "Don't. Let him go."

The Irishman was breathing hard, his spectacles fogged with ire. He pulled away from Richard's grasp, jaw tight. "You have your answer. Satisfied?"

"No," Richard answered softly. "I am far from it."

Leo cast about wildly before snatching up the tankard of ale and downing it in one long swallow. He wiped his mouth with his sleeve and glared at Richard. "I'll find him, Grey," he said through gritted teeth. "You're prolonging the inevitable."

"You gave me your word that you wouldn't tell Thorne yet."

The Irishman looked at him sharply. "You've got brass bollocks to ask for my silence after tonight." At Richard's quiet stare, he curled his lip. "A few days, Grey. That's it.

Because once Thorne hears of this, he and I will find that bastard and float his arse in the Thames." He slammed the empty tankard onto the table and shoved past Richard.

Richard couldn't help but notice how Leo O'Sullivan's hands shook.

39

One day had not made Anne any less afraid.

Once Kendal departed, she lingered in the sitting room, her heart a cage of fluttering birds. Years of mastering her emotions should have served her well, but Anne felt the iron grip of control slipping away. Tremors raked her body until Aileen, the lady's maid, took her hand, murmuring soothing words. It seemed Aileen had a knack for calming distraught souls.

Desperation for fresh air clawed at Anne's chest, the house's walls pressing down on her like a vice, the very air heavy and stifling. Escape was the only solace she sought.

Staggering from the house, she and Owens ventured toward Hyde Park, her steps faltering. No amount of walking could banish the memory of her vulnerability in the drawing room with Kendal. Her mind, sharp as a blade after years in her father's home, was her only defence in this high-stakes masquerade. Yet every moment spent under that roof was a gamble with peril.

Never again would she forget.

The note she had penned to Richard was crushed in her gloved grasp, his lackey nowhere in sight.

Had he forsaken her, then? Left her to face the storm alone?

Owens, sensing her distress, inquired, "Are ye all right, Miss Sheffield?"

Anne swallowed the lump in her throat. "I'm afraid I'm not," she said quietly. "After yesterday…"

Her words trailed into silence. Speaking so candidly before servants whose loyalty lay in their pay was foolish, but her trembling hands and ragged breath betrayed her. She could no more command them than the forces that drove them. Anne was not the actress she'd believed herself to be.

A day was hardly enough to silence the gnawing dread that the duke might reappear and continue his wicked game.

Owens, the stoic sentinel, strolled beside her, his voice a murmur. "I ain't been in service to yer father long, but… I reckon ye a kind sort."

"Much obliged," she murmured. "Your words mean more than you know."

"And it ain't me place, but" – Owens cleared his throat – "'tis plain to see yer duke is a right foul bastard, miss. If ye don't mind me sayin'."

Casting a furtive glance around, she found their path deserted. "Between us… I concur wholeheartedly."

Owens chuckled, incredulous. "And I'm thinkin' yer more clever than ye let on?"

Anne's smile was a flicker of light. "Can you keep a secret, Owens?"

"Aye, miss."

"I loathe hat shopping. I only wished for escape."

He gazed at her, then roared with laughter. "By the gods, clever lady, ye are. Never would've guessed."

As their laughter waned, they strolled in harmonious silence. "Thank you," Anne said. "For yesterday. And today."

Owens grinned. "Anytime, miss."

As they neared the Serpentine Bridge an hour later, Anne spotted Richard's man sauntering along the path. Despite his altered appearance, she'd committed his gait to memory. He ambled leisurely, hands in pockets, blending seamlessly with the park-goers.

Anne exhaled, relief washing over her. He hadn't forsaken her, after all.

Upon crossing paths on the bridge, she seized his hand and – ignoring his startled flinch – slipped the note into his grasp.

It was time to return to her gilded cage.

Anne paced her room, repeating the message she'd written on that small scrap of paper in her mind.

Take this to Mr Grey.

The staff go quiet after midnight. The back garden is protected by a gate that I have left open. The tree outside my window (third floor, directly above the statue of Bacchus) is easily scalable.
Yours,

Anne

Anne was so preoccupied she didn't notice Richard's arrival through the window. She jolted when his arms closed around her from behind.

"Easy," he rumbled, breath ruffling in her hair. "It's only me."

She twisted, dragging him tight against her body and shutting her eyes as she breathed him in. The mingling scents of smoke, soap, brandy, and clean laundry enveloped her – his unique, reassuring aroma. This was sanctuary.

Sensing her yearning for solace, Richard responded in kind. His hand delved into her locks, a low, guttural sound emanating from him as he held her fast.

You're safe, she tried telling herself. *You're safe. He's holding you, and you're safe.*

But the memory of Kendal's touch haunted her. Too recent, too close. He'd stripped her to her soul, his hands cold as they groped and grasped—

As Richard's hands gripped her, she felt a shiver run through her body. "What's wrong?" he asked, concern etched into his features.

She took a deep breath and buried her face in his shoulder, trying to steady herself. "It's nothing," she mumbled.

He ran a soothing hand down her back. "You're trembling. It can't be nothing."

She shook her head – she just wanted to forget. She wanted Richard to distract her and make her feel anything other than the fear gnawing at her.

But when she leaned in to kiss him, he stopped her. "Wait," he said, his voice low and urgent. "There's something I need to tell you about Kendal. Don't be alone with him if you can help it."

Anne froze.

There won't be any servants to save you from my bed.

The sensation of Kendal's hands on her skin returned with vivid clarity. He'd been so emotionless in his inspection of her body – as if she were nothing more than an item he'd purchased at auction.

Take off your clothes.

She shuddered, forcing herself to push away the memories. *You're safe now. You're safe.*

Richard's gentle voice roused Anne from her thoughts, his intense gaze boring into her as if seeking the darkest secrets of her soul. "He's come by, hasn't he?" he whispered, as though the words tasted of ash.

Anne was quiet, a tremor threatening to betray her fear. "The servants helped me."

Richard's hand shot through his hair, the gesture bordering on violence. "Jesus," he muttered under his breath. "Is that why you were trembling?" His piercing gaze settled on her, and she could feel the weight of his words as if they were a physical thing. "It tears me apart to leave you here," he said, raw with emotion. "Do you understand that?"

"I do." She swallowed. Summoning every ounce of bravery within her, she said, "Please, just tell me what you've found."

She knew he struggled to control his anger. She appreciated the restraint, the way he trusted her enough to let her handle herself. "I'm still looking into a few things. Have you ever been to his estate? Or his London house?"

"I've been to the London house a few times," she answered, keeping her voice neutral. "And I went to his estate once with my father."

A muscle twitched in Richard's jaw before he spoke again. "Were there any children around either place?"

An icy tendril of dread slithered up Anne's spine. "Not that I'm aware of." She thought back, trying to recall any detail she may have missed. "It was strange how silent it all was. Kendal only keeps a skeleton staff. Why ask about children?"

"We got a name from St Vincent," Richard said, tracing gentle circles on her cheek. "Thorne's associate did some digging and discovered that Kendal has been adopting orphans from East End rookeries, using Malloy as his go-between. Children no one would miss if they suddenly disappeared." His eyes searched hers for understanding. "Anne... what I'm uncovering might not turn out well for your father. Are you ready for that?"

She shook her head. But somehow, she knew she must prepare herself, anyway.

Richard tenderly pressed a kiss to her forehead and murmured, "I'm so sorry, sweetheart."

Her thoughts swirled in a complicated mess of emotions and longing. Was she a fool to wish for her father's kindness? What kind of life would she have had if he'd shown her even the slightest care? But no amount of wishing could bring Stanton Sheffield any closer to displaying affection – power and wealth had extinguished whatever spirit of tenderness he once may have owned.

Richard's fingers ghosted over her spine. Words of solace and comfort tumbled from his lips like honey, washing away the shadows in her mind. Anne drank him in – his taste, his touch, his voice – and held them close like precious coins. Their bond was forged from the hard-won currency of trust and intimacy, not force or purchase. It was everything to her.

Richard had burrowed into her heart – and she was terrified of losing him.

"Please be careful with Kendal," she whispered. "He's dangerous."

He flashed a grin, his confidence unwavering. "Darling, I've already told you. I'm always careful."

Anne's expression soured. "No, you aren't."

A devilish glint sparked in his eye. "Calling me a liar?"

"You're in politics," she retorted, arching an eyebrow.

Richard leaned forward, and his lips danced a tantalising trail across Anne's collarbone, setting her skin aflame with each kiss. Her breath hitched as his mischievous hand cupped her bottom, eliciting a surprised squeak.

"Mmm," he murmured, the wicked sparkle still in his eyes. "This doesn't feel like politics to me."

"You're trying to distract me," Anne replied as though resigned, but a hint of mirth tinged the edges of her words.

"Yes. Is it working?"

"Only if you admit defeat."

Richard tutted. "Certainly not. You'll have to give me a more convincing argument. Go on."

She shook her head, laughter bubbling up like champagne. "How about this? My father is determined to destroy you, you've a habit of employing confidence artists and thieves, and men are notoriously reckless creatures with little regard for their own lives."

He chuckled, his breath tickling her skin. "Oh, I assure you, I value my life highly. It's the criminals who make it interesting." At her snort, he said, "Fine. You win. As always."

"I love that answer." She hooked an arm around his neck and gave him a quick kiss on the lips. "As victor, what do I get?"

Now his smile was wicked. "I'm sure I can think of something, brilliant girl." As if to illustrate his point, he began pulling the pins out of her hair. "You've been terrifying the devil out of Samuel, by the way. My felonious hireling."

"You must be kidding." Anne pulled back, her curls loose. "You mean to tell me that man was a criminal? You put an actual convict in charge of my protection?"

Richard chortled, discarding her hairpins onto the nightstand. "Trust me. Criminals are reliable hires. Money buys loyalty, and my patronage keeps them off the streets. Samuel is an ex-thief."

"I suppose in the realm of criminality, a rehabilitated thief is preferable to a retired murderer," Anne said.

"A gentleman has to have standards on the sort of brigand he has guarding his lady," Richard agreed. "Samuel's never been noticed before he began watching you. He's starting to think he's losing his touch."

"No, no. He's excellent. It's just—"

"—that you notice everything," Richard finished for her with a wink. "You're so damn clever. Your note said you needed to tell me something?"

She recalled the scrap of paper from Stanton's study. "Have you and Thorne ever menaced someone in Gretna?"

Richard looked at her, puzzled. "Gretna?"

"My father referred to Grey and Thorne being in Gretna on 4 September, 1867."

He wrinkled his brow. "I assure you, I've never had to resort to threats in Scotland. The only thing I want to do there is get married at the anvil – something that has been rather appealing lately."

A smile flickered across her lips at his comment, sending a pleasant tingle through her heart. "Could your sister have anything to do with this?"

"Alexandra?" Richard barked a laugh, as if the idea was so ludicrous it was absurd. "Good God, no. The mere mention of Nicholas Thorne's name once sent her into such a fit of disgust I thought she might retch on the spot."

"And your brother?"

"James? I highly doubt it. The man's all about following the straight and narrow, keeping up appearances, and playing by the rules. I just had to shelter his lover while he learned to grovel for the first time." He chuckled, relishing the guarded look on Anne's face. "Don't tell me you're jealous."

Anne narrowed her eyes. "Not in the slightest."

"Liar," he murmured, his breath hot against her ear as he leaned in close.

"You dare accuse me of—" she started to protest, but a sharp nip at her earlobe cut her off.

"Being a liar? You were raised in a political house," he whispered, nipping again. "And you're jealous as all hellfire. Want me to grovel for you on my knees? Is that it?"

"Rakes don't grovel."

"Reformed ones do." His husky voice slithered over her like a caress of silk, igniting her blood with a thousand tiny pinpricks of delicious fire. "A reformed rake will kneel in supplication at his lady's feet any time she desires. For any reason she desires. Forever and always in service to her pleasure."

A shiver coursed through her body. Hers to command. Hers to have. But only in the fleeting moments before dawn broke – their time together stolen like a breath.

But this mattered: the touch of his fingertips, the taste of his mouth, and the way their bodies fit. Tingles of ecstasy danced under her skin as Anne drew closer to Richard, close enough that he could hear her plea: "I need you."

A low growl stirred within him, and a thunderous thrill shivered through her. Their kiss was passionate yet tender.

"Fuck me," Anne breathed.

Richard's chest rose and fell with exertion, his eyes alight with an intense fire that left her breathless. The surrounding air was heavy with a charged silence until he finally spoke, his voice low and gravelly. "I won't just fuck you," he said, tracing a finger down her throat. "Tonight, I'll worship you. I'll drive you wild with desire." Teeth grazed her pulse, and he whispered, "I'll make love to you."

She froze at those words – words she'd never heard before. But she shouldn't have been surprised; if there was one thing Richard was known for, it was being the ultimate romantic.

"I told you, I'm more than fond of you. I love you." A deep, satisfied chuckle rumbled through him, warming her from the inside out. "The night you stormed into my life? I fell head over heels for you."

Anne gave him better access to the back of her nightgown. "I think you like it when a woman challenges you."

"I'm getting that impression." His voice was darker than midnight, and she felt his need like a brand against her skin.

One hand snaked around her waist, tugging insistently at her bodice and scattering buttons across the floor. His hunger inflamed her, and she responded in kind. Men's clothes were easier, with fewer layers to discard.

She had him naked quickly, clad in nothing but shadows. Anne drank in his form, admiring how the light caressed him like an artist's brush, tracing out divinity in strokes of moonlight. The way his eyes spoke of a possession she was more than willing to grant.

His gaze burned into hers. "I love you," he said, pushing her onto the mattress as his warmth enveloped her. "I love you."

The mood softened. Richard took his time, kissing Anne slowly and deeply as his fingertips traced her curves. Rolling together in a tangle of limbs, they embraced as only lovers could: stroking, licking, biting, tasting each other in their frenzy. They learned the subtle nuances of their desire, exploring every inch of skin with eager touches and lips.

Anne's mind spun with fantasies, hours stretching ahead of them in a blur of passion that would know no bounds. She wanted to savour everything about Richard; the span of his chest beneath her palms, the bones of his hips as they cradled hers, that tantalising line at his pelvis she was desperate to lick down to—

His cock, that was the word Richard had taught Anne. She longed to pleasure him with her mouth.

"You're thinking something sinful," Richard murmured as he pressed atop her. His lips curled in a salacious grin. "I'm intrigued. Tell me."

Anne's smile matched his. "Perhaps it's a secret."

"I want to know all your secrets," he said, nipping at her

lip. "Every last one." She groaned as he rubbed that male appendage against her wet core. "Tell me."

"Mmmm…"

He ground his hips against her, teasing out wild tremors from between her thighs as if he could sense her innermost desires. Then he withdrew, leaving her limp and desperate for more.

"Richard, please."

"Tell me what that naughty mind is thinking, and I'll give it to you."

Anne gasped as frustration mingled with pleasure. She pulled him closer until his warm breath brushed against her ear. "I wanted to get down on my knees and take your cock into my mouth," she whispered in a voice so soft it was almost lost in the darkness of their room.

Richard's body shuddered against hers, vibrating with ecstasy. He groaned and laid his head against her shoulder – a feral hunger and agony in a single sigh.

Laughter bubbled up inside Anne as she shifted beneath him. "Was that a yes?"

"Later," Richard growled before claiming her lips with an all-consuming kiss that left them both gasping for air.

He made some inarticulate noise as her hips arched up to meet him.

Anne gasped as he surged forward and entered her completely, a swell of desire coursing through her veins. Richard's every movement was like a fever, his demands echoing her own. He rocked her body in time to their shared rhythm, fast and slow, hard and gentle.

She could never have enough of him, of this perfect connection between them. Her name was on his lips, a prayer uttered at the very threshold of paradise. His breath shuddered out of him, timed with the urgent staccato of his thrusts.

Then he was whispering something to her – a plea. "*Come. Please come.*"

Pleasure blazed within Anne, each lick a spark that flared until she was lost in a conflagration. She stifled her cry as ecstasy consumed her. Then she felt him shudder against her, his breathing in sync with hers as they reached their peak together.

As the flames ebbed, she lay there, spent and sated, feeling the comforting warmth of his body against hers. He held her tight until slumber finally overtook her.

Hours later, when Anne woke up to find the sunlight streaming through the curtains, Richard was already gone.

All that remained was the lingering heat of where he had slept beside her.

The rookeries had a distinctive smell that made Richard's stomach heave.

It was bodies, smoke, piss, and shit, not to mention the ugly piscine stench of poverty and despair.

He'd only ventured into the East End when he needed information. The criminal underworld was vast, but he hadn't grown up in its dark, winding alleys. His politics had brought him here, for even though the law belonged to Her Majesty, she would never set foot in such a place. It was a world unto itself, anarchic and untamed.

And Nicholas Thorne was king of it all.

Richard had ensured his arrival was noticed; Thorne employed any number of spies in these streets – children, whores, shop owners, especially the street urchins who were always looking for coin in exchange for reports on strangers. Thorne was known to be generous with his patronage.

Soon enough, Richard felt a presence behind him that seemed half-man, half-shadow – and utterly deliberate. He knew Thorne would not hesitate to slice open his throat before he could even blink.

"You wanted to see me, Grey?"

Thorne's voice was like a blade in the night. Richard had never been able to place his accent, no matter how hard he tried. It slipped and slid effortlessly, depending on what Thorne needed it to sound like. Nobleman at St James? He was as blue-blooded as they came. Mingle with criminals in the rookery? Born and bred local.

He glanced over. "Took you long enough."

Thorne shrugged, an indifferent twitch of one shoulder. "Dealing with a situation. I can't abide cheaters."

He stood a head taller than Richard, bigger too – coiled muscle, sleek and dangerous as a leopard on the hunt. Where Richard was fair-haired and blue-eyed, Thorne was dark-as-sin – black locks too long for fashion, like he hadn't had time for a trim recently, eyes so deep brown they seemed like black pools of ink at first glance. In the streets of Whitechapel, he was known for his devil's eyes, yet he was their avenging angel – a protector who showed no mercy to those that crossed him.

"Kill a man, Thorne?"

Thorne's smile was slow. "Maybe. Maybe not. You got a reason to know?"

"Nothing in particular, aside from idle curiosity."

"I don't indulge a nobleman's idle whims in my spare time, Grey. So how about you tell me what you want? Starting with why you're skulking around in the street instead of coming to my office."

"I needed a word and didn't want to be seen at the Brimstone."

That got Thorne's attention. "Interesting. I've already got men working to secure the vote, if that's what you've come to ask. Unless you can't pay 'em, in which case we've got a problem. I don't like men who can't pay up, either."

"I always keep my word," Richard said. "Different business. Two things. One's a favour, and the other's a question."

The ghost of a laugh escaped Thorne's lips as he shook his head in disbelief. "How about we start with the question, and I'll consider the favour."

Richard leaned against the wall of the building and met the other man's gaze. "Why don't you tell me why you've been stopping by my brother's house?"

A strange fire sparked in Thorne's dark gaze, as if Richard had caught him off-guard somehow. Then he shrugged once more. "Pretty area. Thinking about buying a property. The Earl of Kent has a nice one." He peered at Richard through narrowed eyes and added, "Got someone watching me, Grey?"

"Not me, but I'm almost certain Stanton Sheffield is tracking your movements."

"Fucking Tory cunt," Thorne muttered under his breath. "That blundering bastard was a shite hire, besides."

"Hold on," Richard said, "you knew someone was trailing you?"

"'Course I did." Thorne almost looked insulted. "I wasn't trying to keep my comings and goings a secret. St James's isn't exactly a place for clandestine meetings. What's your favour?"

"Context first. The Duke of Kendal has been taking children from your orphanages."

The man's expression turned deadly, and his night-black stare burned with palpable rage. "Was wondering why you were sniffing around the Nichol. You're keeping O'Sullivan from his work, and he gets his dander up every time I ask about it. It's starting to irritate." He paused before adding with a lethal purr, "Your duke have any lackeys working for him?"

So Leo kept quiet about Malloy – at least, that was the only good thing coming out of this conversation thus far. It gave Richard room to negotiate.

"One that I'm aware of. He let slip how many and how much he collected for each child. I went to a few orphanages for more details, but they don't keep records."

"No." Thorne's tone grew colder than the Arctic sea. "For that, they'd have to give a good goddamn." His piercing gaze felt full of malice, with a deep anger emanating from some dark place within his core. Richard understood why people whispered about a demon inside this man. "I'll have his name."

"Thorne—"

"You bloody toffs come here, kidnap children off the streets, and either work 'em to death or rape them." He stepped forward, his hands forming into fists. "Those kids are under my protection, so you'll give me his name, or I'll get it out of O'Sullivan. Your choice."

"Leo gave me his word, and I'll take my favour first."

Thorne's laughter scraped against his throat like broken glass. "'Course you will. So what is it?"

Richard sighed heavily. "I need you to help me search the Duke of Kendal's residence to find out what happened to those children. I think Stanton Sheffield might be covering something up for him."

"Something." Thorne didn't bother hiding his contempt. "Don't mince words, Grey. Murder, you mean."

"It's a distinct possibility, yes," Richard replied sombrely. "You up for it?"

"You've got someone snatching kids right under my nose and killing them? I'm up for it." Thorne fixed him with an icy stare. "And when we're done, you'll give me that name, so I can gut the man who helped your duke like a fucking fish."

The night was their ally. A pitch-black blanket of stars smothered the residence in shadow as Richard and Thorne skulked through Kendal's garden. All the servants should have been asleep by now. The gaslights had been extinguished hours ago.

Kendal himself had vanished, likely to his country estate. His luggage had gone with him, accompanied by a few lackeys who acted as buffers between him and the world. It was the perfect moment to infiltrate the place.

"Let's hurry this along," Thorne murmured beside him as they approached the door leading from the gardens into the main house. He retrieved a kit of tools and began working, giving a derisive snort when the mechanism gave way too easily under his steady hand. "The comfort of you nobs," he said in disgust, pushing the door open.

Silently, they moved through the house, checking each room until they found Kendal's study.

"Search the rest," Richard said. "I'll see what I find here."

Thorne nodded, then vanished into the hallway.

Richard started at the desk, rifling through documents

and ledgers the duke had left behind. Everything seemed in order; meticulous notations littered every page and catalogue, hinting at a man who preferred to handle these matters himself.

That was something of a surprise. The duke had obtained a daunting number of holdings, and the estates alone were enough to disrupt even the most disciplined man. Richard's brother, James, had even resorted to appointing someone to keep up with the ever-growing responsibility.

Richard flipped through the most recent books.

There.

Richard scoured through the archive. Ahh, there it was – Stanton Sheffield's name. Two thousand pounds was quite a hefty sum paid. For what? Kendal had not mentioned a single word about why he would need that much money.

Questioning his prior observation, Richard further regressed into the documentation – two thousand pounds.

Every six months, like clockwork.

Suddenly, a hushed scratching on the door disrupted his focus. Thorne stood at the threshold and signalled him with finality. "Come. Be quick about it."

He followed close behind Thorne as he ascended upstairs to the duke's bedchamber. What was he doing in there?

Then Richard noticed one bookcase slide outwards to reveal a secret passageway. "Bloody hell," he murmured.

"Wait until you see."

Thorne didn't hesitate as he marched down the dimly lit stairs with his lantern. The only illumination came from his feeble flame, casting grotesque shadows along the walls as they descended deeper into the foundation. They eventually reached an abandoned chamber at the bottom of the staircase made entirely of dirt flooring.

"Old wine cellar, perhaps," Richard suggested as his eyes drifted warily. "Though the stairs appear more recently built."

Thorne grunted. "Damn the stairs. Look." He nodded towards a corner of the room and lifted his lamp above their heads.

There, huddled in the darkness, was a little girl.

41

Anne was preparing for bed when Stanton stormed into the room with two servants.

"Get her ready," he commanded. "Pack her things. You have an hour."

Alarm speared through Anne. She staggered to her feet, struggling to keep her wits about her. "What's happening?"

Though her father maintained a calm air, something in his face told her otherwise – flushed and dishevelled, as if torn from some inner struggle.

He met Anne's gaze with a steely one of his own. "We're leaving for Kendal's estate. You're to be married tomorrow morning."

Anne's stomach plummeted. She scrambled to maintain her façade, feigning innocence and stupidity. "But I thought... the wedding isn't until next week." She forced a high-pitched laugh, which sounded more like a squawk to her ears. "Goodness, my dress hasn't even arrived!"

Stanton looked at her in disgust. "Forget the damn dress."

She allowed herself a bemused smile. "Forget the dress? But it's a wedding. It requires a—"

Crack! His hand connected with her cheek, sending her reeling. Her skin seared as she stumbled back, catching the bedpost to keep herself upright.

Her father crossed to her, rage burning in his eyes. His grip was painful as he seized her shoulder. "I said forget the dress!" His voice was filled with panic, a wild animal caught in a snare and lashing out at anything nearby. He shook her hard. "It won't make a bloody difference if your groom is waiting to hang, and we're thrown into the streets with debt. My enemies in Parliament would sooner spit in your face than help you."

Anne froze, staring at her father in astonishment. Even the maids were stunned.

Stanton released her and stepped back, raking his hand through his hair. But Anne could see the anger smouldering beneath his calm façade. His voice was cold, unyielding. "I'll handle this," he gritted out. "In the meantime, you'll marry the duke, do you hear me?" Without bothering to wait for her response, he snapped at the maids, "Get to work. Both of you."

The maids jumped at Stanton's words and began quickly preparing her for the journey to Rosewood, Lord Kendal's estate in Hampshire. It was only hours by coach, and she knew if her father had his way, she'd wed the duke the moment they crossed the threshold.

The dull ache on her cheek reminded her that Stanton wasn't thinking clearly – and that made him dangerous.

She had to warn Richard.

"Excuse me," she said as the maid started dressing her,

"I must…" She pushed past Aileen and strode to the desk, barely registering the mess of letters covering its surface as she grabbed ink, pen, and paper. Her handwriting wavered wildly as she scrawled a quick note.

Richard,

SS sensing his demise. I require your urgent assistance on the road to Rosewood. He will take the main highway. Hurry.

– A

Anne snatched the paper, her knuckles white against the foolscap. She seized Aileen's hands without preamble, staring intently into the girl's wide eyes. "You said you would help me if I asked it of you. Take this outside after I leave. There will be a man looking to go after me in the carriage, but under no circumstances should you let him. Instruct him to deliver this note to Mr Grey immediately. It's imperative that he finds Mr Grey tonight, as quickly as possible."

"Oh, miss, I *can't*—"

"Please." Anne glanced at the other maid, who returned to packing the suitcase as if she hadn't noticed the conversation in the room. "*Please*. I need your help – and his."

Aileen shut her eyes and sighed, but reluctantly accepted her burden. "Yes, miss."

"Thank you. Thank you so much."

All she had to do was hold out until Richard found her.

Richard burst into his brother's residence, startling the devil out of poor Jeffries. "Bit of a crisis, Jeffries."

James's home was closer to Kendal's than Richard's townhouse, and there was no way he would have allowed that child to make the journey to Belgravia in her condition. Thorne cradled the quivering, filthy girl in his arms and shut the door behind him with a swift kick. She hadn't said a word since they left Kendal's, but followed them willingly after they soothed her with offers of help. Exhaustion had melted her, and she could barely move anymore. Richard suspected she hadn't eaten in days, nor had much to drink. She must have been twelve at most – her body weighed nothing more than skin stretched over fragile limbs.

"Jeffries," Richard said, "I need you to take this child to the kitchen. Get her something to eat and drink while Mr Thorne and I talk in the library."

The butler eyed the girl with concern as Thorne set her

down. She clung to his hand, clearly reluctant to let go. "Yes, sir. Shall I… clean her up first?"

"No," Thorne said sharply. "Food and drink. And you'll be gentle with her, or I'll stick your bloody head on a platter." As Jeffries paled, Thorne huffed contentedly and stooped down close to the child. "Don't you worry now, little one. You follow him to the kitchens, and when you're through, have him bring you back to me, all right?" She made a noise of protest. "I know. But he won't hurt you, sweetheart. You're safe." He softly pushed her towards the butler. "Go on now."

Jeffries guided the terrified girl to the kitchen while Richard and Thorne went to the library. Richard poured a finger of brandy into a snifter, then thought better of it. Two fingers.

"Here," he said.

Thorne downed his, then held out his glass for another refill. He grunted something that sounded like a prayer and shoved a hand through his hair. His eyes were like black coals in his pale face, simmering with fury.

"Skin and bone, that one," Thorne muttered. "You bloody toffs. You pull 'em off the street, and—" His voice gave out as he knocked back more liquor.

"Are you all right?" Richard asked. He was shaken himself, seeing the child's condition – bruises marring her frail form and not a spark of light in her haunted gaze. She hadn't uttered a single word since he saw her.

"I'm going to snap his neck," Thorne said, his voice like the scrape of a blade across stone. Richard had never heard Thorne like this – cold enough to commit murder. "Take him to Whitechapel and let the people there finish what I start."

This was Nick Thorne, lord of London's criminal underworld – a man no sane person ever crossed.

"No." Richard steadied himself as best he could as he addressed Thorne. "Justice needs to be done through proper channels."

A mocking laugh escaped Thorne's lips. "Damn your proper channels, Grey."

"Thorne—"

"Richard?" His sister's voice. Alexandra appeared in the doorway, her pale figure swathed in nightclothes, blonde hair loose around her shoulders. "I heard your voice from upstairs. What—" Her eyes widened at Thorne. "Nick?"

Nick?

Richard blinked, bewildered. "Wait. You two know each other?"

His sister's jaw set, and she strode up to an impassive Thorne, deadly rage emanating from her like heat from an inferno. "How dare you show your face here, you rotten bastard."

"Bastard I am," Thorne replied, unfazed. "But you knew that already. Care to raise the stakes? You're an author. Aim higher."

Alexandra balled her hands into fists so tight her knuckles whitened. "I've had enough of your games." Her voice shook with emotion. "Don't think, for one moment, that you can walk back into my life after what you did. You don't get to command me, Nicholas."

"The law might object," Thorne countered, his gaze smouldering.

Alexandra's lip curled in disdain. "As if you listen to the law."

"Would someone kindly explain what the hell is going on here?" Richard interjected.

Thorne and Alexandra shot one another with a look. Two cats in the same corner, neither willing to concede.

Before Richard could get a word out of them, Jeffries knocked on the door. The little girl was behind him. "Sir? The child is fed. She's insisting on seeing that one." He gestured to Thorne.

The Irishman grunted something unintelligible and held out his palm for her. "Come 'ere, love," he said in a gentler tone than Richard had ever heard from him, thickening his accent for the child's benefit. She placed her hand in his hesitantly, comforted by the familiarity of his words. "You know a man from th' rookeries when you see 'im, aye? You remember the name Thorne? I'll keep you safe."

Alexandra stared down at the child with growing alarm. She fell to her knees, so she was at eye level with the little girl, blanching as she took in the fearful expression on the poor thing's face. "Nick," she whispered. "My Lord, she's frightened and ill. Don't tell me she's yours."

Thorne shook his head. "Found 'er at Kendal's."

Alexandra's brows rose in shock. "Kendal, did you say? As in, the *Duke of*?" she demanded incredulously. Her gaze touched both men, searching for answers that neither seemed inclined to give. "You both have a great deal of explaining to do."

"You first," Richard muttered.

Alexandra levelled a scowl at him, then returned her

attention to the child. "Sweet one," she crooned softly. "Would you like to stay with us here and rest?"

"She's from the East End, Alex," Thorne said shortly. "Means she's mine to protect." He looked over at Richard. "I'm takin' her. If you don't do anything about that bloody toff, his life is mine, along with that name you promised."

Alexandra grabbed for his arm, and he tensed beneath her touch. "No. You're not taking her to that gambling den of yours."

He skewered her with an icy stare. "Better there than here. She'll be among her kind." His voice softened almost imperceptibly. "We'll both be."

Alexandra dropped her hand as if it had been burned. "Very well," she said quietly. "But take care of her."

"You wanna come check on her," Thorne challenged, "then you'll have to see my face some other time, won't you?" Alexandra averted her gaze as he scooped up the little girl in his arms and nodded tersely at Richard before Jeffries ushered him out of the room.

After his departure, an unnatural silence descended over the chamber. Alexandra avoided looking at Richard until he spoke up.

"I'm going to ask you to explain," he said slowly. "But I have a horrid feeling I already know what happened."

"Then let's start with you," she said curtly. "How did you find that child at Kendal's residence? And why did she look so terrified and neglected?"

"Alexandra." Richard's voice held a note of warning, and his patience was wearing thin as threadbare fabric after the evening's events. "I asked you a question – one that does not require tact or consideration to answer. Tell me how you appear to be on such intimate terms with Thorne, the lord of the criminal underworld."

She grimaced. "Fine. I only ever knew him as Nicholas Spencer."

Richard blinked in surprise, eyebrows hiked upward. "Nicholas Spencer? The man who writes essays about the working class, who rips your work apart in literature reviews?"

He needed to sit. No, he needed a drink.

Alexandra watched him pour another finger of brandy into his snifter. "Yes, that Nicholas Spencer." She glared at the door Thorne had just left through. "His real name, I discovered later, was Nick Thorne. And he's a liar, thief, criminal, and confidence artist. But by then, it was too late."

Richard's stomach churned uneasily. "Lord almighty. You married him?"

She wrapped a length of ribbon from her clothes around her finger and nodded slowly. "Yes." Her tone dropped to a whisper, and her shoulders trembled under the nightdress. "We've been wed four years now – since I was nineteen."

Richard tossed back his drink, grateful for the burn down his throat. "Holy hell. *Holy hell*. How was it possible I didn't know about this?"

Stanton Sheffield had found out. This was a disaster. Alexandra would be ruined. All of them would be.

"The old earl orchestrated the whole thing," Alexandra said, her voice strained with despair.

Had he heard correctly? "Father. Orchestrated your marriage. To Nicholas Thorne."

His sister sighed. "It's complicated. I'm illegitimate, Richard. He wasn't my father."

This was too much. He needed another drink. Hell, an entire damn bottle. He—

"Sir?" Jeffries was at the door again. "You've another visitor. He says it's urgent. His name is Samuel."

Samuel. He wouldn't have come here unless it had to do with Anne. Something was wrong. As he strode out of the room, he told Alexandra, "We'll talk about this later. First chance I get."

Then he left, steeling himself for whatever awaited him.

∽ 43 ∽

The carriage rocked fretfully along the country road. Anne's knuckles went white as her heart thundered in her chest. Silence hung thick in the air. It was so quiet Anne heard the fabric of their clothing whisper to each other in the darkness.

"You will remain at Rosewood with the duke once we arrive," Stanton said at last, his voice booming like thunder in the small confines of the conveyance. "This is to be your new home."

Anne fought for equanimity. "Will I not return to London?"

He shrugged, his silhouette nothing but a charcoal shadow on the seat opposite her. "Little point. If I need you for political matters, I'll call for you."

Her father had sold her off like livestock and now wanted evidence that she'd obey – something tangible he could accept as repayment for his loss of control over her life. And then there was Kendal – so eager to pry her away from London and into servitude at his estate. All part of his plan to reduce her to mere property, an artefact locked in some dusty cupboard until they called upon it again.

Anne's gaze fell to where Stanton stood in the corner of their carriage prison. Though she could hardly see his face, she felt him watching her intently.

"Are you staying for the wedding?"

A huff of laughter floated through the shadows. "Kendal has a special licence and staff who can serve as witnesses; I have business elsewhere."

So much for being present at his daughter's nuptials.

"What business?" Could Anne ask? Did she dare? What did it matter now? She had been cast aside like a broken toy, her value gone the moment she stepped off that carriage. "In my bedchamber, you seemed troubled."

"I don't believe I asked your opinion." He made a dismissive sound. "Good grief, Kendal will have to work a great deal to undo the Duchess of Hastings' influence. I daresay her instruction is lacking, given the tone of insolence you seem so fond of."

Anne burned to show him who she truly was – not some pliable daughter who sought approval from any quarter. Never that.

"The duchess is my friend," she said.

Stanton raised an eyebrow contemptuously. "Yes, I can tell that much. It will be a cold day in hell before Kendal tolerates your impertinence. You'll have time alone to relearn his lessons if he sees fit."

His lessons. Those horrid liberties no man should take with such a young girl – touches which had opened her eyes to the disgusting things some men believed to be intimacy. And yet her father approved of it all without hesitation.

"I don't care what he thinks. His lessons are an affront to decency."

Stanton looked at her sharply. "Stop whining, Anne – and don't stare at me like that. Look down, for heaven's sake. Have I taught you nothing?"

The fires of fury burned in her veins. The performance was over; she had no further need of the masks and façades. Her mind was her own once more, her memories a deadly weapon that belonged to no one else.

"You've taught me well," she said in a soft voice that cut the air sharp as glass. "Like how to manipulate men. How to gather information." Stanton froze, his expression caught between surprise and consternation, and she twisted the blade one last time. "Where are the children Kendal adopted, Father? Somehow, I think you know."

Before Anne could react, he was across the seat, gripping the fabric of her dress savagely. "Where did you hear about that? You can't—" He let out a brittle laugh, realisation dawning on his face. "Richard Grey. It seems you've been busier than I thought. I'd wondered what prompted him to start looking into Kendal. Should have known it had to do with a woman. I underestimated you, haven't I?"

Anne smiled ruefully at this man who had held her prisoner for years, her sour victory filling the air between them like smoke from a funeral pyre.

"You always have," she said softly.

He gripped her shoulders tightly, his fingers digging into her skin. "Do you have any idea what you've done? You bloody little idiot."

Anne's laughter died in her throat.

She felt his grip tighten and winced, her mind racing.

"What *I've* done?" she asked through gritted teeth. "You're willing to give me away to a man who preys on innocent children. You're willing to hand me over to a monster." Her father remained silent, unmoved. Anne took a deep breath, trying to steady herself. "I knew you lacked empathy, but I didn't realise you were capable of that level of cruelty."

He leaned forward, eyes blazing with a hellish light, and hissed, "I had to. Do you know the funds it takes to become a politician of note? We came from nothing, Anne. No money, no connections. Who do you think has paid for all this?" His mouth contorted in distaste. "If Richard Grey takes all this away, what will you be left with?" With an iron grip, he pulled her closer still until their noses nearly brushed together. "But I'll fix it," he snarled. "Once I tell him I've found out his sister is married to a criminal from the rookeries, he'll keep his trap shut – or she'll face ruin." His lips curled into a cruel smile. "His family is his weakness."

Anne returned her father's chill gaze with a determined one of her own. Her voice was brittle when she spoke. "What if he doesn't?"

A few precious seconds of silence were followed by two cold words that felt like knives. "I'll act."

Murder. He intended to kill Richard.

Anne shoved her father away and tore open the carriage door.

"Anne!"

The road was going fast underneath them. The coach swayed. Stanton held her tight, his fingers like steel around her arm – but Anne fought back, slamming him against the rattling carriage frame.

He released her with a pained howl. "Anne!"

She had to escape.

Before he could stop her, Anne threw herself out of the swaying vehicle.

The impact knocked the breath from her lungs, and her wrist screamed in pain. She staggered to her feet with a silent prayer of thanks that it seemed intact, though she feared tendons might have been torn.

The carriage horses reared, spooked by their master's slipping control, and the coach veered off course, crashing into the ditch.

In the opposite direction, the thunder of hooves grew closer. She looked up to see a man dismounting, blond hair catching the moonlight as he raced towards her.

Richard.

His embrace was savage as he hauled her up, his presence driving away her fears. "Bloody hell," he breathed. "I saw you leap from the carriage and—"

Stanton emerged from the wreckage, a beast unleashed under cover of darkness. His arm hung limp at his side. "Hand her over, Grey."

Richard only held Anne tighter, a blaze of defiance smouldering in his eyes. "You're not taking her," he said, low and steady.

"Try me," came the cold reply. "Or I'll have you arrested for kidnapping."

His voice pierced through the stillness, carried by the chilly wind that whipped through the open fields. Anne felt the coldness seeping into her bones.

Richard flashed a sardonic smile. "Do it," he taunted her father. "It would be my pleasure to tell them all about your sordid cover-ups these past ten years – your twisted attempts at securing political advantage."

"Prove it," Stanton spat.

"Watch me." Hoisting Anne into his arms, he boosted them both onto the horse.

Her father bellowed after them, "I'll find you. I'll ensure everyone knows about your sister and that degenerate she married. *Grey!*"

Anne shuddered against Richard's chest, the crisp night air pricking at her skin. He spurred the horse forward, and she clung tightly to him, her fractured wrist aching with the motion. Her father's voice faded into the distance, and she felt herself relax in Richard's embrace – until his words sent panic soaring anew.

"He'll locate us if he finds a horse," Anne said shakily. "We can't stay on this road."

"We're not." With a tug of the reins, he steered them off course. "Caroline's estate is close; I've sent word we'll sleep there tonight before taking the train to Scotland tomorrow."

But Anne was too distressed to hear him. "Don't you understand? He'll have criminal charges brought against you. He'll have you arrested."

"For what?" Richard flashed a wolfish grin at her. "Would it be kidnapping if I were to abduct my own wife? I suppose if you want me to play the wicked villain to your captured maiden in distress, who am I to refuse such a sweet invitation to performative bed sport?"

Her breath caught as his sinful proposal made understanding dawn on her like an early morning sunbeam. Scotland. They were going to Scotland, where they'd be safe from her father's retribution – for now, at least.

Still, she couldn't help but laugh. "You're such a scoundrel, Mr Grey."

A smile flickered across his face, and he leaned down to peck her forehead. "Comes with the territory, Mrs Grey," he replied.

44

Richard held Anne in a gentle embrace as the train carried them north.

"Hastings agreed to meet us in Edinburgh," Caroline said once they had settled into her private rail carriage. The train was already gliding across the countryside, and Richard felt a weight in his chest lighten with each passing mile. Anne was safe – for now, at least. "His cable was quite terse."

Anne stirred against Richard before he tightened his arms around her protectively. He'd been up all night, holding Anne close and shielding her from the horrors that awaited if they were discovered.

"Cables are always terse," he reassured the duchess. "It's the nature of the telegraph."

"Yes, well. This simply said, *fine*. One word. *Fine*. I'll wring his neck if he doesn't have someone to perform the ceremony." Caroline glanced at Anne, who'd barely slept for fear her father would break down the duchess's door with the authorities. "Poor dear," the duchess said. "To have no one in the world…"

"She has me," Richard insisted.

Caroline held his gaze, steady and determined. "Yes. Yes, she has you." She sat back and watched the countryside roll by outside the window, her voice low and contemplative as she continued, "A husband should treasure his wife."

He met her eyes without hesitation. "All my life."

Caroline nodded once, satisfied. "Good."

It was raining when the butler received them at the Duke of Hastings' Edinburgh residence. As Caroline gave him her coat, she asked, "And where is my husband? Is he at home?"

"Yes, Your Grace. He's right—"

"Here," a voice interrupted.

The duke descended the stairs like a knight of old, his form illuminated by the golden light of the setting sun streaming through the windows. Richard had met with Hastings often enough to be familiar with the formidable lord's visage, but he had a presence that filled an entire room. His intimidating size and strength, earned from countless hours at his boxing club, only added to the gravity of his cold grey eyes. Even hardened lords in Parliament had trouble looking him straight in the face.

"Hello, Julian," Caroline said softly.

A flash of tenderness softened the duke's countenance for the briefest moment. "Hello, Linnie."

Caroline stiffened as if hearing her pet name from him was an unwelcome jibe. She quickly dismissed the butler and gestured in Richard's direction. "Will you allow me to introduce you to—"

"Grey," Hastings finished for her. "We're already quite familiar with each other from Parliament." He turned his steely gaze on Anne and offered a slight nod. "Miss Sheffield, I must admit this is a surprise. The last time I saw you, you pretended to read in a window seat as your father discussed matters not fitting for a young daughter's ears."

Anne lifted her head, a challenge in her gaze. "It depends on the daughter. I thought your position on the reform bill was quite admirable. It's rare to hear a titled gentleman advocating for working-class men's right to vote."

Hastings tilted his head a fraction. "I take it you don't agree with your father."

"No. I do not."

"Interesting."

Caroline stepped in front of Anne. "Enough. Do you have someone to perform the ceremony? I'm afraid your single-word cable didn't indicate."

He gave her a cool look in response. "In the library," he said with a stiff nod toward the room in question. "When it's done, you have a great deal to explain."

Caroline's smile was sweet. "My darling husband, when it's done, we shall have a wedding dinner for my friends, and I'll explain when I damn well feel like it." She grasped her skirts and strode into the library, followed by Anne.

Richard lingered behind and cut Hastings a glare. "Do try not being an utter arse about it, would you?"

The ice in Hastings' eyes hardened further. "One might also suggest you mind your own damn business," he said coolly before striding away.

★ ★ ★

The vicar spoke the ancient words, and Richard recited his vows in a low baritone. He meant them; he'd promised to love and cherish Anne for as long as they lived. But when it came to a particular vow – "With my body I thee worship" – his breath caught.

Anne blushed, her dimple flashing on her cheek, adorable as ever.

He'd kissed her tenderly and smiled as he felt her warm lips beneath his own. He knew that choosing to marry Anne was the best decision he had ever made in his scandalous life.

When they finally retired for the night, Richard left directly for Anne's bedchamber and summoned her maid away.

Anne exhaled when he stepped behind her, loosening the chignon that had held her hair prisoner all day.

"That was lovely," she said dreamily. "But you did shock the vicar when you kissed me."

"I'm a reformed rake, sweetheart, not an impotent one," Richard said, kissing her exposed skin. "And don't think I didn't notice the look you gave Caroline and Hastings during dinner."

"Look?" She feigned innocence, her lips tilted in a coy smile.

Richard rolled his eyes in fond exasperation. "Spare me your false naïveté. I know precisely the wheels churning in your impossibly clever brain," Richard murmured against the curve of her shoulder, punctuating his words with a devilishly intimate kiss.

"Now, that's not true." Anne shifted beneath him, a playful glint in her eye. "What look would that be?"

"The one that said, 'if only I could help them as easily as they helped us.'"

He understood why she was so concerned; Caroline had done an admirable job keeping a brave face throughout the wedding celebration. But there was a strain between Caroline and Hastings; despite Anne having softened him enough to produce a smile, the duke still couldn't look at his wife directly.

Anne nestled closer. "All I want is for everyone to be as happy as I am."

"Yes." He began to unfasten her nightdress buttons. "But it's not over for us, either. When we get back home, your father—"

"Shh." She pressed a finger to his lips. "Let's worry about it later."

It wasn't long before he had her in bed naked, his kisses and caresses conveying the love he couldn't put into words. Richard worshipped her body, each stroke and caress a blessing and benediction. Trailing his mouth across her skin, he whispered hushed verses in the language of touch. A heated union that spoke wordlessly of eternity.

"I love you," he vowed, breathless, his heart pounding against hers as if to prove the truth of his words. "God above, I love you."

Her back arched off the mattress, a pained sigh twisted with pleasure like a prayer to some carnal deity. Her fingers tangled in his hair as she moaned her own vow – that she loved him, too.

Richard drifted off to sleep with a satisfied smile.

⌒ **45** ⌒

During the night, Anne woke in Richard's embrace. The city lights spilled through the window, enough to reveal his handsome features in slumber.

She smiled. Not so agitated now, was he?

Anne pressed her lips to his temple and unwound herself from his hold to reach for the water on the bedside table – but found the glass empty.

"Drat," she whispered.

"Mmm? What is it?" Richard murmured, his voice roughened with exhaustion.

A wave of affection washed over her as Anne stroked his hair. "Just need to get some water. Go back to sleep."

Her husband caught her hand and kissed her palm before settling deeper into their bedding. "Hurry back." He yawned. "I have plans involving you. And this bed. And playing the role of your wicked captor."

Anne chuckled, reluctant to leave the comfort of their sheets after hours of exploring each other with kisses and touches. Their lovemaking blended pain and pleasure in perfect harmony. Anne still couldn't believe that this man was hers; he should be in her arms each morning when the sun rose to light up the beauty of his face.

With a sigh, she threw on her wrapper and headed downstairs to the kitchens, candlelight flickering like a baton of gold in her hand. Early spring in Edinburgh was colder than in London, and she shivered against the chill.

At the bottom of the stairs, someone clamped an iron grip around her and dragged a palm over her lips.

"Shh. No screaming."

Stanton.

He wrenched her arm between her shoulder blades until pain crackled through her body like lightning. "Did you believe I wouldn't track you down?" he snarled. "Did you think that seeking the aid of the Duke and Duchess of Hastings would keep you safe from me? Do you take me for a fool?" He yanked her closer, making her whimper. "Be still. I don't want to hurt you, but I will if I have to. You'll come with me to my horse outside, slow and quiet. Understand?"

Anne shook her head, holding up the hand with her ring to show why she wouldn't leave peacefully. Richard had run out to purchase that simple band just after their ceremony, which now glittered in defiance against this brute's intentions.

"That ring means nothing to me," he sneered. "Do you think I lack the power to annul this marriage?"

A low voice answered from the shadows of the stairs. "Not for much longer."

Anne's relief was palpable as Richard stepped into the

light, his gaze seeking hers for reassurance. Unspoken but clear, his eyes silently asked: *Are you all right?*

Without hesitation, Anne nodded in response.

Turning to her father, Richard fixed him with an icy stare. "Release my wife," he commanded. "Or I swear upon all that is holy, your blood will stain these walls."

"She's my daughter," Stanton sneered. "I won't stand by and watch you snatch away an innocent woman – and force her to marry under duress."

Richard smiled, though there was no kindness in it. "Well done. Quite the dramatic statement. Did you make all that up yourself?"

"It's what I'll tell everyone after I clean up this mess. You wouldn't be the first loose end I've tied up in my history, would you?" Anne felt her breath catch as he pulled out the pistol behind his back.

At Anne's stifled gasp, Stanton yanked her close against him. "You should have kept your mouth shut, Anne."

Richard lifted both hands in a gesture of surrender – yet Anne noted how his chest moved quickly beneath his shirt. "Think on this, Stanton. You're standing in the home of the Duke and Duchess of Hastings. And if they hear a shot go off, will they become two more loose ends for you to take care of? What about their servants? Put down the pistol. Now."

Anne held her breath, knowing she was staring into the maw of fate. Stanton's beastly demons had finally caught up with him, and he could run no farther. He had spilled too much blood, broken too many hearts, and hurt too many souls. It was as if a wild animal were cornered. His only thought? Survival.

"You're right," he breathed, lowering his gun.

But as Anne allowed a flicker of hope to flare within her chest – thinking that perhaps he was about to let her go – Stanton grabbed the candle from her trembling hand and hurled it towards Richard.

The result was immediate – the fire devouring hungrily at the window curtains as they billowed and cast sparks in a frenzied dance over the floorboards. Richard's shouts cut through the air. The flames licked dangerously close to the stairs, and Anne could no longer make out his form through the smoke.

With brute strength, Stanton seized Anne once again. She fought back with gritted teeth and nails digging into his flesh, but he held fast.

"Richard!" The fire's roar drowned out her scream.

In retaliation, Stanton snarled and struck her hard across the cheek, sending bright lights swimming through her vision. Anne ignored the pain and bucked as he dragged her towards the foyer.

She refused to give up without a fight.

"Damn it, Anne!"

He slammed her against the wood frame of the doorway, and Anne sagged in his grip. With ease, he hoisted her up and carried her through the house as another set of shouts echoed off the walls. Was Richard warning everyone? Was everyone safe? That didn't matter now.

She had to focus on herself. With newfound determination coursing through her veins, Anne managed to wriggle free from Stanton's control again. He swore, lunging forward with renewed vigour as he reached for her. But Anne was faster.

Fight. Think!

And there it was – a heavy candlestick on a table just within reach of her fingers. The weighing force of retribution in her grasp. In a moment of clarity and rage, Anne grabbed it and smashed it against Stanton's temple.

Her father staggered. "You bitch."

She swung the candlestick once more, and he went down hard. She took notice that he was still breathing.

Richard.

Where was Richard?

Smoke was filling the room fast now, and Anne heard shouting on the other side of the house, but couldn't make out whom they belonged to above the roar of the fire. "Richard!"

Hands clamped onto her shoulders, dragging her back.

"Anne. It's just me." Richard's arms were around her. Warm. Safe. "Give me your hand. We'll escape outside through the servants' quarters."

"Wait!" She glanced desperately at where Stanton lay unconscious and bleeding on the floor. "My father – we can't leave him."

Richard looked tempted – she knew *she* was – but shook his head with a rueful frown. "You're lucky I'm in no mood to be a murderer today." He grasped Stanton and hauled the other man up onto his broad shoulder. "And the bastard weighs a bloody tonne," he muttered. "Come. Quickly. The others are already awake."

They raced past the inferno, smoke and heat engulfing them as they careened down the blackened hall. Their feet slipped on ash from the cinders raining from above.

Richard hurled open the door to the back garden and

stumbled outside. The clanging bells of the fire brigade echoed off distant hills. Servants lined up like ghosts, coughing and pointing at the lake of flames consuming the house.

The duke was there, too – soot-covered, his clothes smouldering as if he'd tried to put out the blaze himself. He looked up in a start as Richard dumped Stanton none too gently on the grass. "I have several questions about why you just threw Stanton Sheffield at my feet," he growled, "but first, where is my wife?"

Richard shot him a horrified look. "I thought she was with you."

Hastings' eyes locked on the burning building, realisation dawning across his face. "Hell," he whispered.

Without another word, Hastings abandoned them, sprinting back into the house to find his duchess.

Anne clung to Richard as the inferno built. It had spread through the manor now, licking at the walls and windows like a slavering beast.

Smoke lanced through her lungs like a blade. Yet she could spare no concern for herself – not while the Duke and Duchess of Hastings were still in there. How would she live with herself if her father was responsible for their deaths?

Richard stroked her spine, but she knew he was worried too; Anne pressed her face to his chest and felt the frantic beat of his pulse quicken with each crash as another lamp burst apart in the heat. Her heart matched his.

Please don't die. Please don't die. Please don't—

The kitchen door flew open.

The duke staggered into the night air with Caroline in his arms, her body limp. They were both filthy; Hastings was coughing hard as he set his wife in the grass. "You there!" He bared his teeth in a desperate snarl at the nearest servant. "Send for a doctor!"

No subtlety coloured his voice, only raw command and the promise of retribution should it go unheeded. Terror-struck, the maid broke into a run.

Anne and Richard hurried over to where the duke cradled his unconscious wife. Caroline's skin appeared almost translucent in the moonlight; she looked barely alive.

Richard yanked his dressing robe free and draped it over Caroline's motionless form. "Where did you find her?" he asked.

"Goddamn farthest wing of the house," Hastings said through clenched teeth, caressing Linnie's face tenderly. "She wouldn't have heard our shouts there." He gathered her against his chest, rocking on his knees. "Linnie. *Linnie.* Wake up, love." He shook her softly. "Wake up, and you can go back to being furious with me. *Scream* at me. Just—" He held her close. "Damn it, Linnie, don't die."

The silence clung to the air like some kind of deathly fog, smothering them all in its suffocating grasp.

And then – like a miracle – a faint noise shuddered through the darkness. A sound that made Anne nearly collapse with relief.

Caroline was coughing. Weak and broken, but alive. The duke gathered her to his chest as she trembled, his face pale.

"Linnie?" Hastings' tone was filled with concern. "God, are you all right?"

"Where's Richard?" Caroline wheezed as she twisted in his grip.

Hastings seemed to be fighting an internal battle over releasing his wife even while his gaze frosted over.

Richard's gruff voice was choked with emotion as he spoke. "I'm here, Caro."

The duchess slumped to the ground at his words and shut her eyes once more. "Take me home, Richard. Take me to Ravenhill. I want to go home."

"I'll take you as soon as I can," he promised.

Caroline smiled softly in response. "Good. I trust you."

Hastings flinched, and Anne noticed Richard stiffen with a sudden sympathy for the duke. The awkward moment was broken by the doctor's arrival, who immediately set about examining the duchess.

When it seemed she would make it through, Richard pulled Anne aside. He spoke quietly but decisively. "We're making a detour at Ravenhill before returning to London. I need to send an urgent message to my contacts in the police force regarding your father."

Anne felt her heart lurch at the mention of Stanton and glanced at his still form on the ground beside them. She swallowed hard before replying, "I know. I'll worry about that when we come to it."

Richard tugged her into an embrace, his voice a whisper of velvet. "I'll be with you every step of the way," he vowed.

Anne thought of the Duke and Duchess of Hastings and their troubled marriage. How could love falter so suddenly? What could be so insurmountable that it destroyed trust?

She tipped her head back and searched the fathomless depths of Richard's gaze. "Do you promise?" she breathed.

He cupped her chin, a tender gesture that sent warmth

radiating through her body. His lips brushed hers in a kiss as gentle as a summer breeze.

"I'm with you until my dying days, wife," he murmured against her mouth.

∽ 46 ∽

Thorne loomed behind his desk at the Brimstone, a smirk playing across that wickedly handsome face. He surveyed Anne and Richard with something like admiration. "You two have certainly caused a stir in these parts, haven't you?"

Anne flushed and looked away, recalling how her father had been arrested after attempting to murder the Duke and Duchess of Hastings. Kendal had been caught trying to flee the country after police discovered a cache of bones buried in his cellar, damning evidence of his abhorrent crimes over the years.

Richard met Anne's gaze as he replied. "I see that as a good thing."

Her flush deepened. "Even though your sister paid the price?"

Stanton had revealed Alexandra Grey's secret marriage to Nicholas Thorne – right before he'd been dragged away to prison in chains. His final act of vengeance had reduced

Alexandra to shreds, destroying her reputation and any chance of inhabiting the lofty society circles she had once occupied.

"Alexandra said it was worth it," Richard insisted.

Thorne's low hum might have been agreement or dismissal, but Richard had no more time to dwell on it. "Your sister never puts herself first, does she?"

"No," Richard agreed with a note of fondness. "But you ought to see her. Perhaps treat her as if she were your wife? Just an idle thought."

Thorne leaned back in his chair, midnight eyes gleaming with some emotion Anne couldn't quite decipher. Though he had helped Anne and Richard, she could not shake her discomfort. Here, within the East End, Thorne ruled supreme – like a fallen angel living in hell and relishing in his power. His smirk was edged in cynicism. "You trying to play matchmaker now, Grey?"

"Just making sure my sister knows her husband isn't an irredeemable bastard."

At that, Thorne let out a hard laugh. "Your sister knows better than anyone the depths of my depravity. You should ask her about it sometime." He gestured towards the study door with a careless wave. "Now, if that is all, I have important matters to attend to – running a club and planning a murder is time-consuming."

Richard shook his head. "I gave you that name as a courtesy. I could still have Malloy arrested and taken to the gaol."

The smile vanished from Thorne's face, and he appeared every inch the devil incarnate. "I'm not nice, Grey. I enjoy seeing certain men get what they deserve. Keep that in mind when entertaining any notions that I might be good enough for your sister." He straightened in his chair and brushed invisible lint off his jacket sleeve, his voice sharp and cold. "Now get out."

Once back in the carriage, Anne slid across the seat and curled against Richard's side. "Your promise to stay out of other couples' affairs was short-lived," she said.

Richard kept his gaze on the window. "I'm not meddling. I'm giving Thorne a chance to do right by Alexandra before I smash his face in."

Her husband was so beautiful. Anne kissed him, then smiled at the prospect of waking up to his gorgeous face each morning. "If he has feelings for her, he'd march through hellfire just to be with her – like I would for you."

Richard drew her close so that she fit snugly between his thighs. His mouth moved from her ear down to her neck, sending shivers of delight coursing through her. "Let's forget about our friends and their troubles, shall we? I believe I have some obligations due this afternoon."

"What obligations?" She arched against him as each touch seared into her skin.

Richard flashed a devilish grin. "Don't you recall? You wanted me, a reformed rake, to kneel at your feet."

"I told you," she said between kisses. "Rakes don't grovel."

His laugh was pure wickedness. "I won't be getting down on my knees to grovel."

AUTHOR'S NOTE

The Ballot Act of 1872 was the law that made election ballots secret. Before that, landlords, employers, and other men of influence could easily affect people's votes. Not only could they be present during voting to ensure obedience, but they also sent representatives to make sure tenants and employees voted a certain way.

Many powerful men supported keeping ballots public. In fact, it was considered radical (and cowardly) to suggest casting votes in secret. Britain introduced several changes to elections in the 1860s–1880s due to corruption in politics. Election spending was unlimited, voters took bribes, and men in power could intimidate people into compliance.

The Ballot Act was an important step in attempting to end corruption during the election process.

ACKNOWLEDGEMENTS

I have so many people to thank for this one. It's such a strange and terrifying thing to write in a new genre, but my friend Tess Sharpe said, "You should do it!" Her unwavering support and encouragement helped me take the plunge into romance after decades of saying, "God, I want to write a romance."

This series began its life as a self-published side-project, and I never could have imagined the phenomenal reception it would receive. So thank you to my agent, Danny Baror, for taking this series to my publisher and being its fierce advocate.

My editor, Rosie de Courcy, took this series under her wing and helped me shape it into something I am even more proud of. The team at Aria and Head of Zeus who worked on this series deserve a standing ovation, including Bianca Gillam and the brilliant copyedits by Charlotte Hayes-Clemens, and I just know I am missing others by name, but thank you all so much for the warm welcome and all your hard work.

And to my husband—my love, my chocolate-bringer-in-bed. He puts up with my endless nights of writing, and kisses me soundly every morning. I adore you.

Lastly, to my readers: you all are so amazing. Thank you for falling in love with these characters like I did. Your support means the world to me.

ABOUT THE AUTHOR

KATRINA KENDRICK is the romance pen name for *Sunday Times* bestselling science fiction and fantasy author Elizabeth May. She is Californian by birth and Scottish by choice, and holds a Ph.D. from the University of St Andrews. She currently resides on an eighteenth-century farm in the Scottish countryside with her husband, three cats, and a lively hive of honey bees that live in the wall of her old farmhouse.

www.katrinakendrick.com